Welcon

Adolescence is never easy. An ... bewildering. Brought up by pa... surrounded by teenagers all too ... wonder she feels like a social ano.....y.

Her father, Hugh, is struggling to keep his property business afloat. 'When there's a recession on, you have to keep an eye on the figures,' he once said – if only he'd listened to his own advice... Her mother, Millie, hoped her daughter would become her best gal pal. Instead, her fondest communications reach Freya in the form of notes left on the fridge door: 'Feed rabbits', 'Cheese in fridge only one day out of date', 'Be less scary'.

When her parents break dramatically with marital convention, they leave Freya in turmoil as she realizes that, for Millie and Hugh, three is not a crowd. In desperation, Freya goes looking for love in all the wrong places...

Alice de Smith was born in Cambridge, educated at Oxford and now lives in Newcastle-upon-Tyne, where she writes for Live Theatre. She has written for publications including *The Times*, the *Mail on Sunday*, and *Cosmopolitan*. *Welcome to Life* is her first novel.

Publicity enquiries: Fran Owen
Tel: 020 7269 1623 Fax: 020 7430 0916
Email: francesowen@groveatlantic.co.uk

Sales: Joanna Lord
Tel: 020 7269 1618 Fax: 020 7430 0916
Email: joannalord@groveatlantic.co.uk

Atlantic Books, Ormond House,
26–27 Boswell Street, London, WC1N 3JZ
Tel: 020 7269 1610 Fax: 020 7430 0916
Email: enquiries@groveatlantic.co.uk

Welcome to Life

Alice de Smith

Atlantic Books

LONDON

First published in hardback and export and airside trade paperback in Great Britain in 2009 by Atlantic Books, an imprint of Grove Atlantic Ltd.

1 3 5 7 9 10 8 6 4 2

A CIP catalogue record for this book is available from the British Library.

Hardback ISBN: 978 1 84887 016 1
Export and airside trade paperback ISBN: 978 1 84354 983 3

Printed in Great Britain

Atlantic Books
An imprint of Grove Atlantic Ltd
Ormond House
26–27 Boswell Street
London WC1N 3JZ

www.atlantic-books.co.uk

✳ one ✳

Now that my mother is dishonoured and has been variously denounced as degenerate, irresponsible, a lush and a whore, it's hard to believe that once she ruled my life with whimsied severity. Every night Millie wrote us a list, which she placed at the end of the bed. She could easily have confined herself to daily tasks, such as swim, feed rabbits, pick up repeat prescription. But she couldn't help but include not-very-nice suggestions for personal development – smile more, stand up straight. No comeback or discussion was permitted. The year was 1989, the time when sale posters started hanging in shop windows all year round, not just in January. I, aged fourteen, had a long wait ahead before I could deal my mother her come-uppance.

We were supposed to throw the lists away, but I preferred to keep them, items left ostentatiously unticked. Hugh says he married Millie because of her lists, but he has to be lying. No one would choose a wife like that. As for me, I wished for a single day when I could just wake and breathe. Maybe she'd get bored. She'd realise it was stupid to corral our universe and control of our lives would be devolved to us at last. The tiny scraps of paper, written on the backs of envelopes, Post-It notes and fast food menus, penned in her curlicued hand, lie desiccating in my bedroom, like so many leaves of filo pastry. Even now, half a lifetime later, when I come in the front door, I half expect to find a querulous message printed across a piece of junk mail, insisting I declog the drain in the upstairs bathroom.

Those lists were permanent proof of Millie's state of mind. Other parents could pretend they'd never promised to buy a pony or cancel Christmas. But even at fourteen I could cross-reference anything my mother said to an irrefutable, contemporaneous document. I never drew her attention to inconsistencies, however. I simply took note of them, knowing that one day, I'd be able to call her to account. Sadly, I waited too long for this day of reckoning. I missed my chance.

Now that I'm older I've started reading and rereading the lists, questing for subtext. The subject matter is revealing. For example, she emphasised the importance of swimming. I believe she was urging me away from her own bad habits. My mother couldn't make it to the newsagent's and back without getting breathless. 'Everyone's got their own idea of fun,' she'd say. 'Yours, Freya, is a crime scene or something. God knows. Nothing normal, at any rate. Mine's a bit more traditional – booze and fags. S'not like I'm hurting anyone.' Safe to say, she wasn't like other people's mothers.

When I'd ask my father why she was different he always said the same thing: 'Can't be helped, sweetheart. It's because she used to be working-class.'

When she wrote 'feed rabbits,' she was encouraging me to nurture — never her favourite activity. I'd taken on the rabbits in question so I could investigate the Harmisteads next door. Mrs H dressed like Lady Di and whistled through her teeth when she spoke. Her husband was a doctor who wore navy-blue blazers. 'He's not a very good doctor,' Millie told me. 'Only an anaesthetist. They don't really count.' The Harmisteads' rodents were a new addition, since their youngest son had gone to university. 'Only a redbrick. Just goes to show,' said my mother, unimpressed, as per. When we went round their house for Christmas drinks, the Harmisteads talked about congestion on the A14 and other road routes. My parents joined in with enthusiasm, like they were in a boring contest, with cash prizes.

Mrs H had decided to keep rabbits instead of children and to sell them through small ads in the Cambridge Evening News. I'd only have them in the back garden for a week, while she and her husband were off on a FlyDrive to Canada, but the animals didn't like being trapped in a cage and I wasn't allowed to set them free. The bunnies, with their half-blind vulnerability, made me queasy. I was scared to touch them in case somehow they'd be crushed. I wanted to cuddle them, but they were the wrong size. They didn't have the chunky robustness of a cat or a dog.

'You poor little thing.' Mrs H ruffled my lank hair. 'No brothers, no sisters, no pets. Bit of bunny love — that's what you need.' Mrs H hadn't noticed that I was five foot eight and could already get served in pubs. She'd have been shocked if

3

she knew what I thought when I watched Sasha, the best-looking boy in town, cycle down the main road. Just seeing him gliding past, no hands on the handlebars, made me feel funny all over. But still, the rabbits were a nice thought. I couldn't help wishing they were something more manageable, that gave me a better return on my emotional investment. My father taught me the importance of investing wisely, in all areas of life. It was a knack he'd picked up in the property game. 'When there's a recession on, you have to keep an eye on the figures,' he'd say. I just wish he'd listened to his own advice. If he had, then none of what I'm about to tell would've happened.

Some of Millie's directives were totally unfair. 'Be less scary,' for instance. How could I be less scary when no one feared me? I even got 'pleasant disposition,' on my last report card, along with 'consistently co-operative attitude.' But she found me inscrutable and therefore sinister. She thought, as if by magic, when I hit adolescence we'd become the bestest gal pals, all gossip and home manicures, even though she chewed her cuticles and I bit my nails to the quick. Still, I can't say she never taught me a thing or two. She advised me that car exhaust fumes melted fifteen denier tights and when I wore foundation, not to forget the tip of my nose. This was pretty much the limit of her feminine wisdom, though. She hung out in pubs, not restaurants. She preferred football to tennis and crack open a walnut with one hand. That was my mother for you.

Her lists were just the beginning of the records I kept. I took note of my family's bank statements and numbers most frequently dialled. I knew which songs they whistled without even realising it, and that while Hugh trimmed his own nose hair on a daily basis, his eyebrows were Millie's responsibility. Hugh said I was like one of those children who denounced their parents to the Stasi for muttering sedition in their sleep. He called me Miss Moneypenny, which was him trying to be nice but which I considered insulting, because she was only a secretary and never went on any missions.

The problem with my so-called care givers was that being so accessible, they were barely worth the effort of investigation. They seldom left the house except to go to work and they spent their evenings reading middle-brow novels or watching detective series. They were nearly as dull as the Harmisteads. Whatever social lives they had took place outside of the home, apart from each other and unobservable by me, in the form of after-work drinks. The boredom and disappointment they selfishly inflicted upon me forced my attention towards better parents, other lives.

The Glinkas lived half a mile down the road from us, where the city petered out, in a grotty farmhouse they'd bought on the cheap. There was no point them doing it up, since they didn't even own the land it was built on. The yellow brick exterior looked like it'd been chewed by a giant rat. 'Very poor investment,' said Hugh, as he passed his hand over his closely cropped grey scalp. The gesture looked as though it dated from some past time, when his hair had been longer and more luxuriant.

The Glinkas' was a domestic Shangri-La, a buffer between school and home. It was always Mrs Glinka I talked to – never Roman, her husband. I'd never have dreamt of speaking to Sasha, her son, because every time he came near me I could feel my blood cells crashing against each other like erotically charged dodgems. But that Tuesday afternoon at the fag-end of the summer term, on a day so hot that steam rose from The Fens, I got the attention I craved. For a moment, at least.

Roman Glinka had once been Russian, the distant descendent of a poet I'd never heard of. He was also a poet, but not a famous one, or one who made any money. He'd arrived in Cambridge during the Seventies, when his recitals got standing ovations, even though the audience didn't understand a word. Now there were no more ovations. Mr Glinka ran a dress shop in town which sold clothes for the larger lady.

Mrs Glinka came from somewhere horrible like Lowestoft, and spoke with a faint East Anglian accent. You could hear it most when she said noice instead of nice. With her baroque earrings and hair the colour of melted sunshine, it was her not her husband who was Slavic and mysterious. Her father had been a minor nobleman from Tallinn, stranded in England after the revolution. He married the daughter of a sub-post-master and together they'd run an unsuccessful chicken farm. In her union to Roman, Mrs Glinka was restoring the family to its former eminence.

She wore full dark skirts and tight synthetic blouses. When she got emotional, the blouse buttons strained and burst open, even. She often spoke with her husband's grammar, in choppy little sentences, forgetting to use 'a' and 'the'. 'Just because you ask question, doesn't mean you get answer' – that's what she told me when I overstepped the mark.

I could always find her in her tiny, gadget-free kitchen, with its formica furniture and cast iron stock pots. Here she cooked, sewed, embroidered and cleaned. She was constantly in motion, feet gliding, arms jerky. She'd have been perfectly at home telling the hour in a clock in Austria.

'You'll see.' She fixed upon me her stern dark eyes. 'When you have kiddie winkies of your own. Home – that's what counts. I was going to be a lawyer, or finish my PhD. But soon as I held little Sasha in my arms, that was it. I knew I'd spend the rest of my life at home with my ryebyonok.' But now her ryebyonok was eighteen years old and Mrs Glinka was starting to look a bit mad. But then, if I'd ever held her Sasha in my arms, I might have felt the same.

Sasha, like his father, was functionally mute and I almost hoped he'd stay that way. He was boy band beautiful, with white blond hair and a honeyed tan. Whenever he walked into the kitchen, he saw me and didn't see me – both at the same time. He possessed the doleful grey eyes of a prince bereft of his kingdom. In my mind, the unspoken bond between us was so powerful, that if ever we ever got round to having an actual conversation, the sky might splinter. I'm not sure what he thought of me. He probably didn't think of me at all. He most likely thought about motorbikes or beer.

I knew Sasha by sight long before I ever actually met him. His blondness, his confidence, his ubiquity – that made him unmissable. Sasha was special. Mr Cambridge, Jessica called him. He was always lounging in the corner of Berlucci's, my favourite café, cadging a free slice of torta al cioccolato off of Rosalina the waitress. His laughs, dank and sooty, were pitched just under the general noise of the café. He'd pick stuff up off the table – a salt cellar, a wallet, a hat, and juggle with them – sometimes one-handed, even. I tried juggling at home but I couldn't, not even with only two objects and using both hands. Where had he learned to convey such confidence? Even if he was just copying some style from a mag or a bloke he'd seen walking down Carnaby Street, Sasha was, as Miss Gillis, my Class Civ teacher, would say, sui generis.

That afternoon, Mrs Glinka snowed her kitchen table with flour. She kneaded bread which was soft and plump as her bare arms. 'This,' she said, as she punished the dough with furious hands, 'this is happiness. Caring for family. Most important job in the world. Total fulfilment.'

While she glazed the loaves with an egg wash, she told me that unemployment was high because young people were lazy. When I asked her about the global economic downturn she just said glasnost was a stupid idea which would end up with England flooded by low-class Soviets who spat in the street. Premarital sex was a sin, she said. She was Catholic and her husband was pravoslavni, but on this matter, they were in agreement. 'Atalanta,' she said. 'There's a role model for you.

Be like Atalanta. Running fast fast, beating all the boys. Only no stopping to pick up the apple.' Mrs Glinka had a degree in Classics – the real thing, not Class Civ like we did at school – but it wasn't like she'd done anything with her education. My parents, who'd hardly an exam between them, got to make important decisions and drive nice cars, but Mrs Glinka stayed home not working, making no money, influencing nothing.

During those moments of stillness while we waited for the bread to rise, she told me about her menopause, about posture, about men's carnality. She thought poor people should have their benefits taken off of them, that dogs shouldn't be castrated, that tramps should be given a clear choice – sober up, or voluntary euthanasia. I admired the fact that Mrs Glinka had bothered to think through the problems of society: it was just her solutions that I didn't like. I smiled and didn't listen, but that didn't seem to bother her. She'd work on me slowly, like rain on a stone. Recently, it had occurred to me that Mrs Glinka might be rather old-fashioned, even by Eastern European standards. Yugoslavia, after all, had just won the Eurovision Song Contest, and although the band hadn't been cool in any way, they'd looked and sounded pretty up-to-date for people who lived behind an Iron Curtain. I suppose it didn't matter that Mrs Glinka disapproved of humanity in general and modern Western mores in particular. At least she approved of me.

That afternoon she took a lock of my hair in her hands.

'Beautiful, beautiful,' she murmured. But I knew my hair was not beautiful. It was neither dark like my mother's nor fair like hers. Mine was somewhere in between, as if God had simply not bothered to make me descript. Sitting at her kitchen table, though, I knew I was being treated as I should be, with total concentration. My own mother noticed only if I was home or not, clean or dirty, fed or hungry. Mrs Glinka, though, she massaged my shoulders when they grew stiff. She remembered everything I told her.

'How's school?' she asked.

'OK,' I lied. 'Millie got me a new skirt. I don't like it.'

She stared at my new uniform. 'A-line! Unbelievable. You're ten years out of date. Take it off. I'll fix it.'

I hesitated. I wasn't sure I wanted to take fashion advice from such a dubious source. Every since I had first met Mrs Glinka two years previously at a Saturday morning screening of Andrei Rublov, where we were the only two members of the audience, I'd never known her to pay the teensiest bit of attention to what she wore. Not like Millie, who bought new outfits each season, saying, 'Otherwise, I'll look like a freak.'

Mrs Glinka must have seen me scanning her ten-year old co-ordinating separates. 'At my age and size, you find a style you can fit into and stick with it. Do as I say, not as I do.'

Even if I let her change my skirt, I didn't want to be sitting in my undies. What if Mr Glinka or, God forbid, Sasha came home? But in this, as in other matters, Mrs Glinka gave me no choice. 'Off! Off! I'll fix it. Won't take a minute.'

She whipped my skirt away to the sewing machine in the

corner where she stitched two new seams, one down each side of the burgundy serge. I sat on a cold chair in my pants while she urged the pedal up and down. At the kitchen window, out of the corner of my eye, I could see the blur of a face. Sasha. Had to be. I blushed at the thought of him looking at me with my bare legs, dressed only a shirt and a pair of navy cotton knickers. He should know when not to look. I turned my head to meet his gaze, head on. For a slow second our eyes met. I crossed my legs. I waited to feel my inevitable, shameful blush, but my skin stayed cool and pale and my stare remained fixed. Only the sick astonishment in my mouth told me what a very terrible thing was happening. It couldn't be real that he was standing there watching me and that I was letting him. Then he pressed his nose to the window, turning it into a nasty porcine snout. I must have looked like a pig myself just then, with my thighs splayed out on the seat of the chair, which would make them look much fatter than they actually were. I laughed, even though he wasn't funny.

Soon as she saw my mouth twitch, Mrs Glinka shot a glance towards the window. But Sasha had already disappeared, leaving only a smudge of grease and breath where his face had been.

Ten minutes later, my skirt, updated, hugged my legs. I modelled, to Mrs Glinka's applause.

'I had legs like yours,' she said, 'when I used to be a dancer. Just like yours. Don't you dance? You must! You were born to dance. Anyone can see that.'

I knew if I stayed I'd get hot bread dipped in runny homemade jam. I could smell the loaves in the oven, sending my stomach crazy, but they'd not be done for an hour yet, and Millie liked me there when she got home from work. When the late afternoon made the cornfields rusty, I said my goodbyes.

I wheeled my bike out along the dirt track which led to the main road. Sasha was lolling on the front lawn, reading a motorbike magazine. His fringe flopped in front of his eyes so he kept having to brush it aside, slowly, lazily. He was naked except for a pair of khaki shorts. Above the waist band, on his lower back, the sunlit fuzz was brittle as spun sugar. As he propped himself up on his elbows, I had an uninterrupted view of his chest, with its subtle undulations of muscle and bone.

'Hey,' he said.

'Hey.' I stood in front of him, shielding my eyes from the sun. His voice, just the sound of one syllable, gave me vertigo.

'Want to see something, Freya?' He rose to his feet and gestured toward the garden shed.

No one had ever invited me behind a shed before. At primary school, boys had looked inside each other's shorts. Girls weren't really allowed, though, because they'd get into trouble, which seemed unfair, because the boys never did. Then in senior school the girls went behind the classroom to have a fag and they thought no one knew, but anybody with half a nose could tell what they'd been up to. So whatever eighteen-year-olds like Sasha did behind sheds must be far worse than looking down shorts of a puff or two of Silk Cut. Whatever he was offering, it was something I shouldn't be having.

He took my silence as a yes. He threw down his magazine and strolled away from the house. I hesitated for a few numbed seconds, then I laid my bike down on the path and followed him.

Behind the shed we were hidden both from the house and the road. He leaned against the lichened woodwork, took a tin from his pocket, pulled out a pre-rolled cigarette and offered it to me.

I shook my head. 'I don't smoke.'

He leaned closer. He smelled of alcohol from where he'd been lying on the half-fermented grass. He rolled the cigarette between his forefinger and thumb, like he was testing the rustle of a half corona.

'It's not a cigarette,' he said.

'A rollie, then.'

'Nah-uh. You a div or something? Can't you work it out?'

I should've replied with a laugh or a witty riposte, but I didn't know what I was riposting. He tore off the twisted end of his roll-up, then lit it. He dragged on the filter, inhaled deeply, exhaled slowly. The smoke had the same aniseedy whiff that hung around the Strawberry Fair on Midsummer Common.

When offered it to me, I shook my head.

'One drag.'

'Not interested.'

He smiled. 'No fun alone. One drag, and I won't tell my mum on you.'

'What d'you mean?'

'How you've turned up here, trying to corrupt me with illegal substances.'

'She won't believe you.'

'She can see your dark side. She's got the power. Rumours're all true – witchcraft alive and well. Me, though, I am without stain. The chosen one. I can do no wrong.'

'Dob me in, then,' I said. 'Nothing to tell.'

He paused, then grinned. 'You're right. Even if there was – something to tell, I mean – I still wouldn't. Not a dickie bird.' He leaned yet an inch closer. 'Perfect gentleman, me.'

'I'm not doing it.'

'Well, don't then. But think about it. You're bound to try spliff eventually, because everybody does. Even the Queen and Prince Philip and stuff.'

'They do not.'

'Don't be so naïve. You might as well try it while you're in safe hands, not pissed at a party or in some stinky tent at Glastonbury or a dodgy caff in Amsterdam.'

I couldn't imagine myself pissed at a party, let alone the other scenarios. Sasha's reasoning was just like my mother's was about alcohol, that administered by a knowledgeable adult, intoxicating substances lost their power to harm.

He held the joint to my lips.

I knew I'd be able to smoke it, because that was a genetic ability I'd have inherited from my mother. I'd watched her smoke for years. How hard could it be? I had no curiosity about the drug or its effects. I was sure, just like booze or anything else, it made people more stupid, and there was no need for that when people were really quite stupid already. But if I said no absolutely then Sasha might never speak to me again. Just a little try, just me pretending, that was all I'd need to do to keep the conversation going.

I took a tiny drag. I waited to feel choked, to cough and flounder. But instead, I gently let go of my breath. The merest thread of smoke unfurled from my parted lips.

'Clean lungs,' he said. 'Soaked it up like a sponge. Very nice.'

Beyond the shed, parti-coloured fields splayed flat before us – muzzy saffron tufts of oilseed rape. I could feel him next to me, his skin now only millimetres away from the fragile nylon of my shirt. He reached out his hand then ran his forefinger up the back of my neck, stroking the hairs the wrong way, so that every follicle prickled.

'Sasha! Phone!' Mrs Glinka shouted from inside the house.

He pushed me out into the sunlight. 'Go do your home-work.'

I was blinking – dazed.

'Go on. Shovey offy.' He made a shooing gesture towards my bike. 'Go home to your own mummy. You do have one, don't you?'

He turned on his heel and ambled towards the house.

He thought he'd got the better of me, but I didn't care. I'd seen the same thing in him that I felt in me: he was lonely.

I cycled down towards the main road, propelling myself as fast as I could along the raised centre between the ruts in the earth. Stones jolted the wheels beneath me, but I kept my balance. I didn't look back.

Sasha, I reminded myself, only had one over on me because he was half grown up already and could do what he liked. Apart from that, everything about me was better. He might have an IQ of 168, but because of his emotional problems, he couldn't even pass his exams. Plus my parents were richer, with a better house. Where you lived was very important – maybe the most important thing of all. Hugh was right about that.

Chez Hugh stood white and proud near the utmost edge of the city, where country gave way to town. The neighbours complained when we built it, but my father had a friend in the council planning office.

'I know!' he said. 'So out of sync with all the Edwardian round about. Bit naughty, really. But that's what makes it such very good fun.'

The most vital thing for my father was that our home should be tasteful. We had nothing furry or fluffy and absolutely no animal prints. No amateur stencilling round the walls, no furniture that wasn't either black, white or made of wood, and no carpets, wallpaper or radiators, even, because our heating came from beneath quarry floor tiles. Our walls weren't even plastered. Exposed brick, it was called, painted white and shiny.

'Very smart,' according to Hugh.

The wallpaper, fitted carpets and chandeliers preferred by

our donnish neighbours – these were not smart.

On the rare occasions we entertained, everyone told Hugh how contemporary he was. How amazing! How surprising! They were jealous, obviously. Sometimes they made nasty comments. Heating must cost a fortune. But you don't have any storage space. Doesn't look very lived-in. Gorgeous, yes, but not really a family home.

'But what is a family?' said Hugh. 'What is a home?'

That shut them up. My father was the expert. He understood what people really wanted and no one ever gave him credit for that.

I ran up into my bedroom, slipped off my shoes and flopped down on the bed. The humidity in the room squeezed against my ears. Sasha, I decided, was insignificant. It was his mother I came to see, not him. He had nothing to do with anything.

Downstairs the front door slammed. Millie's high heels clunked as she threw them on the floor and changed into the clogs Hugh hated because they reminded him of dinner ladies. Her footsteps, at first deafening, softened as she shuffled into the kitchen. I knew she'd be taking a bottle of wine from the fridge, then popping it open. Bin-end Chardonnay, she was guzzling back then, which was a bit of a come-down. A few years before, when Hugh was raking it in, she drank only champagne.

The back door opened then banged shut. My mother liked to sit outside on the lawn, luxuriating in her first proper drink of the day. She wouldn't come find me for ages yet: she needed her quiet time. Then she screamed. The noise was faint at first, distant, like the yelling in a swimming pool. Then I heard the back door flung open again. The noise grew louder.

'Freya!' she shouted.

I didn't move. I'd wait till she stopped her noise. I was still replaying Sasha's teasing. I'd forgive him, I supposed, because at least he'd spoken to me. And he'd given me drugs and he'd seen me without a skirt on and stroked my neck, which was more excitement really than I'd ever had in my life. I wished there was someone at school I dare tell about it.

'FREYA!' She shouted louder.

I got up slowly and walked downstairs, the wooden steps sticky against my bare feet.

She stood in the hallway. 'I'm sorry, sweetheart. So sorry.'

She reached out her hands. At first, I thought she was going to hug me, even though she never hugged me because that was my father's job. Then I saw how her fingers were smudged with blood. The blood looked wrong. My mother never handled meat because she didn't like the feel of it. If we had mince, she plonked it straight from the packet into the pan. Even when I was little and cut myself she dabbed on antiseptic with cotton wool so everything was clean, soon as. She never kissed it better. She must be sick or she'd hurt herself, perhaps, and I wished Hugh were there. My mother was terrible when she was ill. She'd never stay in her bedroom. She lay on the sofa in the sitting room, moaning and writhing. My father didn't mind getting her drinks and aspirin, but I hated it because I thought she was putting it on. So why the blood on her hands? What if she'd hurt herself on purpose so I'd feel guilty? Slit her wrists so I knew what a bad daughter I was? I wanted her to disappear.

'A dog must have got them,' she said. 'A fox, perhaps. Don't go out.'

'What d'you mean?'

'The…the outside. The rabbits.'

As I walked past her she tried to block my path, but I ducked underneath her arms, ran through the kitchen and out of the back door. I was cross with her then, because she should have just told me what'd happened. And she should never have tried to bar my way. I didn't care about the rabbits, but they were mine to look after. She'd no business interfering.

Out in the garden, the first thing wrong was their cage lying open. Then the air, which should have been loud with rabbity scratching, was silent.

The rabbits could've run, but they hadn't. Most were still lying in the cage, quiet and still. One of them just looked like it was sleeping, but when I touched it, its fur was cold.

The grass round the cage was covered with blood and fur and baby rabbits with their heads bitten off, or their bottom halves missing. I couldn't remember how many of them there'd been. I didn't know if it was worth putting them back together again, trying to work out if perhaps just one of them had escaped the carnage.

I closed my eyes. I thought when I looked again, the scene might have changed and they'd still be alive. But when I raised my eyelids, they were still lying there, mauled and terrified.

I felt the heat of my mother's body as she stood behind me. Her breath was harsh. I waited for her to lay her hand on my shoulder, letting me know that whatever had happened, I was still her little girl. Instead, she inched back minutely, as if she'd thought of touching me, but changed her mind.

I never even fed them that morning. I forgot, even though it was on my list. Perhaps it didn't matter. The fox came in the night, so in the morning, they were already dead, before I left for school.

But what if the fox came later?

Then the rabbits had died hungry.

My mother sighed and said, 'At least they had a nice life, while it lasted. I expect you'll still be wanting your dinner.'

✳ two ✳

Cambridge in summer looks nice enough on postcards, all punting down the river and Granchester cream teas, straw boaters and floppy sun hats – but none of that meant anything to me. From June to September, tourists clogged the pavements. They sat on any available bench or piece of wall, occupied every seat in every café, turning my town into a place to be looked at and not one where people did things. My family never went punting because we didn't know how. My father, I think, was too scared to try in case he looked like an idiot. In summer, 'specially since we had outdoor space as well as indoor, we retreated even further than usual into our own territory. This was supposed to be fun for me, because children liked gardens, but how, at my age, was I supposed to get excited by an anthill or a ladybird? Nevertheless, soon as the evenings grew light, my mother, father and I would sit outside during the televisual vacuum between the six o'clock news and dinner, bracing ourselves against the chill with cardigans and car rugs. My mother regarded our al fresco moments as a luxury of middle class life, which she could only dream of when she was growing up.

It's all very well for me to do her down, but Millie never had any privileges. Not to make allowances for that would just be churlish. She'd left school without any qualifications.

'Never did me any harm,' she said. 'Now, I suppose, you need a degree to scrub a bloody floor.' She never spoke of her schooldays, except to highlight some occasional horror. 'We went on a trip to the V and A. Had to bring a packed lunch. Bread and dripping, my mother gave me. Everybody laughed.' When she talked about her childhood, she was all hint and anecdote. She came from London, where we hardly ever went, even though I thought it was brilliant. 'Spend enough time in Croydon,' she said, 'and you'll change your mind.'

My parents weren't Cambridge people and there was nothing they liked about university life. They couldn't believe that people could go out to a lecture and call that entertainment. But even so, they'd decided that Cambridge was better than where they'd come from.

Hugh would say, 'You might not appreciate it here, but London's a shit hole. You've had a lucky escape.'

Whatever had happened to them in our nation's capital, they couldn't go back. They were refugees, almost as bad as Mr Glinka. Millie's family left London after her father died, which was before I was born.

'Liver cancer,' she told me. 'Does awful things to your breath. The old boy snuffed it six weeks later. Never complained. Never said he was in pain. Just told us he loved us, then he lay down and died.' Her dad collected toy cars and my mother wanted one to keep – nothing pricey – just a little

London bus or something. But my grandma sold the whole lot to some bloke who came to the funeral.

When I asked about my grandma, my mother said things like, 'Oh, she's marvellous. You'd love her. In fact, you remind me of her a bit.' But Millie hadn't spoken to her in years.

Hugh once said, when he was pissed, 'Your grandma, I'm afraid, is a bit of a bitch.' He'd only met her the once. 'She had dyed hair – squirrel red. Put her hand on my knee.' He paused to wink. 'Like mother like daughter.'

After Grandpa died, Grandma decided to have some fun. She sold the family house and went off and did things which Millie didn't like. Now she lived abroad, in Spain, maybe, but Millie always denied having her address or phone number. Maybe I'll go see her one day. My mother had a brother and a sister, too, Uncle Dave and Auntie Karen. I met them when I was little, but I couldn't remember them. 'Lucky you,' said Millie.

On the anniversary of her father's death, when she remembered, she bought a bottle of Scotch, even though she didn't like it, and drank it, because that's what her father would have wanted. She had her first drink when she was five, when her mother put brandy in her bedtime milk. Then, when her aunties came round, she'd have sip of their port and lemon. Later, when she was my age, she started going out on her own. No one noticed because her father was on shifts while her mother worked in a restaurant, taking reservations. Millie wishes she hadn't gone out now. She wishes she'd stayed in and done her homework. That's why I had to be different.

Grandpa didn't like having a wife who worked, but working is what women in my family do.

'You've got to work,' said Millie. 'Otherwise, how d'you get your running-away money? My mum had hers stashed under the bed. Half her friends did 'n' all.'

I'd looked under her bed and knew there was nothing there. 'Where's your running away money?' I asked.

She laughed. 'There are other ways.'

I wondered, if she ran away, would she take me with her?

My mother grew up fast, like I did. When she was my age she wore her mum's clothes. Then she went out to pubs and never needed any cash because the men bought her gin and tonics. In those days, no one ever expected a woman to put her hand in her pocket, she told me. 'By the time you're grown-up, it'll probably be the other way around. Blokes'll be sat there, looking pretty, while you're the one going to the bar.'

The girls in my class were downwardly mobile. Their grandparents said 'awf' when they meant 'off', just like Prince Charles. Millie's parents said 'orf', according to her, so at least my family were improving themselves. My mother poshed herself up when she started in the wine trade and since she'd come to Cambridge, she'd kept on poshing. She was always improving her appearance, too, which was very annoying of her, because I was supposed to be the pretty one by then. The way she viewed it, she was simply getting what she deserved. 'I'm in my prime, darling. I'm owed, see. Wasn't much to look at when I was younger.'

I'd seen a photo of her, from when she was working in a bar in Marble Arch. Her dark hair hangs limply down each side of face. Her face is puffy. She wears a pale suit – baby-blue, she told me. You can't tell on the picture, because it's black and white. Her plump fingers clutch onto a tiny purse. Her legs are straight, up and down, the same from thigh to ankle.

She grimaced when she showed me the picture, saying, 'The Sixties were living hell. I never cut it as a waif. Thank God for the Seventies, when you were finally allowed to have tits.' Now she was thin, but with hips and bust. 'Don't worry, Freya. You'll be the same. Watch and wait. Play the long game. And remember the secret to great boobs – never get fat and don't for God's sakes breastfeed.' I was never allowed anything that might be a bit tarty, but my mother needed to wear short skirts, tight tops and high heels, because where she worked they were all men. 'Sloanes, arseholes and wideboys,' she said. 'Most of them are all three.' If she didn't look attractive, the men wouldn't take her seriously. She complained a lot about work. They had management consultants in, who told her she wasn't efficient. 'They suggested I take a shower in the morning to wake myself up and maybe do yoga after work. Brilliant, aren't they? For this, they're paid two hundred pounds a day. Two hundred pounds.'

She had to work because somebody in the house needed a proper job: those readymade lasagnes from Sainsbury's didn't pay for themselves. Hugh was sometimes rich, sometimes poor. When he was rich his constantly updated cars never lost their delicious industrial perfume. But the trouble with him being in business was that when everyone else was strapped, so was he. Even in our town there were clever people with good degrees who couldn't get a job, not even one that was beneath them. His car had stopped smelling lovely a couple of years ago, and my latest bike was second hand out of the paper, which meant it was probably nicked. I never asked my father for money for school trips to stately homes, or to the theatre. I mostly just helped myself out of his change bowl. Proper mothers might not work, but they had lots of children – two or three at least. Samantha Burgess was number three out of seven and her father was a professor of medieval history. She should have been at Braxton Girls', but like me, she needed a scholarship. She told me, 'Daddy's so clever that a couple of children would be a waste of his genetic material. Thick people have loads of kids and clever people don't have enough. That's why society's gone down the tubes.'

The only problem with what Samantha was saying was that you needed two clever parents, if possible. Loads of the academic dads, though, they married thick women. That way, when there was an argument at home, they could always be right. When I told Mrs Glinka my theory, she nodded enthu-siastically. She'd thought exactly the same thing.

'That's right, Freya! They think baby will have daddy's brains and mummy's legs.'

'And baby ends up with mummy's brains and daddy's legs?'

'Precisely. You know what the Greeks thought? That cere-bral, spinal and seminal fluid were all the same thing. The mother was a hatchery. She only provided the physical body of the child, whereas mind and spirit came from dear old dad.'

'But the Greeks were wrong,' I said.

Mrs Glinka shrugged. 'Look at the evidence. Biology is cruel.'

Lots of families had five or six children and they weren't Catholics even. If you only had a couple of kids, then how could you prove what good parents you were? Hugh and Millie had let the side down with only having one. Maybe they didn't think their genes were worth more than one go. And probably, although they denied it, I was a mistake. I didn't know any other families where there were more children than parents, except for the Glinkas, and it wasn't their fault.

'I wanted legions of them,' said Mrs Glinka. 'But my cervix, it made too much acid.'

Millie lounged on the lawn sipping her after-work sundowner. 'Lovely. First the day blurs. Then slowly, the fuzz. Like swallowing a duvet. Soft. Safe.' The lawn was clean now, since Hugh had gone at it with the hose. Plus it'd rained a couple of times. I still didn't like going out there, but Millie said I had to: otherwise I'd get a phobia and I'd never recover, because there was no way we could afford a shrink. My mother's pay check must have just hit her bank account, because she was drinking kir royale made with almost real champagne. She stretched out her long bare legs. She wore a short skirt and a diaphanous pink georgette blouse, and you could see how she was wearing a lacy bra. I was never allowed to have my bra showing.

She offered me her glass, but I shook my head.

She helped herself to another three inches of bubbles. 'You should get used it. Social lubrication and all that. That's why my mum always let me drink at home. So my first taste of strong liquor wouldn't come from the hands of a man.' She glugged back the rest of her glass.

My mother drank for a living – literally. Her firm supplied wines to colleges, and she tasted it, bought it, sold it. 'Plonk, mostly. Atrocious crates of Fitou they flog at the buttery to students who should know better. High table's not much better. Bit of claret, buckets of port. Good stuff only comes out for feasts.'

'I thought the colleges were rich. Thought they had cellars worth thousands,' I said.

'Some do. Trinity. Corpus. Kings. They'll send the wine butler down to London to get patronised by some toff. Our ones – Robinson and Fitz – they're the modern afterthoughts full of kids from comps. We get some nervous Chemistry tutor on a tight budget, trying to bargain us down. They're all alkies round here. Acceptable vice in this town. You're not a drunk, are you, if you only drink fine wines?'

Most people's parents drank, as I'd learned from the girls at school, but not until after homework. The mothers regarded their children's homework as theirs as well. The dads helped with the maths, while the mothers read set texts and discussed essays. The girls didn't get better marks than I did, though, which suggested their parents weren't as clever as they thought. When the daughters got Bs and Cs, the parents went spare, rang the school and demanded to know why. The parents with the highest standards had the maddest kids. Two girls in my year were already rexic. They were perfectionists, according to Connie. One of them was a baby bird with feathers for hair. She wore two jumpers, one on top of the other, no matter how hot it was.

Hugh strode out onto the lawn, glass in hand, and sat on the chair next to Millie's. He helped himself to a generous glug of wine. As he set the bottle down, his hands trembled.

Now that my parents were half-sozzled, I considered mentioning my school's summer fête. They wouldn't want to come, but at the same time, for reasons I failed to understand, they'd be offended if I didn't invite them. St Joan's annual open day promised several unappealing entertainments – a performance from the school dance troupe, Daughters of Terpsichore and an Andrew Lloyd Webber medley played by the orchestra. My mother usually took such invitations as a personal slight. For instance, if I ever said anything about Sports Day, she went mental. 'Sports Day! Watch you run around all day and never win anything? Wearing some hideous pair of burgundy knickers? You can't seriously expect me to take time off work for that? Don't any of the other bloody mothers have a job?'

The end of the academic year was a bad time if you wanted to keep your parents away from school. Sports Day, concerts, charity auctions – they all blurred the happy divide between my life and theirs. Even when I was at primary school, my mother didn't look right. I was always proud of Hugh, of course, but fathers didn't really count. Girls judged each other by their mothers: they were who we were going to be when we grew up.

Other girls' mothers didn't work, or if they did, they didn't do much. They spent a couple of hours each week giving supervisions to undergrads. They could only teach boring stuff no one else cared about, like mediaeval French, or they did part-time secretarial work for their husbands. Other girls got home from school to find a glass of milk and homemade peanut butter cookies, or Jaffa cakes, at the very least. Then they got tested on their French irregular verbs before dinner. Other girls were shocked that I came back to an empty house and processed food. Millie didn't cook. We were the first family in our street to own a microwave. Back then, I was a tragic anomaly.

'You eat chips! Made in an oven?' Jessica nearly passed out when I told her.

What can I say? I was ahead of my time.

Whenever Millie and Hugh came back from parents' evenings, they'd never bothered to see all my teachers and they claimed not to remember a word of what had been said about me. My parents were both total epsilons at school, so they didn't really care about how I was doing.

'Steady or stellar, darling,' said my father. 'Just as long as you're happy.'

Of course, I wasn't happy. But that was a separate issue.

Whenever they came to St Joan's, Hugh complained about the hard chairs, and Millie raged about the crappy refreshments. My mother couldn't believe how appallingly my teachers dressed. 'Where do they get their clothes? Second hand shops wouldn't dare sell such horrors. Catalogues, maybe? From Eastern Europe?' This, I felt, was a dig at the Glinkas. 'What's more,' she added, 'you don't appear to be taught by a single person who has a waist.'

My teachers spent their days in an almost completely female environment, so fashion didn't really matter. That was good, I thought.

St Joan's had only two male teachers: Mr Lewis who taught German and Mr Simms, our head of Maths. Mr Lewis was so old, Tutenkamun was probably his best friend at school. He was single, the girls in the year above said, because of some medical condition which meant that he could never have a full married life.

The other man, Mr Simms, did have a married life, though nobody knew if it was full or not. In his forties, Mr Simms looked at the world through sad, bored eyes. Like most of our teachers, he clearly loathed his job. Although school dress code was really strict about footwear – for staff and pupils – he wore trainers, not shoes – ones with Velcro on. His suits were brown – a size too large, as if he hoped to grow into them. He had knitted ties and yellow shirts that were a bit shiny. 'They're polycotton,' said Jane Delaware, who was doing needlework for GCSE. 'You shouldn't wear that for work. Makes you smell.' We weren't likely to fall in love with either of the men at St Joan's. That's probably why they were hired.

The last time Millie and Hugh came to school, they went to a play that one of the English teachers wrote. A group of English schoolgirls was washed up on a desert island and then they had to escape before the cannibals ate them. My parents were really embarrassing. They didn't like it when the cannibals were played by two Asian girls and Mimi from Nigeria.

Millie whispered, way too loudly, in my ear. 'I'm hardly PC, but this really takes the biscuit.'

When the big cauldron for boiling the white girls came on, my parents stormed out of the hall and made me come with them. Then the next Monday, I had go in to see the deputy head, while she explained that Saleema and Jaswinder and Mimi were all really happy to be cannibals in the play, so there wasn't a problem. Next time, Hugh and Millie weren't coming, no matter what. Of course the play was racist, but only unintentionally – anyone could see that. My parents had simply used some dubious moral principle as an excuse to leave.

Of all the school events my mother despised, the fête was definitely in the top three.

'Fête worse than death,' she said, every year, then laughed at her own joke.

Even though I had a scholarship, my parents still had to pay some school fees. Then, for the fête, Millie, who never cooked – not really – was supposed to make fairy cakes for the sale. Then people wouldn't even buy her cakes, not until last, because they weren't as good as the ones the proper mothers made. Last year, Samantha Burgess looked at the wonky coffee layer sponge Millie had made out of a packet and said, 'It's really all right, Freya. She just doesn't have the time. When I have children, I won't be working. What's the point in having kids if you never even see them?'

The final insult for Millie was that she was supposed to buy other mothers' cakes. So my parents ended up paying for the fête three times over, once through school fees, then by making cakes, and then by buying other cakes, which they never even ate. My mother tended to prefer her carbohydrates in liquid form.

I decided to try reverse psychology, like we learned in History and Society.

I told them, 'You really don't have to be there, but it'd be great if you did. The fête only lasts a couple of hours. And there'll be a cake sale. Everybody else's parents are coming.'

My mother flinched. The thing I said about everybody else's parents, that really annoyed her. Anything that everybody else did was bad. But that afternoon, Hugh saw Millie's wince. He gave her a stern look. She glared back at him, but it was no good. She'd made a mistake and so had I.

He gave me his most encouraging smile. 'Course we'll come, Freya. It'll be marvellous, I'm sure. Are you dressing up?'

School was my life – the job I never applied for. It was torture: the long assemblies, arcane sports, projects about the rubber tapping industry in Malaysia. I wanted to fall asleep and wake up when I was eighteen.

St Joan's was mediocre – out and proud. The best girls' school in Cambridge was Braxton Girls'. At Braxton Girls', the daughters of academics sweated blood for seven years straight so they could go to Oxbridge, preferably to a good college – not a women's one. But Braxton Girls' didn't give scholarships because it didn't need to. When I was eleven and I should've been going to Braxton Girls', Hugh was already tightening his belt. He enrolled me at St Joan's, a school famous for turning farmers' daughters into young ladies. I begged him not to make me go. I'd rather've gone to a comprehensive, even. But Millie backed him up.

'Freya,' she said, 'No child of ours is ending up a pikey.'

St Joan's was an edifice without presence. Squeezed among a cluster of pokey urban streets, from the outside it was nothing more than a few tall spindly terraced houses, with unpainted brickwork the colour of weak tea. Inside, the building was slightly too small. The corridors, which smelled permanently of chicken, were so narrow that we had to walk to the left, like we were driving a car. Later architectural innovations had been less than successful. The music block was a cube of congealed blood. We studied low prestige subjects like needlework in portakabins. Portakabin was a euphemism, I soon realised, for shed. These prefab shacks were better suited to builders' fag breaks then the edification of impressionable girls.

When it was founded, St Joan's taught three main subjects – French, needlework and piano. A hundred years later, these were still the core curriculum. Needlework was the worst. I spent three years sewing one bolero jacket. When I finished

34

it, it was puckered, pie-bald, and out of fashion.

Millie told me to put up with it. 'They only have needle-work so the thick girls can be good at something.'

On fête day, lessons ended at morning break so we'd have time to theme our rooms. My form chose the Wild West, which meant we laid out our choc chip muffins on gingham table cloths and labelled them Cowboy Cakes. Millie, instead of baking, gave a bottle of Jack Daniel's to the raffle.

My father was instantly worried about our contribution. 'Bit mean, isn't it? Shouldn't we be giving half a case or something?'

'No!' I said. 'Please don't. You can't afford it. And if you give too much, you look flash. That's why you do cakes, which aren't supposed to cost anything, even if they do.'

Although people in Cambridge were quite well-off, you could never tell by looking at them. Like my teachers, most parents were scruffy. They never had perms or highlights and if they dyed their hair, they did it at home. The only giveaway they'd got cash was that they had nice teeth and never wore tracksuits except when they were exercising. They drove second-hand cars and only did home improvements when bits started falling off of their house. The idea was that the worse you looked, the cleverer you must be.

The girls in my form still cared about how they looked, though. We'd been talking about what to wear for the fête for ages now. Wild West wasn't really very good for costumes. We only had a few choices. Cowboys (too butch), Indians (something not quite right about that), or jailbait saloon girls. And of course, we wanted to look pretty.

If Miss Castellano, our form teacher, found it disturbing to see twenty underage girls got up as strumpets, she didn't let on. My classmates wore fishnet stockings with their skirts safety-pinned up, so you could see their suspender tops and slim white thighs. Connie Darke wore false eyelashes which she'd stuck on with a special glue, one by one. She looked about thirty. She jiggled her corseted boobs in my direction. 'What you gawping at, Freya? Like what you see?'

Connie was a friend – on paper, at least – so I couldn't object.

Jessica, who was my actual friend – not just on paper – hadn't chosen her oufit well. She'd bought her crushed velvet gown which hugged every one of her childish curves. Her tummy stuck out in front of her like the belly of one of those starving children from Ethiopia. The scarlet she'd painted her mouth made her skin and teeth look yellow. But although you were supposed to tell your best friend the truth, I couldn't bring myself. She might return the favour.

On the day of the fête, I didn't look as gross as I thought I would. Because I didn't dress up as a whore, I didn't compete with the other girls, who were planting ostrich feathers in their hair and tearing holes in each other's fishnets. Two other girls had dressed as a cowboy as well – Trisha Montague, who was too porky to look decent in a skirt, and Rachel Larson, who everyone said was a lezza.

I was a bit upset with Mrs Glinka, because she hadn't just shortened Sasha's jeans, but she'd put a tasselled fringe on as well, along the outside legs, so now I looked a bit like I was trying too hard. Also, she decided that Hugh's belt was no good. Instead, she got me a string of cartridges.

'Sasha's dyedushka wore them at the siege of Leningrad,' she said.

At one o'clock the fête started and our customers drifted through the classroom. They bought up the lemon drizzle cakes really really fast, and some of them pinned the tail on the sheriff's horse. Every class was supposed to compete to raise the most money, but I could tell my form wasn't really trying. We were too old for that already.

I hadn't bothered to get a good job, like being on the cake sale stand. I didn't want to sell stuff, anyhow. To do that, you had to use customer service skills, which I was pretty sure I didn't have, so I said I'd set up stalls and clear up rubbish. Connie and Jessica were bar room floozies, draping their legs over tables and grinning at alarmed dads. The parents were like one cloned parent, stumbling through our classroom again and again. The mothers wore Laura Ashley dresses – flowery and drippy. The fathers wore suits, like they'd just rushed from work, and the whole fête thing was just a monster waste of time and children were an unutterable inconvenience.

When Hugh and Millie arrived, I spotted them instantly. In the meadow of flowers, my mother was all in black, harsh as an exclamation mark. She looked around her and sniggered.

'What's the theme? Vicars and tarts? Or brothel a go-go? You're a pimp, I suppose, Freya. Good choice.'

As soon as they came within sniffing distance, I could tell they were two sheets to the wind. They had flushed cheeks and glassy teddy bear eyes. Millie must've taken a half day off work then swung by Hugh's office. I could picture the scene. 'Shall we go for lunch, darling? My treat. Nice bottle of Bordeaux.'

She was 'on' that day at the fête — smiling, laughing, waving to any of my classmates she recognised. She paused to chat with my form teacher.

'Marvellous blouse, Miss Castellano. How retro! Where did you find it?'

Miss Castellano's blouse that day was particularly horrible, with a swirly pattern the colour of sick. That meant my mother was being a total bitch.

When Millie and Hugh finished their walkabout they meandered out of my form room and into the one next door, thank God. Soon it'd be the raffle, and that meant the end of the day. I was hoping we could leave before the orchestra started on Joseph and his Technicolour Dreamcoat.

Connie watched my mother leave. 'She's gorgeous. Amazing skin.'

I'd never thought of my mother's skin as amazing or not. It was just this stuff that covered her body. 'You think she's pretty?' I said.

'God, yes!' Connie nodded. 'She doesn't look like you at all.'

I didn't believe that Connie was trying to be mean when she

said that. It was like they told us in the Welcome to Life section of our On Being a Young Woman course. If you're not sure whether someone's being nasty or not, then it's a good idea to assume they're actually being nice. If you pretend that the world is a good place, then the world will be a good place.

I took off the cartridge belt and stowed it in my schoolbag then trudged downstairs to the garden. Because I went to a girls' school stuck in the centre of town, we didn't have nice grounds. We didn't even have a sports field, which meant we had to play hockey at the boys' school down the road. But we did have a garden – a couple of acres of lawn. Occasionally, in Biology, they let us root around the bedding plants, lifting rocks to count the woodlice. And in summer, Miss Gillis, my Class Civ teacher, sometimes let us have our lesson outdoors. 'Why read about nature when we can experience nature?' she said.

I found my father right away, lounging up against a tree, reading a pamphlet. He glanced up as I approached.

'Look what I've bought,' he said. 'Solution of how to do a Rubik's cube.'

'But no one does them anymore. No one's done them for years.'

'You can still buy them, though. You never wanted one, but I did. I'm going to get one. Won't that be fun?'

Hugh could be strange sometimes. It wasn't my fault if he'd missed out on the Rubik's cube, when he was a grown-up who could buy any stupid thing he wanted.

'Where's Millie?' I asked. 'I want to go.'

'Roundabout some place. Find her, then we'll skedaddle. I saw her heading that way.' He pointed in the direction of the needlework block.

It wasn't like there were lots of places she could be. We didn't even have any big trees to hide behind, because they all blew down in the storm of '82.

The needlework annexe comprised of two low-slung portakabins wedged behind the netball courts. The lights were off and the doors were locked, which meant no one was there. I was turning back when I heard a laugh – my mother's laugh, rasping and seductive – the laugh of a cute pony.

There, in the gap between the classroom and the school wall, Millie stood, puffing on a cigarette. Next to her, smoking too, was my Maths teacher, Mr Simms. His baldness shone in the sunlight. Every time a cloud went past it changed the pattern of light and shade on his head. Mr Simms looked like a man who'd just told a very funny joke.

I stood watching, waiting for them to notice me. They were going to feel very guilty very soon.

I coughed.

Millie giggled when she saw me. 'Naughty mummy.' She stamped her fag into the tarmac beneath her feet. 'Just couldn't wait. I was gasping.'

Mr Simms sniggered. 'Me, too. If we'd been out here much longer, half the staff room would have joined us. You're a lucky girl, Freya. Your mum just about saved my life.'

He threw his cigarette end on the ground. He tried to put it out with his Velcro-fastened trainer, but it rolled away. He flashed a grin at my mother before walking off.

Millie gave him a little wave goodbye, then turned back to me. 'No scowly nasty face. This is life, darling. We all have feet of clay. Although with some of us, of course, it's not just the feet.'

'What about Daddy? Won't he mind?'

I thought of her flirtatious glances at Mr Simms. I wished my mother could read my mind. She'd shrivel up if she could. She'd throw herself down on the ground and beg my forgiveness.

She sighed. 'Your Daddy...Daddy doesn't mind about anything. And that, my darling, is rather the problem.'

✳ three ✳

Some men fall in love with their daughters. One day she's not an annoying kid any more – instead, she becomes a beauty to be entertained, treated, guarded. I was still waiting to become Hugh's princess, because as yet Millie was the only woman in his life. At best, I was my father's buddy – at worst, his side-kick. When he made a joke, it was my job to laugh or a raise my eyebrows. We were a couple of down-to-earth chaps kidding around, while Millie was some crazy chick we had to keep in line.

My mother merely found my puberty amusing, I think. When I was eight and my unwelcome breasts appeared, she sniggered about my joining the club of womanhood. I cringed, especially since membership of this particular society seemed to offer no advantages whatsoever. The other girls never stopped staring at me. By the time I was ten, the zip at the front of my gymslip strained with the pressure from my not-flat-enough chest, while the skirt skimmed my crotch. Builders whistled at me on my way to primary school. When Mary Collingwood came up to me and said, 'I feel sorry for you,' she was only saying what everybody else thought. My father went through a brief phase of uneasy protectiveness, so when I opened the door to the postman, say, he'd hover in the background, glowering at this potentially predatory male. Soon as he saw I wasn't about to be abducted into the white slave trade, he went back to telling me about football and the history of the Second World War (specialist subject British naval vessels).

By his own admission, my father was going into decline. The early Eighties, he said, was his floruit. This meant it was the time when he did all his important stuff.

'Look at Renaissance artists,' he told me. 'Five years, ten years. All their greatness, packed into less than a hundred months. Everything before and everything after – futile, spent.' I think he'd seen some documentary or other and the point hit home.

'We work our whole lives, Freya. Unless we're dossers. Most of us'll never do anything worth a bean. And for those of us who do make it, the great work, the real work, it happens in a moment.'

1982 to 1987 were his golden years. He looked at Cambridge and saw opportunity. Back then, like now, there weren't enough family houses. Dons, till the twentieth century, lived in college and were supposed to be celibate. The university owned most of the undeveloped land and planned on keeping it that way. Then in the Eighties, when the colleges turned their plots on the outskirts of town into science parks, that was the beginning of proper money. If I was Thatcher's child, Hugh was her boyfriend. At Mrs Thatcher's say-so, he bought big and sold bigger. In tree-lined avenues he replaced old fireplaces and papered the walls with Victorian prints. In the urban pads he built for the new technocracy, he painted the walls white and ripped out skirting boards, picture rails and ceiling roses.

All the while, he was building our fantasy house. To some it appeared scary – a blanched fortress. But inside, the high ceilings and cosy bedrooms provided us with luxurious comfort. Our house told the world that we were shamelessly nouveau riche. Two Nobel Prize winners lived on our street (one Physics, one Medicine), but Hugh made more money than either of them. Millie used to have a go at him.

'But sweetie, why are we bothering? We will simply never fit in.'

He patted her knee. 'Grain of sand, sweetheart. That's what makes the pearl.'

The comparison didn't quite work for me. Hugh was the grit, not the oyster. But no one likes to see themselves as grit.

The weekend before Hugh and I were going down to Eastbourne to see his father, in our On Becoming a Young Woman course, Mrs Rally decided to teach us about life and death. Mrs Rally was a pink-cheeked RE teacher who wore mint green Bennetton jumpers, pleated tartan skirts and sensible sandals. 'What are we all here for?' she asked.

'We just are,' said Samantha Burgess. 'Life has no purpose.' Samantha Burgess was an existentialist, even though the school had a definite policy against atheism.

'We're here have fun,' said Connie.

'We're here to be nice to other people,' said Lucy Saville. That was a wet answer, deliberately aimed at buttering up the teacher.

Mrs Rally shook her head in disappointment. 'We're here because God made us. Our life and death are in his hands. Our real life only starts after our death – that's what Jesus died to give us.'

'And what if we don't believe in Jesus?' asked Connie.

Mrs Rally looked very sad just then. 'I'm afraid, in that case, then you won't be going to heaven.'

Samantha Burgess burst into tears.

It was Hugh's dad who started him in the property game. Grandpa Eric lived in Eastbourne – the necropolis, Millie called it. Grandpa Eric had rosy pink cheeks same as my father's when he'd been drinking. He mostly sat and watched television with a solemn, inquiring look on his face, like he was a Roman emperor who'd been set down in the wrong century and was now wondering what to do next. His straggly eyebrows enhanced his regal air. I thought the eyebrows were rather sweet, but they made Millie furious. 'Nurses should trim the poor old sod. They obviously don't give a toss.' My mother got rid of all Hugh's weird hair as soon as it appeared, because it was bad for business. I wouldn't be inheriting it, though, because unwanted face fluff was like haemophilia. As my mother said, 'Women carry the gene, men carry the can.'

Hugh usually visited his father alone, but once a year I came with. It didn't really occur to me that Grandpa Eric was too young to be in a home. I knew other people's grandpas still had jobs or went to India to spread the word of the Lord, or won prizes for growing oversized marrows.

'Who's this, Bertie? New girlfriend?

'I'm Freya,' I corrected him. I didn't know whether he was joking or not. True, I was an early developer. (I hated that phrase. It wasn't a compliment.) But no way did I look like someone's girlfriend.

My father whispered in my ear. 'He's got a lot worse. Thinks I'm his brother, Bertie. I know Bertie liked them young, but I didn't think he was a paedophile.'

Grandpa Eric whistled the tune of a music hall song he used to sing before he forgot the words. 'You've let yourself go, Bertie. Great shame. Great shame.'

I asked my father once whether he liked my grandpa.

'Tricky one that,' he replied. 'He's my role model, so if I hate him…Well…'

Grandpa Eric and Grandma Lily had once lived in Brighton, where my father grew up. When asked him whether he'd enjoyed it, he'd shrug and say, 'Never thought about it. The town's changed quite a bit, you know. Back then it was cheap and grotty, all flaking Georgian grandeur and nasty little shops selling knocked-off antiques. Not much for a kid 'cept swimming in the sea the two times a year I wouldn't get frost-bite. Can't imagine moving back, specially not now it's gone chi-chi – all juice bars and his 'n' his leather hotpants.'

My father was born in South Kensington in a red brick purpose-built flat with a communal garden and a French patisserie over the road. It's rather grand, I know, because he took me there once. He wanted to show me what Grandpa Eric had pissed up the wall. Grandpa Eric had money, from the property he'd inherited from his father.

'Rich enough,' said Hugh, 'to be a gentleman.'

Grandpa Eric's father, my great grandfather, who barely went to school and never had a leg-up in life, thought his son would be a success. He thought Eric would become an MP or at least be called to the Bar. But Eric went to some posh school where he didn't learn that much, but met a lot of people who were richer than him. Eric learned from the other boys how to spend money, something he turned out to be very good at.

'It's not like he blew it on loose women and coke,' my father told me once. 'He's incompetent, not venal.'

Jessica said it was OK to have a few bad eggs in the family fridge. She told us, 'My Great Uncle Cosmo was a transvestite. He had parties for it and everything. Total scandal at the time. The ladies were very jealous of his slim calves.'

When we'd learned about tolerance at school, Mrs Rally had told us that we weren't to make jokes about minorities, even if the jokes were funny. I wondered whether transvestites were a minority. Transvestism was clearly OK if you were a woman – like me dressing up as a cowboy wasn't funny or strange. But if you were a man, it was some kind of perversion or slur on women. I didn't really understand that.

*

Eric's wife, my grandmother Lily, died years before I was born.

'Why aren't there any women in this family?' I asked.

In my house, women outnumbered men by two to one, but I didn't have any grandmas, or aunties – not ones I knew – or even girl cousins.

Hugh said that girls were a bother. 'Same at any age. Just ask around.'

'So you'd rather I was a boy?'

'Course not,' he said.

I wasn't convinced.

He wasn't clear about exactly how Eric had squandered our fortune. It all took a long while – so long that even Eric didn't notice. Hugh never saw his father much. 'My father was a useless piece of shit. But frankly, I don't blame him. Mummy didn't help. She was very demanding. Depression, it was. In those days, they called it nerves.'

Hugh went to his father's old boarding school, even though it was rubbish, he said. 'Everyone hates those places – anyone with an ounce of sense. Fathers develop this fear. If their sons don't go to the same dreadful place and suffer like they did, then they won't be able to understand them. And so it goes on.'

When he came home in the holidays, he saw things going quietly to pot. Summer in France in a decent little hotel became summer in Scotland somewhere not quite so decent. No more tea at The Savoy: now it was scones at home instead. One summer holiday he came home to a different house, in Notting Hill, not South Ken. Then they moved further west, to a semi in Ealing. In the end, they left for Brighton, and not to a nice bit. There was no more money for boarding school and Hugh got sent to the local one instead. At least it was a grammar: he'd have been crucified at a secondary mod.

Grandma Lily didn't care where she was living, since life under one duvet was much the same as another. One day she never came out from the duvet at all. 'Mothers little helpers.' My father got teary. 'Doctor should've been horsewhipped.' Grandma Lily was cold and still and not yet forty – not even as old as Millie. My father was philosophical about it. 'A shitty childhood was pretty much standard issues in those days. Kids weren't supposed to have fun. Besides, who wants to be too happy growing up? Adulthood's a horror. Best get used to it, soon as.'

Maybe it's ancestral, my family's poor relationship with the medical profession. My parents had a no-illness policy which meant only my mother had permission to be poorly or have days off work. I'd been allowed to have chicken pox and whooping cough when I was younger but I'd never been able to miss school, not since Millie went back to work full-time. Now I'm grown-up, I never go to hospital. I had to take a friend in once when she broke her ankle jumping over a wall when we were pissed. I made the jump and she didn't, so it somehow became my fault. We sat waiting for X-ray for so many hours I thought I'd scream. She kept asking me to get her hot chocolates from the vending machine, but just the smell of them made me want to be sick. My revulsion made her upset and I didn't have the words to tell her why.

Eric smiled when Hugh handed him a pair of socks, clumpy, green and flecked with orange. 'Wool?' He sat the socks on his laps and stroked them like they were a cat.

'Had them knitted specially.' My father patted Eric's hand. Eric's skin was thin as the rice paper Mrs Glinka put at the base of her macaroons.

'Good boy. You were always a good boy.'

Hugh leaned forward, kissed his father on the cheek. I did the same.

'You'll be back tomorrow?' said Eric, as we got up to leave.

'Soon,' said Hugh. 'Soon.'

We went down to the seafront and Hugh bought us chips. At home we only ever had oven chips, white and floppy. These ones were made out of real potatoes, Hugh said. They were fat and heavy and stuck to the bag.

'Not crispy, though,' he said. 'They've only fried them once, not twice.'

We sat on a bench and stared out towards the beach. I could smell salt, but I wasn't sure whether it came from the chips or the sea.

'Does he know whether we come back next week or next year?' I asked.

'Possibly. He'll start fading faster, that's what the nurses say.'

'Why does he live down here? We could visit him more often if he lived nearer.'

'He wouldn't like to move, not now. Still thinks he's in South Ken. And he's a handful. Mind like a sieve, legs like

Tonto. He's always running off and then they have to track him down in some amusement arcade. Couldn't bring him up our way, stick him in the middle of a field.'

I tried to imagine Grandpa Eric stuck in a field like some confused scarecrow. I'd looked up Alzheimer's in our home medical dictionary so I knew it was hereditary, maybe, and I could well end up like that myself. Euthanasia might be legal by then, though, so I could opt out all together. I'd already made my parents get rid of our aluminium milk pan, because aluminium makes you go senile, but we still had cakes made of cake mixes and they were full of the stuff. Mentally, I was on borrowed time.

I turned to my father. 'When you're old I'll have to look after both of you, won't I? It was a bit selfish of you to have just one kid.'

I expected him to laugh, but instead his mouth went thin. 'We did have a natter about that, your mum and me. We'll just stagger along, propping each other up till one of us drops off the perch. Then whoever's left'll just get on with it.'

I thought of my parents being together till death did they part. 'But what if you stagger apart, not together? What'd I do then?'

'Your mother and I – we do have the odd tiff, but who does-n't? Sorry if we've ever worried you, sweetheart. We're soulmates, her and me. There's nothing I wouldn't do for her. Do you believe me?'

I did believe him, more or less, because I saw the way he looked at her sometimes, with this silly look on his face. But

I'd rather they held hands more, or went out on date night, like Jessica's parents did. They were highly deficient in public displays of affection and should've made more effort in this regard, if only to reassure me.

'Did Grandpa Eric love Grandma Lily?' I asked.

He stared out into the English Channel. 'He loved her very much, I think. Never remarried after she died, though he had his chances. Never considered divorce, even when things were dicey, to say the least. No one in our family ever gets divorced. We take our vows seriously.'

He was trying to reassure me, but actually he was freaking me out. I wasn't sure I'd ever want forever with anyone – not even Sasha. When would I have time to be me?

I didn't finish my chips. The ketchup on them was sour and dribbly.

'If you could have chosen which one would die,' I asked, 'Would it have been your mother or him?'

'Used to think I was lucky to have any kind of parents. Now I suppose I'd rather not be bothered any more. Does that seem very terrible to you, Freya?'

I met his gaze. 'No. I understand completely.'

While Millie poshed herself up, Hugh had to do the opposite. In Brighton my father flattened his public school vowels into Estuary English, or whatever came before it. His father, once a property owner, was now a commercial estate agent. Eric drove round all day, scouting out empty hairdressers' and newsagents'. At night, instead of doing his homework, Hugh sat next to his dad with a thesaurus open. He read out adjectives to put in property details – words like 'capacious' and 'sympathetically-decorated.'

There was no university for my father. That was the Sixties, he explained. 'No one bothered.'

Maybe Eric had already started losing his marbles. It'd explain why all the money disappeared.

At eighteen, my father ran away to the south of France. He tells loads of stories about those lost years and most of it, I think, is a lie. He says he worked as a gigolo, living on yachts and mixing Snowballs for the wives of wealthy businessmen. They paid him, he said, in cigarette cases and one time, with a motorbike. My father shouldn't have told me he was once a prostitute, I don't think. Maybe there was one woman and one cigarette case. He does have quite a good French accent. Plus women seem to like him – women in shops and restaurants. He dresses OK and he's not got fat and he does Norwegian army physical jerks every morning. When he came back to England, Grandpa Eric's estate agency was nigh-on kaput, so my father seized the reins while Eric made the tea. He started getting up early and working late, doing sums on the backs of envelopes, spending all day on the phone. He's done that ever since, pretty much. Other girls' fathers mostly have jobs, but Hugh never has – not really. My father always made things happen. And when everything went tits up, he never made a fuss. He was used to it. 'Respect the chaos,' he said.

When I looked deep into his eyes I saw more than a yellowing cornea with broken blood vessels. The bright silver flecks in his hazel eyes were the stars which guided me. My father, those eyes said, was special. If I stuck with him, I'd always be safe and one day he'd tell me all the secrets of the universe.

Looking back, it seems like the housing crash happened overnight, but when you lived through it, it happened little by little. First houses got snapped up. Then they took a couple of weeks to sell. Then a month, then more than a month and so on. At home, the same thing happened. We didn't get poor all at once – just bit by bit.

My going to St Joan's rather than Braxton Girls' was simply my father being careful, though. When I started senior school he was riding high on the hog – he just didn't like the thought of shelling out seven years' full-rate school fees. To a businessman, it looked like a poor deal with no guaranteed return. It wasn't like I had grandparents who'd sub my education. When I looked around me, I saw the depth of the other girls' wealth. It wasn't just their dads who earned good money: all their family were comfortable and middle or even upper-class. Uncles, aunts, cousins – they knew how to sail, tie a bow-tie and that port went one way, snuff the other. My family had no safety net. Interest rates were rocketing and our future was mortgaged up to the hilt.

Millie fumed about the school uniform she was expected to buy. I needed two pairs of shoes – one outdoors, one indoors – plus a blazer, jumper, skirt, three shirts, three summer dresses, one duffel coat, one mac, white socks, burgundy woolly tights, plus gym kit, hockey stick, tennis racket, swimming costume, goggles, hat, and so on and so on. I found the PE gear particularly revolting. For games we had a red aertex shirt and a tiny pleated skirt. The skirt provided no warmth whatsoever and made my thighs look horrifically chunky. Plus wearing it meant I had to shave the top bit of my legs which gave me ingrown hairs that looked like blackheads. I hated my gym shirt. I was supposed to take it home after ever PE lesson to be washed but I nearly always forgot, so by the end of term I smelled like cat litter.

About that time, the new clothes stopped. I wore the same skirt for three years, even though I'd grown and it was way too short. Millie only got me a new one because of decency and teachers making comments.

I told her I could get hand-me-downs off of Jessica probably, because she was always getting new stuff. But Millie said not to tell anyone we were strapped. 'Consumer confidence – it applies to people as much as business.'

Other changes were small but still really downlifting. I used to go for six-monthly check-ups with a private dentist who played classical music when he prodded my molars. My upper canines were a bit skewiff and he was going to refer me to an orthodontist. But then I got switched to an NHS dentist who had a mouthful of metal. He said my wonky teeth were 'an acceptable irregularity'. We cancelled our private medical insurance as well. When Millie got this weird mole on her shoulder, she had to wait months to get it taken off on the NHS, even though she could've had cancer.

My mother went for her weekly shop at Sainsbury's just the

same, but she brought back own-brand cereals and instant coffee. We still ate ready-meals, but more often than not, they came from the freezer section, not the chilled cabinets. I hated the pizzas because the tomato sauce was sweet as ketchup and the cheese had the texture of Playdough. Millie said this was rubbish – no way could I tell the difference. Same went for generic beans and Heinz. But that wasn't true. I'd been brought up to appreciate the finer things in life. I already knew the difference between a Cabernet Sauvignon and a Chardonnay by smell alone. It wasn't like I could just forget.

One day, Hugh got me digging down the back of the sofa so he could pay the milkman.

'Why can't we sell the house?' I asked him.

'We can't sell. No one can. Boom and bust – that's capital-ism. Those East Germans, they'll find out soon enough. Think twice before you go into business. Become a cardiac surgeon, maybe.'

'Science is boring,' I said.

'Maybe so. But people will always have hearts.'

People always needed houses, too, but that didn't seem to matter. My father stopped building and stopped buying. He got rid of a couple of staff, then another couple, until it was just him, Jackie the seccie, and some new guy who was desperate enough to work for peanuts.

Black dog, my father called his sadness. I liked that idea. His dark mood might follow him round, but then maybe it'd roll over so I could tickle its tummy. But it didn't work like that, he said.

He did lots of staying up all night and boozing. Then he stopped working so much and he got a bit better. His forehead, which had started to look like a screwed up papyrus, became smoother. Usually I cycled to school, but now he sometimes he gave me a lift. He liked listening to Radio 2 in the rush hour and laughing at the other parents' driving. Some days, he sat downstairs while I got ready for school. He wore his dressing gown and ate toast and did the quick crossword in the paper. It took him ages, but he seemed to enjoy it anyway. Once, at the weekend, he even suggested we go out into the country, cycling to Wandlebury, where we could walk in the woods and search for badgers.

I quite liked my new less suave father with his imaginary pet dog, but my mother didn't. She'd never planned on being the breadwinner. Her salary was there to be splurged on nifty jackets and dazzling earrings and instead, she eked it out to pay gas bills and car tax. A few years ago, we'd had two holidays a year – in spring, a city break in a European capital, and in summer, a fortnight at a five star hotel on the Med. At weekends we'd gone to nice restaurants with proper cloth napkins and I'd been allowed to order a la carte. At the time our little luxuries meant nothing to me, but now they were gone, I'd an inkling of what life without ordinary pleasure might be like.

In our On Becoming a Young Woman class we'd had a discussion about unemployment. Mrs Rally said that working was a privilege and it wasn't possible to live a useful life if you didn't have a job.

'What about housewives?' Jessica asked. 'My mother says that looking after children is the most important job in the world.'

Mrs Rally seemed interested by this. 'But what if she wants money for a new handbag? Then what does she do?'

Jessica didn't know. 'I think she just goes out and gets one.'

'But with your father's money?'

Jessica nodded.

Mrs Rally sighed. 'We don't want to end up like that, do we girls? When you grow up, you'll want to be able to have as many handbags as you want, without having to ask your husband about it.'

Everyone looked at Jessica like her mother was a very sad person indeed.

I couldn't believe the unemployed people on the news would ever be me. I'd spent most of my childhood going to school or doing homework – never having any real fun – so it'd be totally unfair if all my hard work failed to pay off. Sometimes I felt like I was really important and destined for something amazing, but then I remembered that I was just an ant on the face of the planet and I didn't really matter at all. I was sick of being an ant. I wanted to be important – not some time in the future, economic conditions permitting – but right now. People my age were already movie stars or Olympic swimmers or had records out. I'd never done anything worth mentioning. Quite possibly, I'd never amount to anything at all.

*

I was in the kitchen late one afternoon not long after the summer fête and the world had died. In the sky shreds of clouds hung about, cast-off remnants of some greater atmospheric manifestation. I was getting myself some toast and Marmite and all I could hear was the ugly scrape of my knife against burnt bread. I paused for a moment, straining to hear birdsong even, to prove I wasn't alone. Then I heard the screak of brakes as outside a learner driver practised their emergency stop. My mother's clogs stormed into the kitchen.

'Where's your dad?' she said.

'In the sitting room.' I felt like I'd ratted him out.

She dropped her handbag on the kitchen floor. She didn't even stop to pour herself a glass of Chardonnay. She marched straight out through the corridor and into the sitting room, slamming the door behind her.

The shouting started right away — no warm-up. I heard 'cash-point' and 'arsehole' and 'fucking sick of it.' It wasn't much of a stretch to work out that her card had been eaten by a hole in the wall. The same thing'd happened a few weeks before. It was horrible, listening to my father pleading. His voice was so soft, I couldn't catch his words, even when I pressed my ear to the door. My mother shouldn't have been so nasty to him. He built our house, not quite with his bare hands, but near as. This wasn't his fault.

Millie shouted. 'What, then? What?'

Then the noise stopped.

I crept upstairs, where I ate my toast as softly as I could. My mouth was dry.

I lay on my bed and stared out of the window. Rain fell with ruthless enthusiasm, promising more where it came from. In the cherry tree outside my window, an old carrier bag hung limp and shredded, like the clothes of a Victorian orphan. It might as well be winter. Then I'd be in the Upper Fifth – one step closer to my freedom. I couldn't hear anything from downstairs – no voices, no telly, no stereo. Usually they stopped shouting and put the telly on – that's how I knew the row was over. They'd been at it a long time.

I opened up my Class Civ set text, The Oresteia. I'd an essay to write: Is the end of The Oresteia fair? There were only five of us in the class. We were only there because we didn't want to do pottery. Handling clay was vile, I thought, and it made me feel sick. In Class Civ we had loads of reading and essays and tests, but Miss Gillis taught it, so I suppose it was OK.

Miss Gillis was a post-structuralist and a feminist. She didn't believe in teaching the work of dead white men, but she said we had to know who they were – how else could we object to them? Teaching was her fallback position. Eventually she was actually going to become an academic, but so far the patriarchy had refused to fund her PhD.

Far as I could see, none of The Oresteia was fair. Agamemnon had to kill his daughter Iphigenia to win the Trojan War, and then his wife Clytemnestra killed him and his girlfriend in vengeance, with the help of her boyfriend Aegisthus. Then her son Orestes had to kill Clytemnestra and get pursued by Furies till the end of time. Eventually, Apollo let Orestes off the hook, on the grounds that it didn't really matter who your mother was, so killing her wasn't a big deal. Fairness didn't come into it. Everyone did what they had to do and they had no choice. They were made what they were by who their family was, and what the gods decided. Even Aegisthus, who didn't have much to do with anything, was fuelled by ancient rage because Atreus, Agamemenon's father, had killed his father Thyestes' other sons, then fed them to him at a banquet. So how could I blame Aegisthus? Or was Aeschylus saying that some time or another, you just have to let stuff slide? I didn't get it.

Someone knocked at my door. My father – had to be. Millie never knocked.

'What?' I called out.

The door edged open. 'Can I come in?' said Hugh.

He sat down on the end of my bed. He toyed with a stray thread in the duvet. His thick fingers struggled to grasp at the wispy cotton.

'There's an old proverb,' he said. 'Every problem has a solution.'

I carefully replaced the lid of my pen. 'But first, Hugh, you have to work out what the problem is.'

I thought he'd laugh, but he didn't. He looked serious. I wondered if I was going to get the speech I'd heard about from other girls. Usually it was both parents together delivering the news. They looked guilty and sad. 'We've tried so hard,' they said. 'We still love you and it's not your fault.'

There were a couple of girls at school who were on assisted

places because they lived with mothers who'd been totally screwed by Daddy's divorce lawyer, so that Daddy could buy a big new house for his new family, even though he was in the wrong. In the last year or so, a few other parents had just stopped loving each other and said they weren't going to live a lie any more, no matter how hard their daughters begged them.

'We need to talk,' said my father. 'You're old enough to make decisions. This is about you as well.'

'You told me you'd never get a divorce. You said divorces were suburban.'

Hugh laughed. 'Did I? Well, I dare say I had a point. But no. No divorce.'

'What, then?'

I hated it when he did this – strung me along. At least Millie shouted stuff straight in your face. With her, you never had to guess – not much.

'You've noticed that things have been tight,' he said.

I twisted my mouth. 'I don't mind. I don't mind any of it. Just no more own-brand baked beans. They're hard. Maybe we could just buy stuff and cook it. That would work.'

He smiled. 'If you want us to cook stuff, then we can. We used to, when you were little, but you wouldn't eat it.'

'That's because I was little. Don't blame me. You and Mummy, you're used to being poor. I'm not. You should've thought of that.'

He leaned forward. 'This is a big house, isn't it?'

I nodded.

'And you know we can't really move, don't you? Not without losing lots of money.'

I nodded again.

'So we thought we might put the old place to work.'

I sat up a little straighter. I tried to imagine how this might happen. Would we become a bed and breakfast, with Hugh getting up early to serve sausages and bacon, a tea towel draped raffishly over one shoulder? We'd finally get carpets, every room with a different swirling pattern. We'd scrap the blinds and have curtains like everyone else. A rack in the hallway would display brochures for double decker bus tours of the American War Cemetery. I wondered what the neighbours would say about the vacancies sign we'd plant in the front garden. Isla Godfrey at school, her family ran a hotel. She could never walk past anything – a banister or a table, and not dust it with her sleeve. Force of habit, she said. I didn't like dusting.

'Don't look so worried.' My father pinched my cheek. 'It's just for the summer. It'll be fun. Trust me.'

He left the room and I wrote my essay. Yes, I said. The Oresteia was fair. Everybody got what was coming to them.

The next day, after school, that's when it happened. A tall young man who wore badly-ironed trousers moved into our house.

His name was Edward.

✳ four ✳

My mother's lists, which usually abated during the holidays, started springing up unexpected on my bedside table, on the mantelpiece in the sitting room and inside kitchen white goods, even. Some client had given her this huge box of Belgian chocolates, which she'd stowed in bottom of the fridge so they didn't melt, but when I sneaked to get one, there was a great big Post-It stuck to the inside of the lid: Do Not Eat — Chocolates Poisoned. I'm sure my mother thought this was hilariously amusing, but really, it was very unfair of her, since she didn't even like chocolates, and I was the only family member who was young enough to metabolise them efficiently. Food was my principle pleasure and now, even during the holidays when I should have been allowed to gorge as I liked, my desire was being thwarted. The day before, she'd pinched the back of my calves and tutted. She said instead of eating I could read a book or brush my teeth or make a phone call: I'd plenty other ways of occupying myself.

If there'd been more going on in my life then I'd never have got lured into Mrs Glinka's power. But just at the time when some girls were getting really popular, I only had one proper friend and no boys interested in me whatsoever.

I was only Jessica Rose's second-best friend. None of my friends were particularly good. I was choosy and so, it turned out, were other people. Jessica was one of the rank and file, bread and butter girls – chubby, mousy, neither clever nor stupid. She liked ponies and Duran Duran and when she giggled, other people giggled too. If there was anything wrong with her, it was her improbably high level of niceness. She didn't need for us to be soulmates. It was simply enough that we sat there at her kitchen table sharing our coloured pencils, and that her mother had bought us Chelsea buns from Fitzbillies. There was a weird atmosphere around Jessica – pinkish and welcoming. Perhaps it was warmth.

When St Joan's girls decided what kind of teenager they could be, there were two main choices. First, Tory piglet – which meant horse riding, stripy shirts with the collar turned up, Young Farmers' discos, Bennetton jumpers and toilet humour. Or alternatively, CND activist – anti-capitalist, hunt protesting, baggy clothes and no humour whatsoever. The cool kids at school were the worthy ones. They wouldn't let their parents buy shares in newly privatised public industries and they dreamed of going to Sierra Leone to rehabilitate child soldiers. But like me, Jessica had chosen to fit into neither group. She hadn't embraced adolescence at all – not really. For Jessica, leaving her childhood behind was tantamount to death and she was already wistful about the children's telly programmes of her toddlerhood.

'D'you remember Bagpuss?' she'd say. 'What happened to

Bagpuss? Why isn't he on any more?'

I always found the lugubrious pink and white cat rather sinister and was only too pleased to see the back of him.

Jessica sighed whenever a bakery started selling generic fried chicken, or a corner shop became a bathroom emporium full of snazzy vertical radiators. 'Why can't everything stay the same?' she said

Since our town was pretty much a living museum, I didn't see she had much to moan on about. The present might be bleak, but the past had been worse. Childhood for me meant being short and not being able to get things out of cupboards.

For the past two years, ever since Jessica and I sat out hockey together and discovered we'd both always wanted to be private detectives, being her friend had been the height of my social aspirations. I knew that if a nuclear bomb went off, when the five minute warning went, I'd want to be with her. She was my ticket to normality, acceptability and membership of the human race in general.

Connie Darke was Jessica's first best friend. Connie was short for Constance, as in Lady Chatterley's Lover. Her parents probably thought that was funny, naming their little baby after the heroine in a mucky book. Connie was cooler than we were, but she hadn't had much choice of friends, because she came as a new girl half way through the year, so she pretty much had to make do and mend. Connie was half Jewish – her mother's half – which was the right way round, according to her, because it meant she wasn't lumbered with some awful surname. Plus she looked like an English rose, she said, so if anyone ever invaded Britain and rounded everyone up, like they did to Anne Frank, she'd probably be all right.

It was a Saturday in June, three weeks before the end of term, when me and Connie were round Jessica's, wondering what to do. Jessica's was a proper teenager's bedroom like they had on television, with posters of pop stars and a sound system with CDs, which must have cost a fortune. She had a cork board where she'd pinned up tickets from all the stuff she'd been to, plus photos of friends – even some of me. I looked about ten years older than the rest of them. Jessica was a happy pony club girl, while I was more like a bored pony club mother.

'Oh for God's sakes,' said Millie. 'You're growing into yourself. Just sweat it out. The women in our family peak in later life. You'll see.'

Jessica didn't believe in waiting for nature to take its course. 'I've just started plucking my eyebrows. Can you tell?'

They certainly looked a bit weaselly.

'Only below the brow and never above.' She took out a pair of tweezers. 'You could really do with some shaping. I don't mind sorting you out.'

I had a look at myself in Jessica's mirror, which was surrounded by light bulbs like backstage in the theatre. I supposed I did have a few stray hairs.

Jessica certainly sounded like she knew what she was doing. 'I'm going on a professional make-up course when I finish my GCSEs. Mummy promised.'

'I'm scared,' I said.

'Christ on a stick, Freya.' Connie stretched out her legs on a pink fluffy beanbag. 'You are such a big girl.'

Connie had massive eyebrows, so I didn't know why Jessica didn't do her instead.

'Please!' Jessica and her tweezers lurched towards me.

'I'll let you do a bit,' I said.

She glowed with victory. 'On the bed, then.'

She kneeled beside me and leaned over my face. Her hair was sweet, all bubblegum and daisies. She propped herself up on her elbows. I could see down her blouse to where she was wearing a tiny white cotton bra that she didn't need, because she had no boobs whatsoever. I closed my eyes. She must have grabbed hold of one of my eyebrow hairs because I felt a tug, then another tug, then pain. 'Ow!' I flinched away.

Jessica tutted. 'Don't move! You'll make it worse. Never does that with mine. Yours must be made of badger bristle or something.'

When I checked in the mirror, I saw a red bleeding hole in the side of my face.

'You should've put a hot towel on first,' said Connie. 'Shall we go out?'

Because Jessica lived in the centre, going out was easy. No one really lived in the centre of town except for students, but Jessica's dad was old money. They had this ancestral residence behind Jesus College, a house with two staircases – one for servants and one for proper people. The walls sloped inwards and outwards at funny angles and all the furniture was old and had been in the family for donkeys' years, except things that'd be unhygienic, like beds and sofas. Jessica thought that was a shame. 'You can restuff them, but it's cheaper to buy new. Pity, though. New things are so nasty.' Jessica, though, didn't seem to mind all the new things she had, like clothes and make-up and the same eyebrow tweezers as Oprah Winfrey.

To Hugh and Millie, it was old things that were nasty. When I wanted to buy some apostle spoons from an antique shop, my mother said, 'Please, darling. Don't start with all that. Just because it's old doesn't make it nice. Nothing makes me more angry than going round someone's house and look-ing at their ugly, tatty old rubbish and having them give me a five-hour-long history on where every bloody thing came from.'

So I didn't buy the spoons. Hugh and Millie had no history: everything they had was bought new between them. They even got rid of the new stuff when it became dated. I wept when they binned the urine-yellow tweed curtains that'd hung round our windows since I was a baby. They were like part of me, those curtains, but out they went and in came blinds, dove grey, instead.

My parents weren't alone in their aesthetic sensibilities – you only had to look at the new buildings in town. Next to seventeenth century cloisters they'd plonked stacks of higgledy-piggledy white blocks, Lego constructed by a giant baby. The hideousness must've been deliberate. According to my father, the dons were all grammar-school educated meritocrats who voted for raw modernism as an insult to the ivory towers.

Dr Tourneville from three doors down thought that women were the problem. 'Soon as we let them in, we had nowhere to put them. That's how all the colleges got ruined.'

Though I'd been reared to be clean and smart, I could see how people might think that Jessica's house was better than ours. Chipped paintwork, faded carpets and scuffed armchairs – they told of a family that'd lived for centuries in the same space surrounded by the same things. Their DNA was imprinted in wood and plaster. My family were like organisms in a Petri dish. We got almost nothing from our surroundings: all our life came from us.

Jessica's parents bought her pretty much anything she wanted, but they kept her short of cash. 'I've only got a fiver,' she said.

I took a deep breath. 'I can pay.' Hugh always said that it's nice to share, but I never had anybody to share with. I looked through my purse and pulled out a twenty.

'Oo la la!' Connie batted her eyelashes.

Jessica laughed. 'What are you, Connie? A can-can dancer or something?'

Connie hitched up her skirt to reveal her long spindly legs. 'You know, Daddy wants me to be a research scientist so's I can cure cancer or something, but really, I'd like to be in a chorus line. Do they still have chorus lines? D'you think that's really sexist of me?'

Jessica sighed. 'Let's just go to Berlucci's.'

It was the height of our sophistication to drink a cappuccino at Berlucci's. In the teen mags like Jackie and Just 17 girls hung out in youth clubs and met boys round the snooker table. I don't think we had anything like that. Maybe there was a youth club up in the Arbury, the council estate, but nobody we knew ever went there: they'd probably get mugged. We didn't really have anywhere to go. Jessica and Connie looked too young to get served in pubs, although I didn't, obviously and I could get into 18 films as well. Since I was tall and had cheekbones, I was able to watch actors dry humping each other or cutting each other into bits, neither of which I found very entertaining.

Berlucci's, a shabby, glass-fronted Italian café, unlicensed and open in the early evenings, was our usual hangout. This was a townie place – tourists and students keep out. No cloying olde tea shoppeness here. The waitress – Rosalina, according to her name badge – dressed like Madonna in Desperately Seeking Susan, with her dark curly hair piled high on top of her head and an all-black outfit – low cut lycra top, skin-tight skirt, legwarmers and ankle boots. Her eyeliner swooped outwards, Cleopatra style, while her lips so red they were almost purple. When she spoke –'Hello, darling!' – her Italian accent sounded like a parody. She was everything glorious about the late Nineteen Eighties.

Rosalina, the permatanned Mediterranean goddess in the heart of pallid academe, was the person I most wanted to be, even thought I knew deep down that after a week of saying

71

'hello darling' in a silly voice, I'd be bored. She was the first adult I'd ever known, however superficially, who seemed constantly happy. She talked all day, switching between Italian and English. She and her family worked together from ten in the morning 'til ten at night, every day except Christmas and New Year. Her father frothed cappuccinos, her brother toasted panini, while her cousin, like her, worked the till, sliced cake and cleared tables. They never rowed or scowled at each other.

I went to Berlucci's for lunch one day with my mother. She didn't believe in Rosalina. 'No one's that happy. She's just doing it to get tips.'

The other reason I liked Berlucci's was that Sasha went there, even though he never talked to me. He was still as far from me as if he was living in his mother's native Lowestoft, or his father's Leningrad.

The café was mobbed by language students that day, so we didn't get any chat from Rosalina. The scent of congealed cheese and Silk Cut hung in the air, but at least we got a break from the packed summer streets. We looked through the window out onto the melting snake of the tarmac beyond.

We ate chocolate cake which wasn't like an English one at all: high and light and creamy, with lots of layers. Mrs Glinka said her cakes were like The Fens – flat and moist. She said that Russians didn't really have cakes, because why eat cakes when you could have blini, which were far superior, and hot, besides.

Connie took a forkful. 'You know – if you eat twenty of

these at once, you can have an orgasm.'

I was about to point out her error, when I saw him, leaning against the counter, waiting to be served. He wore frayed jeans and a faded T shirt which said Metallica. Sasha was with a couple of friends – both tall like him. One had silky straight hair which skimmed his eyebrows. The other one had a pony tail, which meant he must be older. No school would let him go round like that, not even the comprehensives.

I imagined Sasha and his mates coming to sit with us, but we were crammed round a little table meant for two.

They got coffees then sat down in the café's Siberia, by the door. Sasha had seen me, I was sure, but he was behaving, as usual, like he hadn't.

'Your boyfriend's not talking to you today,' said Jessica, like she was reading my mind.

'You've never got a boyfriend! That's ridiculous,' said Connie.

'That's not very nice of you, Connie,' said Jessica. 'Freya can look quite nice when she tries. I did her hair in ringlets and she looked just like Kate Moss in that Marie Claire Caribbean photoshoot, but a bit fatter.'

I'd been very wrong, I thought, to pay for their cappuccinos.

Connie rolled her eyes. 'What I meant was, the only girls at school've got boyfriends are the slags who wear blue eyeliner and smoke dope on the way to games.'

I felt a pang at the mention of dope. I was halfway to being one of those girls now, I supposed. 'Can we go?' I asked. I couldn't bear Sasha ignoring me any longer. I must seem totally disgusting to him, especially with the scabby hole where an eyebrow hair once was. If I'd been more like my mother, I'd have got his attention. Millie at my age could stroll into a bar and have the blokes fighting to buy her a vodka tonic. 'There are ways you can let a man know he's interested, but so he still thinks he's made the first move.' She told me that when we were cleaning the tops of doors with a damp sponge. 'Just give him a look, then look away. Easy as pie.'

Mrs Rally had talked to us about dating. She'd said, 'Like it or not, we still live in man's world. In the olden days, when a woman fancied a chap, she couldn't do a thing about it, except drop her handkerchief and wait for him to pick it up. I'm afraid the same holds true today.'

'But what kind of man's going to pick up a Kleenex?' said Connie. Everyone laughed.

We stood and walked towards the door, weaving past the tables, the hard backs of chairs squeezing at our thighs. I didn't so much as glance at Sasha, except out of the corner of my eye, so I wouldn't bump into him.

I'd no handkerchief to drop. But then I thought about Millie and her looks and I wondered if it worked. I edged past Sasha's table, then hesitated, then glanced over my shoulder. I stared him straight in the eye and he stared right back at me. I didn't smile. Then I turned away and headed towards the door. I was nearly out of the café when I heard my name.

'Freya?'

I turned round, too quickly, too keenly.

'Didn't recognise you out of your school uniform,' he said.

'Yeah. I….'

'What you doing in here?'

I wasn't sure how to reply. 'We were sitting. And now we're going.'

He laughed. 'I'm celebrating. Just passed my driving test.'

I didn't want to be impressed, but I was. 'I'd love to be able to drive.'

'I could teach you if you liked. Dad says I can use the Volvo.'

I couldn't tell if he was joking or not. 'That'd be illegal.'

'Not on private land.'

'But wouldn't it be dangerous?'

He sighed. 'It was only an offer.'

It was only then that I understood I'd said no when I'd wanted to say yes. My look had met with success, but I'd thrown it away. In the meantime, Jessica and Connie had sidled up beside me.

'I'd like driving lessons,' Jessica said.

'Me, too,' said Connie.

Sasha grinned at them. 'I'm not a bloody instructor, you know.'

Connie and Jessica and Sasha's friends all laughed a lot, but I didn't. They had no right to be talking to Sasha at all. It was me who'd found him and Mrs Glinka. They were my property.

'We better go.' I glared at Jessica and Connie.

'Au revoir.' Sasha gave us a little wave. 'And by the way, Mum mentioned she wanted to talk to yours.'

'She can't.' I thought of all the things I'd told Mrs Glinka and how if Millie knew about them, she'd go mental and never let me forget it.

He must have seen my fear. 'Just to be polite.'

'But why?'

'Don't ask me. P'rhaps they're going to fight over who you belong to.'

'Are not. Don't be silly.'

'Am not being silly.' Sasha mimicked my disapproving pout. 'They're going to mud-wrestle for you. Tug-of-love teen.'

'Oh. OK.'

'OK?' Sasha was taking the piss out of me again and there was nothing I could do about it. 'So high noon approaches. I'm really looking forward to it.'

'Right.' Finally I mustered some sarcasm. 'I'll be really looking forward to it, too.'

As we meandered in the direction of Lion Yard, Connie had a go, as per. 'You could've introduced us. We were just standing there like a couple of dills. I mean, they might have asked us to sit down or something.'

'There wasn't room,' I said.

'It's OK being emotionally stunted,' said Jessica. 'I mean, she's only fifteen. There's still time.'

'Fourteen.' I corrected her.

'Urgh!' Connie rolled her eyes. 'Baby. Hothousing's really bad for kids, you know. Just look at that Ruth Lawrence, the Maths prodigy. She might be a genius, but her and her dad on that tandem. I mean…'

'My birthday's soon. I'm nearly fifteen,' I said.

'Nearly legal, then,' said Connie.

Jessica tutted. 'You're obsessed. Come on. I want to go to the market. Buy a hat, maybe.'

'Thought you didn't have any money,' I said.

'There's always the hole in the wall. My Grandma gives me a twenty quid for every A I get in my exams.'

Jessica didn't get that many As, but she must've got at least four or so, which could buy quite a lot of cappuccinos and at least two or three hats.

Connie peeked up at the sky. 'Come on. I'm getting sunburn.'

'Can we hang around a minute and look at Snowy?' I asked.

Snowy was an old man with a bushy white beard and a red ringmaster's tailcoat who stood around all day in the centre of town, but unlike the tramps and the CND protestors, he seemed to enjoy himself. He had a white cat sitting on the crown of his top hat and little white mice running round the brim. The cat never once tried to scoff the mice. I wondered if that was because Snowy gave the cats loads of Whiskas before they all went out. However he managed it, he'd proved that cats could get on with mice, if given the right incentives.

Connie winced. 'You can't hang round him. He's probably an alky. And those animals are vermin.'

Even Jessica had to protest. 'That really isn't very fair, Connie. He's not a boozer. He's actually quite saintly and collects money for the blind.'

But Connie was already half way to the Market Square. Where she led, we followed.

There was nothing to buy, so we sat on the stone fountain behind the hotdog stand. The hotdogs smelled boiled and plasticky, like if a Cindy doll was getting barbecued. All the people walking past looked slightly familiar. We must've seen them every Saturday afternoon for the whole of our lives.

'Jesus, look at that cellulite!' Connie virtually shouted out when a woman waddled past in a mint green terry towelling all-in-one.

I didn't have cellulite, I thought. Not yet, at any rate. But I decided to double check when I got home.

'Gross.' Jessica looked nervously down at her own thighs, which splayed sideways across the stone step.

'When I grow up, I want to live in an octagonal room,' said Connie.

'That'd be so cool.' Jessica gazed at Connie as if she'd said something really clever.

I pondered how I could make Jessica realise that an octagonal room wasn't such a great idea. It wasn't the sort of thing Hugh would build. Where would you put the wardrobe or the bed? Rooms were square for a reason.

'When I'm grown up,' I said, 'I'm going to live in the house I live in now. A square one, with square rooms. One my dad's built.'

Connie smiled. 'My dad says you've either got taste or you

haven't. And if you're new money, it'll always come off a bit fake.'

'Everyone thinks they've got good taste. Anyhow…' I checked my watch. 'I better get back. My mother will be wondering where I am.'

That was a lie, actually. Millie would still be out and not wondering at all, but I was hungry and I didn't want to have to buy hotdogs for Connie and Jessica. They could buy their own with their own old money.

The day Edward arrived, I had too much skin. My summer dress – gross burgundy gingham which clung at my hips and bagged at the waist – rode up my legs with static and heat. The rest of the Lower Fifth was baring flesh. In the last year, my classmates had shifted from shame to exhibitionism: they untucked their shirts and tied them in a knot below their breasts, slathered their legs with baby oil and lounged on netball court at break time, skirts hoiked up to their knicker line.

I loathed our fascination with each other's bodies. The girls brought in copies of fashion mags which were full of starkas women laid out for other women to ogle. In one photo, a completely naked model, back turned, dangled a thigh-high boot over her shoulder. Why didn't they just take a picture of a boot? How come we were being peddled lesbian soft porn? The school didn't really mind whether or not we were gay. St Joan's, although gaspingly conservative in most respects, regarded sexual relationships between women as the inevitable consequence of men's repulsiveness. For every Miss on the staff who was wedded to her work, there were another two who were wedded to each other. Only the possibility of corruption was frowned upon. Older girls weren't allowed to take younger ones out to Botanical Gardens any more, because they'd been leading them astray.

I was neither repulsed by my own body, nor excited by it. My breasts and buttocks were beginning to take shape, but I was accumulating podge at the tops of my legs, where it wasn't needed. I'd no need to tan, since my olive skin, inherited from Hugh, meant that from May onwards my face was as dark as my hair. Each year, my father laughed at my transformation. 'Touch of the tar-brush there.'

That afternoon, my body was all wrong for me. My inner thighs were sore where they'd chafed from heat and sweat. When I cycled up to the house, in the driveway stood an unfamiliar car – gold, dented, with a long bonnet. Hugh and Millie drove nice smart German cars, while our neighbours had battered Volvos, which were better, apparently, because they weren't made by Nazis. This new car had a back seat full of crisp packets and empty bottles of pop. Mazda 626, it said on the back – Japanese, which I suppose made sense, because its oblong headlights gave it this oriental look.

When I opened our front door, I heard voices and laughter. A strange jacket, houndstooth check that Hugh would never wear, was slung over a chair in the hallway. A holdall, big enough to hold a dead body, lay prone beside the stairs.

Millie heard my key in the door. 'Freya? Come in the

kitchen. Come meet Edward. You remember – Hugh's associate.'

He stood leaning against the cooker, smoothing his floppy hair back from his face. His rumpled blue shirt looked out of place against the smooth white kitchen. Even from across the room I could sense he was different – not like my family. Millie was pungent with tobacco and a torrid sweet perfume which she dabbed behind her ears and the backs of her knees. My father, in the morning, smelled of the coal tar soap he used in the shower and the flowery fabric softener which Millie put in the tumble dryer. By evening he was musty, his hands dry with handling paper all day. Sometimes he'd let me snuggle up to him on the sofa while he watched the evening news. He let me near him more often now, since he'd become a failure. My mother didn't like to snuggle. She didn't like to be kissed, even in greeting, and made sure she always shook hands instead, even with other women.

Edward, when he saw me, stood up straight. He held out his hand and shook mine firmly. I inhaled him clearly now – cooking, like a warm oaty biscuit.

'I brought donuts, look.' He reached behind him on the kitchen counter and brought out a bag from the bakery a few streets away. I'd had these donuts before – too much sugar and not enough jam – but I thought Edward might be hurt if I refused him, so I took a one from the bag. As I bit, warm jam spilled out over my tongue. It didn't taste of any particular fruit – just sweetness. I licked the sugar from my lips and set the rest down on a kitchen towel.

I didn't see why I should talk to this Edward. It was bad enough when we had a gardener outside, digging around, making noise and peering through the French windows. Cleaning ladies were worse – wanting to sit and chat and get in the way. They never stayed long, our cleaning ladies. They were always getting divorced or having nervous breakdowns – and now we couldn't afford one anyway.

The grown-ups went outside to admire the roses, they said, but I hung back. Millie's voice carried across the garden. 'You're a perfect godsend. She's never had a brother or a sister. Bout time she got some competition.'

I hoped she didn't mean what I thought she did. I lingered a few seconds in the doorway, enough time so it wouldn't be obvious I'd overheard. Then I stepped out into the garden, slamming the door shut behind me.

Millie, Hugh and Edward were sitting on deckchairs, but I lay belly-down on the grass, using my jumper as a blanket.

'What d'you want to be when you grow up?' Edward asked me.

'Britain's ambassador to Paris,' I replied, which got a laugh from everybody. The girls from my school, if they joined the Foreign Office, would only do it for a year or two, and then marry another trainee ambassador. That way, if they were lucky and pushy enough, they'd end up as the wife of the ambassador to Paris, and play lots of bridge. That was the best we could hope for.

'What do you want to do when you grow up?' I asked Edward. That got an even bigger laugh, mostly from my mother. Edward looked at Hugh, then back at me. 'Just like your daddy,' he said.

Later, when Edward and Hugh went out to the pub, Millie and I shared a frozen pizza. We sat at the kitchen table, eating our ham and pineapple with our fingers. When Hugh was around we had to use a knife and fork, because no child of his was going to eat like a pleb, or an American or something. As we ate, she gave her opinion on Edward. 'Twenty-eight. But Jesus! He looks so much older. The trauma, I suppose. Though I dare say we all look ancient to you. But you wait. One day you'll look in the mirror and... Your father took him on because he's the only one who'd work for the money. Poor old Edders got sacked from his last place. Couldn't make the sales figures, but there again, at the moment, darling, who can? I'm dying to ask, though I'm far too polite to, obviously, precisely why that girlfriend of his has ditched him. OK, he's no oil painting, but she knew that didn't she? Suppose the crappy job was the final wafer on the camel's whatsit.'

'No oil painting? How d'you mean?' To me, he seemed rather good-looking.

She curled up a soggy, undercooked middle section of pizza into a tube and prepared to feed it into her mouth.

'He's a bit...Well...Funny looking, don't you think? Everything slightly skewiff. Like Picasso wanted to make a cubism thingumywhatsit out of him, then gave up before he did the job properly. He's a nice chap and everything. Course he is. But Hugh'd never have him here if he wasn't a bit challenged in the old fizzog department.' She took a big bite of pizza and gave me a significant look.

'Why not?'

'Oh, please! Don't give me that. You know what I'm talking about, you with your hormones running around. Girls of your…Give me a little credit. Anything with a Y-chromosome is catnip to you.'

'That's not true!'

'He's moving in, Freya. Just for a while. Get used to it.'

I didn't agree with her. Edward's face was battered-looking, a bit like his car, but he was still attractive – although not to me, obviously. Millie sometimes saw ugliness when there wasn't any. She thought trees were too tall, that diamonds were vulgar, that the colleges should be painted, for God's sakes, because why did they all have to be beige beige beige? Edward's eyes were dark and sweet as the forbidden Belgian chocolates in our fridge. When he grinned you could see how large and white and confident his teeth were. He must have grown up drinking milk by the gallon. Charred stubble flecked his chin, cheeks and neck, so either he was lazy or his beard grew fast. Hugh complained about shaving, but to me, it was much worse to shave your legs and armpits, because there was a lot more of them than there was of a chin. Edward was tall as well, which was the most important thing about a man, according to my mother, because otherwise you could never wear heels. Altogether, Edward was really quite nice to look at, although at twenty-eight, he was obviously far too old for me.

But whatever Edward's possible virtues, they didn't make

it all right for him to come and live in my house. Anyone as old as him who wanted to be a lodger must have something wrong with him. He was clearly a bit of a dill if he wasn't very good at his job and was that old and had no one to love him and no house of his own. And anyone who wanted to grow up and be exactly like my father was either sucking up to him or was a nutty as a fruitcake. I knew only one thing: Edward was not staying.

✳ five ✳

No one ever asked me anything. What did I want with an additional family member when I wasn't even allowed a pet? It was optimal, I'd read, for a girl to have a younger brother. Then she'd be a success in later life, because she'd spent her formative years in authority over a man. Edward was no younger brother. How would I explain him? Samantha Burgess's family sometimes had tenants, but they were actors on tour who never stayed long. Samantha's mother had once trod the boards herself, before she got a bun in the oven. The occasional thesp round the house was, apparently, essential to any child's cultural education. Edward could hardly be passed off as artistic nourishment and soon as the girls at school found out about him, they'd realise we were secretly poor.

Was he the beginning of a long line of future tenants? After all, we had four bedrooms, which meant even with our new arrival, we still had room for one more. Long as I could remember, the little room at the back of the house had been the huffy bed, used for Millie to escape Hugh's snoring, and for Hugh to avoid my mother's restless legs and sharp toenails. We could easily fit a foreign language student in there – two even. Or what about a foster child? I quite liked that idea. We'd get some half-wild creature from the estates. I'd teach her to read and stop holding her knife like a pencil. We'd too many grown-ups in the house as it was. Why was it OK for Edward to stay when I wasn't even allowed a French exchange? I tried to remember when we'd ever last had houseguests, even. I'd never had a friend to stay and I wasn't allowed sleepovers. Given my parents' scanty record in hospitality, Edward wouldn't last long.

I was reading thrillers back then, the ones newly in fashion, with detailed descriptions of mutilated bodies, so I'd fall asleep thinking of entrails lying in fridge freezers in labelled plastic bags. But that night, I lay awake. I heard Hugh and Ed roll in from the pub then get ready for bed with lots of clunking about.

If I'd thought ahead, I could've taken one of Millie's pills, but she kept them in her bedroom and anyhow, she noticed if I took them too often. Hot chocolate was the only answer.

I slipped on my terry robe and tiptoed downstairs. I wasn't usually allowed to creep around after my parents had gone to bed. My mother claimed the lightest footfall on the stairs would wake her, although this was blatantly untrue. She was so tanked-up by bed time, I could have torched her duvet and she wouldn't even blink.

When I reached the bottom of the stairs, I saw light bleeding from under the kitchen door. I expected it was my father being mentally disturbed. The last few months he'd had trouble sleeping, so in the morning, we'd come downstairs to find he'd cleaned out the cupboards or regrouted the tiles.

As I pushed open the door, I saw Edward sitting at the kitchen table, his head in his hands. He made a snuffling noise, like the hedgehog did, the one we used to feed outside the back door. We left the hedgehog bread and milk, but then I saw on the telly how we should've given him cat food instead, because bread and milk kills them. The hedgehog never came back and I wept because it'd died for no reason. A hedgehog came the next year and Millie said it was the same one, but I didn't believe her.

Edward heard me come in and jolted. His eyes were porcine, puffed-up.

'Sorry,' he said. 'I didn't mean to...'

He looked away and his snuffling grew louder.

I'd never seen a man cry before except on the telly. Sometimes, in a high wind, Hugh got teary. 'An irritation,' he said. Millie didn't cry either, except at black and white films on a Saturday afternoon. 'I went to see this with your grandma,' she'd say.

At St Joan's, there was a lot of crying – in lessons mainly, when the work was hard, or the teacher was nasty. Sometimes the teachers cried, too. Miss Rolands who taught geography got overwhelmed when she talked about poverty, injustice, or whole countries in Africa where clever people couldn't read or write and had boring jobs for the whole of their lives, which was true in Britain, she said, in bits of it even now, in the North of England. I'd never cry to get someone else to feel sorry for me, or to get them to treat me better, because with my parents, it'd never work, and with other people, they'd just end up despising me. I'd learned to control myself, at least, where Edward had not. I knew I should be nice to him, but it was only Brownie Guides who have to do a good deed every day. I wanted a hot chocolate and a slice of toast and why shouldn't I have them, just because he couldn't get a grip?

His shoulders quivered. He alternately gulped in air through his mouth, then through his snotty nose. He was some lonely monster – homeless and loveless. Two in the morning, and he'd not even got himself into his 'jamas yet. Or maybe he didn't even wear jamas. I took a step towards the fridge and he started, although I'd made only the tiniest of noises.

'D'you want some kitchen roll?' I tore him off a sheet.

'Thanks.'

'D'you want hot chocolate?' I didn't want to make him one but I knew I had to, out of politeness. There was plenty of milk, although that time of year it was often on the turn. I didn't understand why we even got the stuff from the milkman when we could get nicer milk from the supermarket, but Millie said we weren't Europeans yet, whatever the law said.

Edward gave a little laugh. 'I'd love one. Can't remember when someone last offered me a hot choccy. Not in summer, anyway.'

I gave him my special mug which said Property of HM Prison Dartmoor. It really did come from Dartmoor, because in Devon, a maximum security prison counts as a tourist attraction.

I handed him a spoon. 'That's for the skin, although there shouldn't really be a one. I didn't let it come to the boil.'

'Too right. Never let anything come to the boil.'

Edward, thank God, had pulled himself together. Now to look at him, you'd think that he'd just washed his face and dried it too hard with a rough towel.

'I know what you're thinking, but I'm not sad,' he said.

'Yes, you are sad. Crying means sad.'

'OK. A bit sad. I'll give you that. But not just sad.'

'What else could it mean?'

'I used to think crying was just sad, too. But mostly, it's relief. Just such relief to be here, not there. I can't tell you, Freya. Thank you so much. So so much.' He bit his lip, restraining further tears.

'I haven't done anything. You don't thank a person for doing nothing.'

'Sometimes…It's enough just to be.'

That sentence sounded weird. 'You a hippie or something? Don't look like a hippie. I mean, you haven't got long hair or anything.'

He smiled. 'I'm not sure that anyone's a hippie any more. Nothing to drop out of now. No such thing as society, remember.'

That was what Mrs Thatcher said, but I didn't really know what she meant. One thing I was sure of – if there was such a thing as society, I'd never been invited to join. As Edward dried his tears, I said, 'I know I shouldn't ask, but are you heartbroken? And if you are, is that how it feels? That your heart is actually breaking?'

He gazed at his fingers, which had big joints, like if his bones had been stung by a bee. 'Maybe I am heartbroken, but it's not my heart that hurts. It's here.' He pointed to his stomach. 'Like I'm being stamped on.'

'Is that why you keep eating the doughnuts and stuff?'

'Very perspicacious of you, Freya. Dare say you're right.'

He insisted on washing up but he did the job badly, making a racket. I didn't know what perspicacious was but it sounded like a compliment. Edward, I decided, wasn't the kind of person I was used to, but I'd allow him to stay until I found out more.

Edward clearly had his feet under our table, because soon it was July and he hadn't budged and only a week remained before I obtained my freedom. I'd been dreaming of the summer hols ever since January, but now when a month and a half of nothingness approached, I was scared they'd be just that. At least when I was at school, Edward's presence in my house didn't overly bother me.

At school after exam time we just occupied chairs rather than participated in meaningful activity. The heat made my so-called studies physically arduous. I wasn't allowed ankle socks because Millie said they were most unflattering, so as I sat trapped in an airless girl-filled forced labour camp, my nylon knee socks suffocated my calves.

When I came home, Edward would have dinner with us, then afterwards him and my father mostly went to the pub. Millie wasn't happy about this because it cost money. My father claimed it was just for a pint or two and that Edward needed a bit of masculine attention.

Our lodger still had his wistful moments – one afternoon he sat in the garden, clutching a glass of Millie's Chardonnay, but he didn't cry. He just stared into the Cambridge blue of the air above, allowing a ladybird to land on his face. The ladybird should have brought him luck. According to Jessica, if they weed on you, it was even more lucky. Hugh said that Edward had been unlucky in love and it'd take more than ladybird wee to cure that.

I wasn't sure that I fancied being in love myself. Connie claimed that the girl had to make sure the boy was in love with her, not vice versa. It wasn't humiliating for a boy to be in love, but for a girl it was. If I was in love, would I really want to have sex with someone? I was well enough acquainted with the biological facts of the matter, but the actuality sounded nightmarish. Was that why Edward's girlfriend had kicked him out, because the sex had been really awful and she just couldn't face it any more? I didn't think she'd gone off him because of his personality, because he wasn't such poor company as I'd expected. He didn't know much about teenage girls, though. 'Even when I was one, Frey, a boy, I mean, they were a total mystery to me. All giggles and lumps and bumps. Only ever met them at bops in the summer.'

Edward, like me, had endured a single-sex education, but at a boarding school, where he'd been one of the day boys. 'Best that way. You don't want to know what the boarders got up to.'

'I do want to know,' I said.

Edward looked shifty and I knew it was something to do with sex.

'They slept with the teachers?'

'No!' He looked at me, appalled. 'With each other, silly. But don't tell your parents I said that. I'll deny it, anyhow.'

Hugh had been a boarder. He had a friend from school he still kept in touch with, a small-time stockbroker called Millers. Millers was short for something and I couldn't remember what. Millers wore striped pink and blue shirts with cufflinks in them which were also clocks – one for the time in London, and one for the time in New York. I tried to imagine Hugh and Millers young and doing things to each other and I hoped my father would've valued himself more highly than that.

Most of the girls at school were disgusted by their parents' sex lives. Andrea Weston's mother had a baby at the age of forty-five, and Andrea didn't know what made her more furious – the fact that her parents still did it, or the fact that her father was too much of a he-man to wear a johnnie. In other families, infidelity was rife. Daddy was constantly getting told off for fumbling his graduate students and the evening polenta was salted by Mummy's tears. As far as Hugh and Millie went, I assumed that in the bedroom, as in other respects, they were rather dull. The less I knew, the better.

Sex education from Millie was elaborate, clinical and deeply off-putting. My mother had a special sponge bag which contained her equipment. It was made of waterproof plastic and decorated with garish orange and purple flowers. She brought it into my bedroom one night.

'Now darling…' She held up a squashed beige gum drop. 'This is a condom. D'you want me to take it out of the wrapper?'

'We've done that at school,' I lied.

But she was relentless. 'What about a diaphragm, then?' She opened a large plastic pill box and took out another round beige sweetie, only this one was unwrapped, greasy looking, firm round the edges, pouchy in the middle – a leprechaun's swim hat. She flexed it between her forefingers and thumb. 'Some people call it a Dutch cap, but I think that's tacky. You don't use it on its own. You use spermicide. That's in here.' She picked up a wrinkled tube. 'Then, if you're anything like me, it's a bit hard to find, sort of tucked away, but you'll get there in the end, and you slide it up your…'

'Stop!'

'I'm just trying to be a responsible parent.' My mother's cheeks erupted with twin blotches of annoyance.

'They tell us about this stuff at school.'

'You can't rely on them. You should be grateful for this. Women threw themselves under racehorses to be allowed contraception. And what about this AIDS thing? It's not just for the gays.'

'Normal mothers don't do this.'

She snorted. 'What's normal? Nothing is. Nobody is. Don't give me that crap. Spare it for your shrink, for when you're my age, and you're still blaming me. See if I care!' Although storming out is a teenager's prerogative, surely, she stuffed her baby-preventing bits into the washbag and flounced out of my bedroom, slamming the door behind her.

When we came to study women's matters at school, I revised my opinion of my mother's attempt to enlighten me. At St Joan's, we'd skirted round the issue of sex for several years. First, there were earthworms, which reproduced asexually so they were hardly representative. Then there was half a rat – the bottom half – which was mostly intestines. Then, finally, we got onto humans and for ten minutes, we got permission to ask any stupid questions we liked.

'Can you get pregnant by giving someone a blow job?' asked Pippa Wilkins. At least Millie had spared me from public humiliation.

Then Mrs Rally, our RE teacher, gave us the sex talk as part of our On Becoming a Young Woman course. It was impossible to believe that Mrs Rally had any carnal knowledge even though she must be quite old, because a deep double inverted comma was carved into the flesh between her eyes. Rumours about the sex ed session had already filtered down from the girls in the year above.

'Mrs Rally's going to show you how to be a condom on a banana,' they said. 'She's going to tell you how if you're up the duff, the headmistress makes you get rid of it.'

It worried me that sex education had moved from the realms of biology to those of theology. St Joan's, though it sounded like a Catholic school, was a secular institution. Even morning prayers were virtually hymn and prayer free and RE classes shied away from Christianity. We knew the eight Ks of Sikhism, the laws of kashrut, and that Baha'i wasn't an ism at all. But in On Becoming a Young Woman, I suspected that sex was going to be in league with Jesus.

The lesson was held in the crappiest of classrooms, a portakabin which looked like it'd been thrown onto the lawn. The portakabin was Baltic in winter, while in summer, we were like grains of rice being boiled in the bag.

Mrs Rally asked us, 'When is it all right to make love with someone?'

'When you're in love,' someone said. 'When you fancy someone.' 'When you're ready.' 'When you're married.' Maybe six girls in our class had pledged, at some church youth group, not to cross the thin red line. Kissing was allowed, apparently, but hands under the jumper were not.

Mrs Rally nodded as she listened to our answers. Clearly, none of us had hit the nail on the head. She left a dramatic pause, then tilted her head to one side. 'The answer is…it's all right to make love…when it doesn't hurt anyone.'

We murmured in incomprehension.

She continued. 'What I mean is, that you have to think of all the other people we might affect. Not just ourselves, but our teachers, parents…'

I felt sad then, because I realised how I'd been looking forward to this class. I'd wanted to learn something and now that was looking doubtful. Millie was not the kind of woman I planned to be. I simply could never imagine plucking my eyebrows, as she did, into two faint parabolas which swooped over the brow bones. I hated wearing heels. I only wore tights in winter time and could never manage to keep a pair of fifteen denier ones, like Millie wore, ladder-free for more than half an hour. My mother had a sultry air which made me queasy. Mrs Rally could have shown me how to become a better sort of woman, but already she'd failed.

The second half of the class was the medical bit. A woman doctor came in to explain to us various methods of contraception. She created a rustle of horror when she passed round a Femidom, which looked like one of the filmy plastic bags in the supermarket you put loose vegetables in. But the doctor was saving her bombshell for the end of her presentation.

'Of course,' she said, stowing away an intrauterine device, 'your cervix doesn't mature until you're twenty. Up until then, contact between sperm and the immature neck of your uterus can lead to the formation of precancerous cells. So medically, sexual relations in your teenage years are not to be recommended.'

The doctor was telling us that teenage sex could give us cancer. How she thought she was going to get away with this, I had no idea. After all, I'd been reading The Times every day since I was ten. The paper was obsessed with all things medical. No drug advance, no preventative health measure was too dull for a column or two – tea tree oil cures athlete's foot, pumpkin seeds are good for your prostate, coffee may or may not give you heart attacks. So if teenage sex caused cancer, I was pretty sure I'd have heard about it by now. The school, for entirely selfish reasons, was trying to stop us having sex if not for good, then at least until we'd done our A-levels. 'Too late for some,' said Jacintha Bryce. Emily Richards had almost certainly given herself to a Turkish waiter during her half term holiday. Out there, apparently, fifteen was considered to be rather mature.

I could sympathise with poor Mrs Rally, trying to build a moat of fear around the fortress of our sexual potency. St Joan's did have a bit of a reputation for pregnancy. Every year at least one girl, not necessarily a sixth-former, was disappeared. Only months later, when she was spotted wheeling something pink and squealy through the centre of town, did the truth come out. Sex education, I knew from watching TV dramas about comprehensives, was supposed to be entertaining, not terrifying. At St Joan's, nothing was as fun as it should've been.

The day we got handed Femidoms, I was more than usually ecstatic when the final bell of the day rang. I pelted out of the back gate and smelled the free, non-school air. Popular girls had boys waiting for them outside the gates. The boys lounged against the low white-painted fence of the car park opposite. They had gelled up spiky hair, school shirts with upturned collars, jumpers slung casually around their waists. I often fantasised that Sasha would be there waiting for me. It'd be a surprise. Finally, he'd have realised that it was me he wanted to hold hands with in the Botanical Gardens. Once I actually thought I saw him, waiting for me, the ebbing sun igniting his flavid hair. I smiled, started running towards him, but the light had blinded me – it was another golden boy, waiting to slip his hand inside another girl's nylon blouse. After that, I made myself stop. I was good at not expecting things: I'd had plenty of practice.

That day, there was a new boy leaning against the fence. He was taller than the others, and stockier. I don't think he realised that adults weren't allowed on the fence, not by any specific rule, but by tradition. I almost didn't recognise Edward at first because he was in the wrong place. He existed only in my house, and maybe in Hugh's office, but certainly not outside my school. When he saw me, he grinned and waved and I tried, by the power of my mind, to stop him. Other girls looked at me then at him, imagining him to be a pervert with poor taste. Some of the sixth formers had boyfriends his age, I knew, because I'd seem them round town with a man not their brother, too young to be their father, holding hands and laughing, but these men would never dare come to school.

'Who's that?' Connie narrowed her eyes in Edward's direction.

'No one,' I said. 'Family friend.'

I wheeled my bike across the road, determined to shift Edward from the gate before anyone else could see us together. I was scared then that there was another explanation for why he was standing there: something had happened. My parents hadn't picked me up from school for years. When I was seven, even, before I was allowed to cycle, I took the bus into the city centre every day, my ten-trip ticket clutched in my duffel coat pocket. Were Hugh and Millie, even now, lying in a cold morgue?

Edward leaned down and gave me an awkward kiss on the cheek, like he was greeting me at a cocktail party. He must have seen my fear, my rigid arms, my stiffly offered face. 'No need to look like that. I'm not taking you off to boarding school or something. I'm picking you up.'

I looked down at my bike.

'I've thought of that. It'll go in the back of the car,' he said

My bike would certainly not go in Edward's Mazda, not unless we took off the front wheel, or tied it into the boot with a bit of string. But Edward pointed towards the car park behind the white fence, the car park which parents were expressly forbidden to use, ever, because it belonged to the university, and could get us all into trouble. I followed him towards a large green estate car I didn't recognise. He slung my bike into the back, lifting it easily as if it was a child's scooter.

On the back seat sat Millie and Hugh. My mother turned round. She was wearing lipstick the colour of melted strawberry ice cream. 'Hello, darling! Hugh's done a car swap with Pat. You know...The builder man with the wet handshake. We're going on a little trip. Do try to look a teensy bit pleased.'

'What trip?' I got into the front seat beside Edward. Again, this was strange because the front seat was not my place.

Edward grinned. 'Late supper. Picnic. Your dad and I bunked off work early and made sandwiches. Thought we'd go to Audley End. Me and my parents used to visit all the time.'

'Edward offered to take us, darling. Isn't this fun?' said my mother.

I caught sight of my father's face in the rear view mirror. He seemed far away. His knees were jammed up against the seat in front, so he can't have been comfy. He wasn't a man who rode in the back seat, ever in his life.

Edward started the ignition and backed out of the car park. 'D'you go on many trips? We used to, every Sunday. A museum. Car boot sale. But I haven't, not really, not since my dad went to live in Somerset. Now him and my stepmother go down the beach together and sunbathe in the nude. No tan lines.'

In the rear view mirror, I saw Hugh smirking.

I was only used to my parents driving. Hugh was careful but decisive. Millie was aggressive and enjoyed speeding ever so slightly. The police sometimes pulled her over, but she was always nice as pie, so they never gave her a ticket. 'If you're good-looking enough,' she said, 'they never do.' This was before speed cameras, though. Speed cameras didn't care how pretty you were.

We drove south of the city down the long cramped roads which linked the villages. I remembered the journey from a school trip a few years' back.

'What do they do, the people who live here?' I asked.

Hugh wrinkled his nose. 'This is Essex, darling. A dormitory county. They troll to London every day, squashed like sausages in a packet. This isn't a real place, not like Cambridge.'

Girls at school had started telling Essex jokes back then, like, 'What's an Essex girl's idea of romance? Being driven home afterwards.'

But the windy country roads looked quite civilised, to my mind, not as if they were full of people having sex in lay-bys at all.

A grey stone lion stood guarding the front gate, pointing sideways, his sad stiff tail outstretched, as if he didn't care whether we came in or not. It was four thirty by then, when most people were leaving. Even the man at the ticket kiosk thought we'd left it too late. But Edward insisted that we'd plenty of time, and that our picnic would be nicer with fewer people around.

'No time to go to the house. Do you mind?'

'I've seen it,' I said.

Millie scowled. 'It's bloody awful. Stuffed animals and portraits of inbred aristos. For God's sakes, Edward. You can't really be interested in all that tosh.'

He pulled up in the gravelled car park. 'It's nice, I think, that we have old families. They care about their history.'

'All families are old,' said Millie.

We traipsed through the grounds, where peacocks dusted the lawns with their burdensome tails. At the back of the house, bedding plants stood in orderly clumps around a fountain, like the way we stood gathered class by class, out in the school garden during fire practice.

'Can we go up there?' I pointed away from the house, up to

where a scuffed white collection of columns stood on the crown of the hill.

'As your ladyship commands.' Edward doffed an imaginary hat.

Hugh offered to help him with the picnic basket, but Edward insisted on taking it all by himself. The ha-ha, a grassy moat which divided the house from the grounds, sliced through the lawn. Edward and I galloped across the bridge over the ha-ha and up the hill. 'Temple of Concord, it's called.' He pointed towards the folly. 'I had my first kiss in there.'

I tried to imagine Edward kissing and it made me feel funny, so I didn't look at him the rest of the way, even though he kept trying to tell me about the history of the house, and how the owner had embezzled James the First just so he could have the cash for the interior décor he fancied.

We laid out green checked picnic blankets in the shade of the folly. The house looked better far away then close up, like most things did, which was something I didn't understand. I didn't hate the kind of people who lived in the house, not like Millie did. The posh girls at school were just like the rest of us, far as I could see, except more confident and less clever.

Edward served us mini pork pies, carrot sticks, and egg and cress sandwiches made with white bread, which I disapproved of.

'I bought dip, but I must've left it in the fridge,' he said.

He and Millie and Hugh drank cans of beer, while I had lemonade.

For desert, Edward brought out a box of donuts. 'Gooey in

the middle. Like me.'

We all took one, out of politeness. Millie didn't really eat hers. She just licked a bit of sugar off of the edge and then prodded the thing with her finger until the jam bled out. 'I'll feed it to the geese when we go back down,' she said.

Edward ate without licking the sugar off of the outside of his mouth, not until the end, so he sat there with a powdery clown smile plastered to his face. I'd never seen anyone enjoy food as much as he did. My parents ate because they needed to, to stay alive, but Edward was the kind of man who licked the lids of yoghurts.

Millie lit up a cigarette, creating aggressive white clouds that fought their way upwards to join the real ones in the sky.

'Women,' said Edward. 'You're so funny. Just like Jackie at the office with her Ryvita and her cottage cheese. Then come three o'clock, she rushes downstairs and has a Twix. Scoffs it so fast, no wonder she doesn't choke. Least we won't be putting up with that any more.'

Millie stubbed out her cigarette into the turf. 'How d'you mean? What's happened to your seccie?'

Hugh was giving Edward a furious stare. 'Edders. I thought I said… And anyhow, she's an office manager.'

It was too late for Edward to back track. 'It's no biggie. She's left. And we're better off, frankly. She doesn't do much.'

'That's not true, Edward.' Hugh was sitting very upright.

'Yeah. Suppose you're right. Least she stops anyone stealing the chair she sits on.'

'She's the only one who can work the computer.'

'Why didn't you tell me about this?' my mother demanded.

'It was only last week.' Hugh tugged at a tuft of grass, wrenching it out of the earth. 'We thought maybe she'd come back.'

'So what's the problem?' My mother's face was scrunched up. 'Get someone else. Last I heard, seccies were ten a penny.'

Edward took another samosa. 'Sorry, Hugh. I know I shouldn't have... But there's nothing to be ashamed of.'

Millie had a nose for human frailty. She could scent one tiny lie in an evening of honesty. Because of Millie, I never lie: it's never been worth my while. The only way with my mother was not to say anything at all.

Hugh sighed. 'There's always something to be ashamed of. No matter how hard we try, we... Fact is, she resigned.'

Millie shrugged. 'Least you don't have to pay her redundancy, then. Or have her hanging round. Why'd she leave? Rat leaving a sinking ship?'

'It's complicated.'

Millie's nostrils grew so big, you could've stuck a finger up each one. 'What did you do?'

Hugh rubbed a bunch of grass between his fingers, pulping the juice out of the green fronds. 'She's sent a letter. Some ambulance chaser lawyer. Nothing to be worried about. Some stupid stuff about constructive dismissal, sex discrimination. That kind of thing.'

'You stupid fucking bastard.' Millie took a cigarette out of the packet. Her last one. She scrunched up the empty packet and threw it hard onto the ground. It landed in the middle of

Edward's egg and cress sandwiches.

'It'll all come out in the wash,' said Hugh.

She stood up. 'Nice boys' club you've got going now. Don't tell 'er indoors. What she doesn't know can't hurt her.'

'I never meant...' Hugh couldn't look at her.

'Right little game of soggy biscuits. Pissed fumble over the photocopier, was it? Or was it more your full-on shag? One more stain on the office carpet?'

'Wasn't like that.'

'So tell me. What was it like?'

Hugh looked pointedly towards myself and Edward.

'Fine.' She lit her final cigarette and stood up, her heels digging into the turf. 'We're going home. Don't know why we came here in the first place. I hate the bloody countryside.' She strode down the hill towards the car park, an Isadora Duncan scarf of smoke trailing after her.

Hugh watched her for a minute, then followed.

Edward piled his picnic back into the hamper. There seemed to be more food now than there was when he'd unpacked it. I helped him stack together paper plates, smooth cellophane over sandwiches. The cellophane had lost its stickiness.

'We should just bin the lot of it.' He struggled to close basket.

'I'll take it to school tomorrow. For lunch. Share it out with my friends.' I'd nowhere near enough friends to eat this much stuff, but he needn't know that.

'This is all my fault,' he whispered. His lips were trembly.

I hoped he wasn't going to cry again.

'She'd have found out soon enough.' I reached forward and squeezed his hand. He returned the squeeze. His hands were very hot. He let me go, stood up and picked up the picnic hamper. 'Can you manage the rugs?' he said.

As we walked down the hill, we could see my parents maybe fifty yards ahead of us. They weren't shouting, or even talking.

'Thanks for the picnic, Edward. It was nice,' I said.

'No, Freya. It wasn't nice.'

'It was us – my family – who weren't nice. We can't help it.'

He looked confused. Wherever he came from, things must be different.

On the journey home, Edward pointed out the trees that grew by the side of the road. He knew all their names, in English and in Latin. I pretended to listen. I'd learned that much from Millie, that men could be quite boring, but they couldn't ever know it. The knowledge would be more than they could bear.

As Edward was talking, I thought about how my father might have had sex with another woman – a woman far less pretty than my mother. But I'd found out something else even more interesting than that – that the thought of my father's indiscretion made my mother was merely angry. She wasn't in the slightest bit surprised.

✳ six ✳

Our next On Becoming a Young Woman class was all to do with marriage.

'Who should we marry?' asked the teacher.

We called out answers. 'A nice man.' 'A rich man.' 'A man who likes children.'

'It's whom should we marry,' said Samantha Burgess.

Mrs Rally said that all our answers were right, but that none of us had got the full picture. She read us a bit of Plato's Symposium, about how we were once one person, then got divided up and spent all our lives looking for the missing bit, which was equal and completed us.

'What if we can't find that person?' I asked. I usually kept quiet around Mrs Rally because I was sure I didn't have a soul and I worried that once she realised, I'd be put up for compulsory exorcism.

She gave me her kindest look. 'If you can't find the perfect person, it'd be best not to get married, then, wouldn't it?'

She moved on to affairs and the damage they caused. 'If you're married and you have an affair, you're breaking a promise you've made to God.'

Presumably if you got married in a registry office, the way my parents had, then God didn't know about it and wouldn't mind if you got a roving eye.

'Which is worse?' asked Mrs Rally. 'For a man to have an affair, or for a woman?'

Connie said that it was worse for a man. 'Because then they leave the wife and kids and they can't afford piano lessons and things any more.'

Most of the other girls thought that whoever did the dirty, it was pretty much shocking and inexcusable.

Then Mrs Rally told us the answer. 'Infidelity is a very wrong thing. But for a woman to do it is even worse, because then how do you know whose the children are? That's the most terrible thing you can do to your husband – have him bring up another man's child.'

A lot of the teachers at school were married to academics who, if you believed Hugh and Millie, were boring, drank too much, and slept around if they could, because it was the cheapest of all the vices and they were too poor to get a divorce.

'Divorce,' said my father, 'is only OK for the very rich or the very poor. No one else can afford it. That's why the middle-classes carry the moral burden.'

When you read between the lines of the St Joan's magazine, this moral burden seemed pretty heavy. The magazine was mostly full of dull reports about less than stellar sporting achievement, as well as poems from girls in the Upper Third, badly edited by the English teacher in charge of the editorial committee. The most interesting bit was in the back — the news of Old Joanians. Their lives were expressed with lots of exclamation marks. 'Hilda Evans (nee Marchmont) is now living in Dubai! Where her husband works in textiles! She has managed to contract three other ex-pat St Joanians, and they've since formed a bridge four!!!' The average old girl's life went: university, marriage, giving up career, children, affairs, widowhood/divorce, gardening, death. It wasn't much to look forward to.

'I'm having children as soon as I graduate,' said Molly Wilkins, as we sat opposite each other on the packed lunch table.

'But what about your career?' I said. 'What if you get divorced?'

'Christian marriages have a much better success rate than the norm.'

'But what if he dies?'

'That's really not very likely, Freya, now is it?'

I despised girls like Molly Wilkins, but no doubt she'd have the last laugh. She'd choose a nice man from a good family. She'd have her own detached house and her kids'd be off her hands by the time she was forty-five. She'd never regret the raves she hadn't been to or the ski instructors she hadn't slept with, because she'd never wanted any of that in the first place.

At home, nothing more was said of Hugh, his secretary, and whatever'd gone on over the photocopier. I tried to think of my father and his infidelity and hate him for it, but I couldn't bring myself. First, although it was obvious that something had happened, it was unclear what. Actual penetration might not have been involved. Given that it was Jackie, I hoped it wasn't. Hugh could surely do better than that.

My father, I assumed, had strayed because he was sad. Sad people needed comfort and Millie was not comforting. Since my mother hadn't even been that angry, she probably realised it was all her fault.

Edward seemed much happier belonging to my parents than I did. He was delighted with everything on offer. He never made us watch what he wanted on television and instead, he merrily went along with my parents' detective shows and current affairs programmes. He got up early, showered and dressed before anyone else was up. In spite of his healthy physique, he hardly took up any space on chairs or sofas. He'd curl himself up in a corner or lounge on the floor – less a lodger, and more a relaxed hairy pet. Only his food looked like being a problem, because to prove he wasn't greedy – which he was – he had to pretend to be a connoisseur instead.

Having failed to woo us with his donuts, he turned to sandwiches. Usually I made my own for my packed lunch: cheese and tomato or sometimes tuna and cucumber, even though it smelled and Millie never remembered to buy the tuna in brine, not oil. But now Edward decided that all of us should be taking sandwiches to work, and that he would be the one to make them.

On Day One, he made houmous, mango chutney and avocado.

'Too sweet,' said Millie. 'Needs lettuce or something.'

Day two, it was prawn, chilli and fried potato.

'Bit too spicy,' she said.

Day three, he got up super early and made mini calzone, which were like pizzas, except folded over, with the topping inside.

Millie nibbled the corner of one before she went to work. 'Not bad,' she declared.

One day he turned up with a box of cookery books – Thai, Caribbean, wholefood, classic French. His ex, he said, didn't want them in the house. He set out the books in a row on the work surface in the kitchen. I couldn't believe that Hugh would stand for it, because the books created clutter and were a total design no-no.

Then Edward started making breakfast as well – French toast, omelettes, crispy bacon. I usually had a slice of toast for breakfast, which I ate while cycling to school. Millie never had breakfast – only a cup of instant and a fag. Hugh ate at the office – Danish pastries from the shop downstairs, although we never had them at home. Now we all had to get up half an hour earlier and sit down like a family in the adverts. Millie and Hugh were going along with it, but it wouldn't last.

About a week after the picnic, Millie and I were sitting in the kitchen eating Edward's blueberry pancakes. My father was still in bed, doing the crossword. I'd never had blueberries before and I wasn't sure that there was much point to them. They didn't taste of much and they bled black stuff into the batter.

Millie prodded her blueberry mess with a fork. 'Edward, we have to talk about this cooking business.'

He was leaning against the oven, a lobster claw oven mitt on one hand. Clearly, Millie was going to be mean to him, even though he was only trying to be nice.

'Edward, I haven't failed to notice your skills in the kitchen department.'

He blushed. 'Just a…you know….Penelope was never keen, so it rather fell to…'

'I've been thinking. How bout we scale down the breakfasts to weekends only and save your skills for a wider audience?'

He looked confused for a minute, then decided to take her rejection as a compliment. 'Strictly amateur, me. Bit of fun. Did have a job in a pub kitchen one summer, but God it was dull. Chef was a right old…'

'I don't mean jack it all in so's you can go to catering college, you idiot.' She set down her fork and sparked up a Marlboro Light. 'Hugh's fifty next month and I was rather thinking we might have a do. Nibbles. Music. Booze. You know the kind of thing.'

This was the first I'd heard about a party and it didn't sound fair. We'd never had parties in our house, except when I was so little I was practically a foetus.

Edward smiled. 'Fifty, eh? Kept quiet about that. Dare say

I could rustle up the old hedgehog with cheese and pineapple, that kind of thing.'

'Can I invite people?' I asked.

Millie arched her eyebrows. 'You mean you have people to invite? And I thought you were quite the lone wolf. Course, darling. Come one, come all.'

Edward and Millie exchanged a look which I didn't entirely like.

'I'm late for school,' I said.

I hadn't been round to see the Glinkas for ages, not since Edward had provided me with fresh fascination at home. I couldn't wait to show Mrs Glinka the photo of me in my costume, the cowboy one. Plus Sasha might be there, so I could tell him I'd changed my mind about driving lessons.

That afternoon, the bloated air squashed everything flat. I could feel thunder coming, which was a talent I had, though no one ever believed me. Dogs went funny before a storm, so why not me?

In the gunmetal light, the Glinkas' house was lonely, forbidding, a sandy-coloured toad squatting on the shorn field.

Mrs Glinka wore a black blouse strained tight over her chest, a dirndl skirt, and a woolly red and black woven belt tied around her waist. 'From Tallinn,' she said. 'Where they shoot the Russian versions of Sherlock Holmes.'

She was making a sauce.

'You ever made a roux, dushenka? Flour and butter, warmed in the pan. Then add milk, slowly slowly.'

'Millie doesn't believe in cooking – not properly. Once you learn, you can never get out of it.'

'What's the alternative?'

'Someone else does it.'

She tutted. I showed her the photo of me dressed as a cowboy.

'Very nice. All the man. No cooking. Wearing the trousers, just like your mother.'

'My mother only ever wears skirts. And she doesn't have flat shoes even.'

'Not even for playing tennis?'

I tried to imagine my mother playing tennis. I didn't think she'd ever done any exercise in her life, except at school, or ante-natal yoga, which was so boring, she said, no wonder she'd never had another kid. She hated sports like tennis and golf, where you had to have money to play them. 'Tossers,' she said. She hated the fact that men in her business made deals on the golf course.

'Why don't you learn golf?' said Hugh. 'They'd love to teach you, I'm sure.'

She snarled. 'If you can't join them, beat them.'

Mrs Glinka dripped milk into the roux. She performed the operation with care – a mother bird feeding her chick. 'I saw your mother. Couple of days ago.'

'Where? She never said. I didn't think you'd even recognise each other.'

Millie had insisted on picking me up at the Glinkas one time, just so's she could check they were OK.

'We saw her at Sainsbury's. She wasn't buying much.'

'We've got a lodger now. He buys lots of food.'

'She invited us to some party.'

'What? Why? Hugh's fiftieth?'

She shook her head. 'Please don't call your father by his first name.'

'But that's what I call him.'

'It's not right.'

I still couldn't understand why Millie had invited the Glinkas. She must've done it to annoy me. Mrs Glinka was my friend and if she became Millie's friend as well, then that would ruin it. 'She never said anything about meeting you.'

'She must have forgot.' She set the sauce on the back burner. 'It's reducing now. Just a simple béchamel to pour over vegetables. The English, they're not good with sauces. It's as if we have enough wetness. Except in the North. You ever been North?'

'The Edinburgh Festival once. We saw the Military Tattoo.'

'That's not North. I mean the North of England. There, they have gravy on their chips.'

'That's disgusting. You're making that up.' I leaned my chair back against the wall, like I'd never be allowed to at home.

The kitchen door opened and Mr Glinka stood at the threshold. Widthways, he almost filled it. He can't have been tall, maybe five nine – a lot shorter than Sasha or Hugh, or even Edward – but he was broad – shoulders, face, cheek-bones, everything. Although his mouth was sulky, the top half of his face was smiling. His eyebrows swooped upwards, long white hairs mixed in with the dark ones, fluffing out, as if he'd blow-dried them specially. His eyes were steely and alert, same as those on the stuffed eagles in the glass cabinets in Audley End. There was something about him which made me want to look at him. He had a quality, my mother would have said.

'His eyes dance,' was how Mrs Glinka explained the phenomenon. 'It's to do with being a poet and a great man. Englishmen's eyes – they never do that.'

Mr Glinka usually just shuffled through into the larder beyond the kitchen, took some biscuits out of a packet, then shuffled out again. But this time he didn't move.

'Hello,' he said.

I never realised he could speak. I was too stunned to say anything back.

'We saw your mother in Sainsbury's,' he continued. 'She was buying frozen peas.'

'She buys these peas flavoured with mint, which I don't like.'

Mr Glinka laughed. 'So many kinds of peas. So many kinds of trouble.'

I laughed, too, though I didn't see the joke.

Mr Glinka strode across the kitchen into the larder. He picked a packet of Rich Teas off of the shelf and tucked them under his arm. 'Food for thought.' He sauntered out through the kitchen, closing the door softly behind him.

Mrs Glinka gazed in the direction of the closed door. 'He writes and eats. When we met, he was a thin man. A twig man.'

'How did you meet?' I asked.

I knew it was in Cambridge, in some Cold War forbidden love type scenario. I'd always imagined that Mrs Glinka had saved him somehow. She'd taught him English, introduced him to different types of cheese, beer, peas.

'We met in the Spar – you know – the corner shop. I was buying that pasta you mix with water, sauce included.'

'I can't believe you ate that.'

'I was younger then. Roman asked me about washing powder.'

'He chatted you up.'

'Not really. He genuinely didn't know what washing powder to buy. Even though they only had two kinds in the shop, he wasn't used to having any choice at all.'

'That's so lovely!'

'Not what every little girl dreams of. But it's something.'

I laughed, but she didn't laugh back.

'I have things to do now. You'll have to go home.'

I blinked in surprise. Mrs Glinka always had things to do, but she did them while I was there. She lived in a house with two men who didn't have speaking parts, so she needed me, so she wouldn't go mad in the silence.

I got up, slung my satchel over my shoulder. 'Sorry. Didn't realise. See you soon.'

She walked me to the door. 'Sorry, dushenka. If I had my way, I'd have you here all day. But I have to do Roman's accounts.' She lowered her voice. 'He's in a bad mood. Trade's slow, so he's not bringing in the readies and he has no time for his poetry.'

Served him right, I thought, for working in a shop. Mr Glinka had been at it for twenty odd years, so if he was going to make money, he'd have done it by now.

'I suppose you're coming to the party, then?' I tried to make it obvious that I didn't think it was a good idea. 'What'll I tell Millie about it? Are you coming or what?'

'I have pain you cannot understand.'

'What pain?'

Mrs Glinka breathed in, like it hurt her to do so. 'It is possible we will come. Out of respect to you, Freya, of course.'

'I thought everyone liked parties.'

'Do they? Ask me again.' She closed the door to a sliver. 'Ask me when we get there.'

Back home, there was another new car outside our house – a Morris Minor with a cloth top. Hugh always laughed when he saw them. 'Handbag on wheels,' he said. He thought it was super amusing when he saw a man driving one.

I nestled my bike up by the side of the house then went straight through into the back garden. Hugh and Millie and Edward lay poured into deckchairs, their faces ruddy. The air was sticky with booze, cigarette smoke and soft fruit.

My father waved to me. 'Fancy a Pimms? Very nice. Edward made it.'

Edward struggled to hoist himself out of his deckchair. He got me a glass and poured me a little. 'It's mostly fruit and lemmo, anyhow.'

'D'you know why it's called Pimms No. 1?' Hugh slurred.

'There used to be Pimms No1, Pimms No2, Pimms No3 and so on. Four or five of them there were. When I was a barman, way back when. One was based on vodka, one on rum, one on brandy. You get the general idea.'

Millie was sucking on her cigarette like it was the last in the packet. It was the second last, actually. Soon she'd get annoyed, then she'd try and make Hugh to go out and buy her some more. 'Don't talk like that, darling. It's very ageing.'

My father laughed. 'Next to you, I'm always old.'

'So what's this one?' I took a sip. The murky cocktail tasted nothing like as disgusting and Vicks Vapour Rub-like as when my father made it.

'I think it's brandy,' said Edward.

'But the colour's rum-like,' said Hugh.

'For God's sakes!' Millie stubbed her cigarette out onto the lawn. She wasn't killing any grass because she picked a sun-shaven bald patch. 'It's gin. Smell it! Juniper berries. Gin. Gin. Gin!'

Hugh and Edward knew not to contradict Millie, especially not where alcohol was concerned.

In the house, the loo flushed. Footsteps scuffled on the kitchen tiles. Then a tall woman with red hair scrunched out onto the gravel.

Edward stood to greet her. 'Freya, meet Penelope.'

I was standing with my back to the sun, so Penelope had to squint to see me.

'Hello.' She shook me by the hand, not gently, like most women would. She gripped my fingers like a squeegee pressing a damp sponge. I felt the nerve endings clamp then release, right up my arm and into my shoulder.

She splayed herself out on Edward's picnic blanket, the one he'd brought on our trip to Audley End. She had legs nearly as long as Millie's, but more muscular. She must have been a serious sort of person, because she wore sandals made out of recycled tyres, which weren't in the slightest bit pretty, but cost a lot of money all the same. I recognised them because a girl in my year, one who went to junior CND meetings, had special permission to wear cruelty-free shoes to school.

Penelope's hair was curly and hennaed red. Natural dye was rubbish – my mother had taught me that much. More dubious than her Greenham Common hair, even, Edward's ex had a tattoo on her shoulder. I was a bit shocked to see it. I knew they were fashionable on women because I'd seen them in magazines, but never on a woman in Cambridge, at least, not on one who had a degree.

'It's a peacock,' she said, when she noticed me staring.

It was more of a blob, like she'd got it done on the cheap, in prison, perhaps. In magazines, models and actresses got a dolphin or a love heart on their bum or their shoulder. The tattoos were small and arty.

'Why a peacock?' I asked.

'Symbol of Hera, Queen of the Gods.'

So it was some feminist thing. Millie didn't like feminists. She said they gave women a bad name. My teachers at school weren't feminists – they just didn't like men, which was not the same thing.

'Penelope's doing a PhD in philosophy.' Edward smiled at Penelope. She gave a half smile in return.

Millie regarded Penelope with the alarmingly sparkly gaze she reserved for visitors. 'How marvellous to be so clever!'

Penelope looked half pleased and half suspicious. 'I wouldn't say I'm that clever.'

'No need to be modest. So do tell us...What does one do with a philosophy PhD nowadays?'

'Teach, I suppose.'

'How fulfilling!' said my mother.

Penelope screwed up her face. 'Unfortunately, teaching's very time-consuming. And not very well-paid.'

'I suppose what you'd really like to do is sit around and think about things all day.'

'Well, that was the general idea.'

'But I dare say it's a bit tricky to get paid to sit around and think.'

'Impossible, pretty much.' Penelope stared down at the grass. Somehow, in the space of a few sentences, the futility of her existence had been unequivocally revealed. That was one of Millie's talents — to make people realise they were nothing special after all.

My mother reached forward and patted her on the arm. 'Never mind, darling. None of us really ever knows what we want to do when we grow up. I'm sure you'll work it out eventually.'

Penelope recoiled her arm. 'I have worked it out! I am intellectually and emotionally fulfilled. Money isn't everything.

You can't tell me that what you do – flogging booze or what-ever it is – you can't tell me that really makes you happy.'

My mother laughed. 'Gosh, you look so cross! Didn't mean to hit a raw nerve. No offence intended. And as for my job – well, I do find it fun, even if it does have the drawback of being rather well-paid. Does that make me a terribly shallow person?'

Against the raw orange of her hair, Penelope's face was the colour of skimmed milk. Hugh gave her an encouraging smile. 'Fancy another?' He topped up her glass. 'Edward…Why don't you show our guest the blackberry bushes?' He gestured towards the back of the garden. 'Pick some fruit. It'll only go to waste if not.'

I was going to say that the blackberries weren't ripe yet, but Penelope stood up like someone had set fire to the grass she was sitting on. Edward got the hint and swiftly led her across the lawn and out of our sight.

My father gave Millie his sternest disapproving stare.

'Fuck you,' she mouthed in reply.

Our garden was long and thin, so the shrubbery two thirds of the way down made the orchard private, more or less. Orchard was a glorified word for it, but Hugh was proud of this bit of the garden, because it was there before the house and gave our property, he said, a gravitas. It was nothing more than a few cooking apple trees, a pear tree and a couple of bushes – black-berry, redcurrant, and some other thing that was a bit like rosehips but not, which I'd been told not to touch. Sometimes the man in the next street, whose garden backed onto ours, lit a bonfire and turned the orchard air into old treacle.

'So that's Edward's ex-girlfriend?' I asked.

'Don't be nosy,' said my mother.

'We're enjoying high hopes of a reconciliation,' said Hugh.

'Does that mean Edward's moving out?' I said.

'That poor man has shown you nothing but kindness.' My mother looked at me as like I was a snail.

'I was just asking,' I said.

Hugh stared in the direction of the orchard, with this funny look on his face.

'What're you smiling about?' asked Millie.

'Just life. Youth. What it'd be like to be twenty years younger. Marriage. Children. All that to look forward to.'

Millie snorted. 'Marriage and children? Edward's barking up the wrong tree with that one.'

'Don't you think Penelope wants to marry him?' I said.

'What Penelope really wants,' said my mother, 'is a woman with sensible shoes and a lot of cats.'

'So how come she's going out with Edward? If she's actually a lesbian?'

'Was going out,' said Millie. 'And I'm not saying she's a dyke. Just saying she should be, only doesn't know it yet.'

Hugh looked at my mother and slowly shook his head.

In my last On Becoming a Young Woman class, the day before we broke up for the summer, I thought of Edward and Penelope, Hugh and Millie. We were doing money – which was as important as love and sex, according to Mrs Rally. Her financial advice made her sex ed look pretty good. She'd obviously never been self-employed. If you had a job, someone was always making a profit out of you – that's what my father said.

'How do we get money?' she asked.

'Marrying it,' said Connie.

'By curing cancer and winning a Nobel Prize,' said Samantha Burgess.

Getting a Nobel Prize was Samantha's main goal in life. She often said, 'Daddy says that Stephen Hawking's not really a genius, because if he was, he'd have got one by now.' The wider world, I learned, had rather low standards of what constituted a brilliant mind.

Mrs Rally said it was immoral to marry for money, 'But if you happen to fall in love with a rich man, then that's just jolly good luck.'

'What if we end up poor?' asked Molly Wilkins, as if she was reading my mind. Just because we came from nice homes, that didn't mean our homes would be nice, especially not with the economy going to pot. Our parents might end up needing nursing, like Grandpa Eric, and they'd spend our inheritance before we ever got our mitts on it. At the rate my family were going, I might have to make all my money for myself.

Mrs Rally didn't seem bothered by the idea of poverty. 'Jesus was poor, remember. You don't have to have a wonderful job. Just doing a bit of childminding will give you your independence. And remember, if you end up earning more than your husband, you should still do stuff round the house for him, so he thinks he's the boss. That's why Mrs Thatcher makes an omelette for Dennis every morning, even though she's the most important lady in the country.'

All the teachers at school were obsessed with Mrs Thatcher. Mrs Rally saw her as a role model for young girls. We could now do anything: there were no excuses left. The girls who did RE would even be vicars and bishops one day because the Church of England couldn't ban them forever. When we went out to work, the playing field would be level.

But if it was all so easy, then Millie would've been bossing loads of men around at work, which she wasn't, and she wouldn't have to go out drinking with the lads and match them glass for glass and laugh at their jokes. Mrs Rally worked in a women's world, so she didn't know what it was like outside. The trouble with having a female Prime Minister is that now we'd had one, everyone could think that was it. The fact that the next ten or whatever would all be men would then be OK.

The popular girls – the ones who wore DMs at the weekends and put a poster of Che Guevara up in the common room – they all hated Mrs T. They said she wasn't a woman really – she was a man, and that we'd only have equality when society was run along feminine values. If you succeeded as a woman in a man's world, that wasn't really success at all.

There was another poster in the common room, with a woman in a turban on it. It read, 'Women, all around the world, reaching out.' But all I saw at school was women bitching about each other and stabbing each other in the back.

In a world with men in it, like my house, women got treated more nicely.

The last day of term went on for years. We had a long assembly where people got their music certificates handed out and where teachers left to retire or get married. They never left to get a better job – I noticed that. One teacher left to go work in children's TV, but she was only on it once, at breakfast time. Some girls gave each other cards and presents. I got a couple of cards, but only from girls who'd given one to the whole class. Jessica and I didn't do stuff like that. We all had to talk about what we were going to do in the summer, and I was the only girl whose parents hadn't booked yet. Samantha Burgess gasped. 'One year my parents did that, and there was nothing left! We couldn't go on holiday at all!'

Obviously, her parents were lying. You could always go on holiday. Only freaks booked at Christmastime to go in August. Hugh didn't like package holidays because he said he was too old to fly all night to Corfu then get there at four in the morning, then wait another two hours till the room was ready. It was humiliating and you wouldn't treat a veal calf like that. But Millie liked packages because you got a better hotel that way, for less money.

We had to clear our desks, too, because next year it'd be another form in the room. I didn't have much to clear because I'd been sneaking it home, book by book. Most girls took it all in one big wodge because they got picked up by their parents then taken out to lunch, but I never even asked for a lift. My parents had come to the fête, so that was their duty done for the year. They'd probably even forgotten I had a half day.

Everyone got a bit worried about their school reports. Some girls got punished for a bad one because their parents wanted straight As. I worried a bit sometimes. Once our geography teacher wrote 'Freya has approached our studies of the developing world in a dispassionate manner – so much so that it borders upon callousness.' That wasn't very nice. It was because I said that maybe we shouldn't send all that aid to Africa when the people who ran those countries cut the limbs off of babies and had child soldiers and spent half the GDP on coronations and stuff like that. What was the point in me collecting all my pennies for Christian Aid when it went on feeding the soldiers fighting the civil war? Hugh and Millie never even said anything. Maybe they were glad I didn't have a heart.

I cycled home round the back of the Botanical Gardens, beside Hobson's Conduit, one of my favourite buildings. Three times my height, but still clumpy, the octagonal domed mass was made of biscuits and gold, or so it looked. Hobson was the same man from the phrase Hobson's choice. We did him in the Lower Fourth. I told Millie about it, how he got the conduit from Holland to help drain the Fens in Cambridge, so they could graze cattle. And he had stables as well. Before Hobson, if you wanted to hire a horse for the day, the more money you had, the better horse you got, but at Hobson's stables, you had no choice. You got the horse nearest the door, the one that'd rested longest.

'Don't believe it,' said Millie.

'It's true.'

'You can always choose.'

'No, you can't. That's the point of the stables.'

'I bet you it's a myth. If some rich bloke with loads of money waltzed in, they'd give him any old horse he liked.'

'But people would see. The tired horse wasn't worth more money so it'd be cruel to ride it. It makes sense.'

She laughed. 'You! So bloody naïve.'

When I got home, my mother's car was in the drive. If she wasn't at work, she should've been picking me up and I'd like to have made her feel guilty, but she was immune to it. My grandma had made her feel awful all the time, so she got inoculated for life.

The back door was open, which meant my mother must be in the garden. I thought I better check what she was up to before I went and bothered her. There was one room in the house which overlooked the whole garden, just about, even the orchard bit. In Hugh and Millie's bedroom, the back window was high enough so that you could see everything. I wasn't really allowed in my parents' room, but they'd never know.

I eased the window upwards, nervous of the scraping of the sash against the frame, and leaned out. My heart beat fast as a gerbil's. There was a bit of a risk my mother would be able to see me, but it was like that story about Charles the Second hiding in the oak tree – people don't think of looking up.

She sat on the tartan picnic blanket, wearing sunglasses and a black sundress. Next to her was Edward. They were drinking wine. I didn't understand how Edward was there when his car wasn't parked outside. He should be working with my father to save the business, not being home at lunchtime, boozing away with my mother.

One of her hairs had strayed into her mouth, it looked like, so Edward put up his hand to brush it away. She backed away from his touch like she didn't want him near her, like she was angry.

Then she stood up. She was saying something and waving her hands around. She knew not to shout because the Harmisteads next door spent their whole time gardening. Edward looked down and I was glad he was getting it in the neck. She liked telling people off – mainly me. It was something she was good at.

Clearly Edward had been bad in some way, which gave me this bouncy, special feeling inside. He wasn't so perfect after all. When it was just me, Hugh and Millie, I was always the odd one out, but now Edward was here, things might be different. With two men in the house, Millie was bound to get annoyed with them, like this afternoon. Finally, she might start belonging to me.

✳ seven ✳

'You're going to have to be extra nice to your father.' Millie and I were unloading the washing up machine. It was Saturday night and we'd just had Edward's shepherd's pie, which was OK as far as texture went, but he'd put baked beans in and if you cooked with baked beans, the whole thing tasted of them. He should've known that.

'Why do we have to be nice?' I asked.

'Because this tribunal of your father's – it's going to be like in the cultural revolution. You ever do that at school?'

'Which cultural revolution?'

'In China. What other one is there? Where they tie you to a chair and everyone you've ever known, all your friends and family and neighbours and people you work with, they walk round you in a circle and say every nasty thing they've ever thought about you.'

'That's what's going to happen to Daddy?'

'Something like that.'

'But we're not going to join in.'

'Course not.'

'I want to come.'

The stuff with Hugh and his seccie had happened just after Edward came to work there, apparently, but it'd been on the cards for a while. Now Jackie hated my father and was after his blood. She'd put the papers in and now it was going to Industrial Tribunal. Hugh had to hire a lawyer he couldn't afford, but there was no choice.

'A litigant in person has a fool for a client,' he said.

I think that was supposed to be funny.

The navy blue glaze on the shepherd's pie dish was black and crusty, even after it'd been washed. My mother, frowning, picked at a black bit with her fingernail. She got annoyed when the washing-up machine failed her.

'You can't come,' she said.

'But you're going.'

'I have to – for the first couple of days, at any rate. They're saying he hates women, so if I'm not there, it'll look bad.'

'But I'm a woman, too. He needs people on his side and we all are, aren't we? You and me and Edward. We don't care what other people say. We're loyal, no matter what.'

'I'll discuss it with your father.' She dropped the burnt casserole dish into the bin.

On the Monday morning, the first day of the tribunal, we sat in the waiting room for respondents, which meant we were the ones being done. The other side had their own waiting room, separate to ours, so we didn't have to see them. The chairs were orange and the walls were magnolia. Magnolia was absolutely the worst colour to have on walls – I'd learnt that from my father. It was the lowest common denominator of taste and showed no vim, verve or personality. White was a statement, which is why the walls in our house were white. Any other colour just wasn't classic.

Hugh's barrister was a bit younger than my father, but not much because his hair had grey bits in. He wore a pin-striped suit, which is something Hugh never did, because they were vulgar. His shoes were scuffed. When he sat down, you could see where the heels were worn down on one side, which meant he must be walking funny. He was fattish, but in a nice way, with a cosy, saggy-down belly. Millie had already warned me about him.

'He won't be a good barrister,' she said, 'because good barristers work in London, not Cambridge.'

'Why can't we get one from London?' I asked.

'That's what I said. Why spoil the ship for a ha'penny worth of tar? Plus the fact that he's tax deductible. But you know what your father's like.'

The barrister was called William Bloom and he came from the Somerset, but he talked with a normal accent. We had to wait for ages while some other case got settled and William told Hugh about himself, how studied at Cambridge, but he didn't go to a chambers in London because he wasn't interested in the rat race. Millie rolled her eyes when he said that. In our family, the rat race was the only race.

The barrister patted the file on his knee. 'Tricky – cases like this. If you sacked her 'cos she was up the duff, then we'd know where we are. But this kind of thing, it's her word against yours. All a question of whose evidence the panel prefer. Least it's better than if she was black or disabled.'

It was nearly lunch by the time we got called in. Hugh and the barrister sat in front, while Millie and I were at the back, watching.

Jackie, Hugh's ex-secretary, was slumped at the other side of the room. She didn't have a barrister, only a union rep, who was greyhound. He wore a suit, but he didn't look comfy in it. I hadn't seen Jackie that many times before, but when I had, she'd worn shoulder pads, big hair and red lipstick. She didn't look like that now. Her face was scrubbed clean of make up, so that every line showed up in the strip lit courtroom. Her beige suit was creased and baggy, like she'd just lost weight. Her hair was flat, unteased.

The chair of the tribunal was a woman, an older one, and the barrister said he'd been up before her before. She was old and dressed in black and she didn't smile. She was a retired solicitor, apparently, so she might not like barristers, because barristers thought they were better than solicitors, and solicitors knew that. The man and the woman sitting on either side of her were wing members.

William the barrister explained what the wing members were for. 'In theory, they all have an equal vote. But when it comes to the verdict, that's rubbish, obviously.'

I could see why all the parents at school wanted their daughters to be barristers, because there were loads of breaks. The first bit was just an introduction and talking about what documents were allowed and not allowed. William the barrister and the union man both had bundles. Bundle made them sound romantic, like bundles of joy, or the bundle of belongings Dick Whittington had at the end of his stick. In fact the bundle was a big file, like some massively padded history project, full of copied out sections of badly written text books, about how the Spanish Armada limped back to Cadiz. The barrister said how it wasn't a very big bundle at all, which was what you'd expect in this sort of case. 'It's all about witnesses and how they come across. Luckily for us, they're batting first. Gives us time to assess the damage and regroup when we're up.'

Edward gave me a wink that said he knew the barrister was mixing his metaphors.

At lunchtime, Mille and me went to get sandwiches, while the men stayed in the waiting room to talk about the case.

There wasn't anywhere proper to get food, except from a man outside who sold rolls out of a refrigerated wagon. I didn't think we'd be allowed to get them, because I wasn't allowed hotdogs off of market stalls, or eating in the street, because that was infra dig. But Millie said the wagon was fine and that she ate worse things every day, God knows.

'Why didn't Edward make sandwiches?' I asked. 'Wouldn't that've been cheaper?'

'I told him not to bother.' She was dithering between beef and tomato and egg and cress. 'Best knock it on the head for a while.'

'Don't you like his sandwiches?'

My mother turned to me and narrowed her eyes. When she spoke, her voice had a hard London edge. 'Hard to explain this, Frey. But sometimes, when someone does stuff for you, it's nice and that, but it gets on your tits n'all. They scratch your back, so you have to scratch theirs.'

'You don't want to scratch Edward's back?'

She selected a cheddar ploughman's. We got egg salad for the barrister in case he was a vegetarian. Millie said it would-n't matter what we got him. 'Fat people'll eat anything. Just you watch.'

When we got back, Hugh was perkier than he had been in a while. 'It's a relief, frankly, to get it going. The waiting – not knowing what's going to happen – that's what gets to you.'

Millie put her hand on his arm and squeezed it. We were all there, but it was like it was just the two of them just then – her and him. I didn't see my parents together in public very often. At home they spent time in the same room, but my father would be doing his crosswords or his sums while Millie watched telly. If ever we went to a party – which was rare, maybe annual Christmas drinks at the Harmisteads – soon as they got in the front door, they darted off in different direc-tions. They never spent a second with each other all night, not if they could help it.

'Oh, darling,' said Millie, when I protested. 'There's noth-ing so pathetic as couples who cling together for grim death.'

'Maybe they just love each other.'

'Please! That's how they might justify themselves, but it's utter bollocks. That's not why people get married.'

'They do it so they can have children?'

'They're terrified of being alone. Of being themselves. Of people thinking they're gay. They don't want singles' holidays and dinner for one and being pitied. When really, it's the married people who we should feel sorry for. They never had the balls to do it all differently.'

'So you married Daddy because you were scared?'

'Not me. God, no. I had alternatives. A job. Mates. I married your father because he had lovely thick hair and he laughed at my jokes.'

'Is that all?'

'And for other reasons. Private ones.'

I suppose she meant that he was good in bed, which wasn't something I wanted to know.

I wasn't sure whether I'd get married when I grew up. Half the St Joan's teachers were single and they didn't look very well on it, because they were definitely worse-dressed and madder than the married ones. When people didn't do their prep or broke the uniform rules, the misses went mad, like it really mattered.

We did it in history, how people used not to get married so much. In the nineteenth century, fifty per cent of people never got married at all, and no one thought they were gay because they simply couldn't afford it. They were domestic servants or farm labourers and if they'd had children, they wouldn't have been able to feed them. Now, if you were a single woman, you were just sad or lonely. But it was worse for single men. People thought they were gay or serial killers or watched porn all day.

Men could always get someone if they wanted.

After lunch everyone looked happier.

'Always like that,' said the barrister. 'No more first night nerves. Now we're settled in for the duration.'

The one who brought the case had to start it, so Jackie sat down and read out her statement. Hugh must've known what was in it, because he'd been reading the bundle at home in front of the telly.

Jackie's eyes were pink and her voice was trembly. She took off her jacket and you could see how her arms were pink and lumpy, like marshmallows on a skewer.

This is what I remember her saying. The details might be a bit wrong, but I've caught the tone, I think.

I started work for Hugh Baines Associates in January 1986. I was a highly qualified and experienced senior admin officer, but this was my first posting as an office manager. I took a slight pay cut from my previous employment, because Mr Baines assured me that I had excellent prospects for internal promotion within the company, outside of an administrative role.

For the first year of my employment, I worked hard in a busy office, and relations were good between myself and Mr Baines. The business was highly profitable and I received generous bonuses and training opportunities. I was the only female employee.

Last year, the housing market began to cool and Mr Baines changed in his attitude towards me. He took a highly critical view of my work. I worked harder and longer hours in an effort to defer this criticism. Mr Baines was forced to lay off a number of staff and sell properties with negative equity. When the last of his associates left, he decided to advertise a junior position in sales. When I asked if I could be considered for this position, Mr Baines said I didn't have the experience he was looking for. He employed Edward Albany. He told me he was getting him cheap because he had low self-esteem.

Millie laughed. The chair gave her a stern look.

Mr Baines began working longer hours, and we were frequently alone in the office together. I considered leaving, but the job market was increasingly difficult, and I would have found it hard to secure another position at the same rate of pay.

One night Mr Baines asked me out for a drink at the Blue Boar. I agreed, although reluctantly. He bought a bottle of wine and drank most of it on his own. He told me that he didn't have enough money to pay both myself and Edward Albany, and that one of us would have to go. Then he started crying. I patted his hand to comfort him and he put his arms around me. We hugged. I regarded this as a purely professional act of compassion on my part. But then he moved in and kissed me. I didn't want him to kiss me, but I was too scared of the consequences to reject him. As far as I could see, my job depended on it. Then he tried to cup my breast. I was shocked and terrified.

When Jackie burst into sobs, the Chair looked dismayed. 'I suggest we adjourn for the day, if the respondent is amenable.'

We waited while the panel walked out, then we went back to our little room.

William the barrister looked pleased. 'Not bad. If she can't get through reading her own witness statement, it's bonanza time for us. She looks completely crackers.'

'What happens tomorrow?' asked Hugh.

'I'll just grind through, challenging her on points of fact. I won't be going at her all guns blazing, if that's what you're expecting. That's not my style – the whole sneering, sarcastic attitude.'

My father seemed worried. 'But you will go for her, won't you? I mean, we will win?'

'Balance of probabilities. There's a natural sympathy for the defendant, but that can be eroded pretty sharpish. And a female chair, she's not going to have much time for a woman she thinks is using her gender out of malice.'

Hugh's prospects, then, were better than I'd thought. First of all, he had a proper lawyer. Secondly, Jackie was a lot madder than I remembered. It was funny how her statement said she stayed late at the office, because at Bring Your Daughter to Work Day, she told me she never stayed late, not unless it was an emergency, because she had to have 'me time' – whatever that meant.

The barrister looked at his watch. 'Tomorrow ten am. Get here fifteen minutes before.'

'How long will this thing last?' asked Hugh.

The barrister cost hundreds of pounds a day, which is why it was cheaper to settle than go to court. But I think they must've tried that already, because I'd heard Millie on the phone to this woman, Sandra, who she met at antenatal yoga and had lunch with once a year.

My mother had sounded disgusted. 'She won't settle. She's not in it for the money, apparently. She's doing it as a point of principle. For all women.'

On the way home, I sat in the back with Edward. He'd had been quiet all day. Millie told me that was because he wasn't like us – he was sensitive.

'I'm looking forward to tomorrow,' I told them. 'I mean, it's not a holiday, but it's more interesting. And when I go back to school, they'll be so jealous.'

Millie spun round. 'You never talk about this to anyone. Family loyalty. You don't breath a word, not about this, not about anything. You're only coming to court because I can't leave you alone in the house. And cos you've got no aunties, no uncles, no sodding grandparents, and we've no bloody money to pay for someone to check you don't set the place on fire. So you keep quiet. For ever. D'you hear?'

I didn't usually blush when Millie shouted at me, because I was used to it, but it was worse that time because we were in the car, where it sounded a lot louder and where I couldn't escape. The absolutely worst thing was that Edward was there. Millie was always really careful not to shout at me in front of strangers. She tutted when red-faced women with their bra straps showing had a go at their kids in the street. That was vulgar. That's what her mother used to do.

I looked out the window. We were going down Fen Causeway where the cows stood, great black and white blotches on a fluffy snooker table of grass. A female cow was trying to get on top of a male cow. Perhaps she was trying to attract his attention. I'd read in the paper how more people every year get killed by cows than by taking Ecstasy, but still, cows were legal and Ecstasy wasn't.

When we got home we had takeaway pizzas. This was supposed to be a treat, but it wasn't really, because when they came they were cold. No one was eating much, except for me. Millie opened two bottles of wine at once and she and Edward and Hugh all drank a couple of glasses really quickly.

'Haven't you got homework?' asked Millie.

'It's the holidays. I've got a project to do, but I'm not going to start, not for ages yet.'

'Well, go upstairs and work on it for a bit.'

I took the pizza box through to the kitchen. They'd ordered my favourite, Hawaiian with extra chilli, but now looking at the leftovers made me sick.

I went upstairs and read a novel I'd been banned from getting. It was supposed to be about a Swiss finishing school, but really it was about whether it was OK to be a virgin or not. As far as I could tell, no one was supposed to be a virgin anymore. It wasn't like you could capture unicorns, because they didn't exist, but if having sex was anything like in this book, I wasn't sure I fancied it. The whole goldfish thing was particularly disgusting. If anyone put a goldfish anywhere near me, I'd run a mile. Plus it was cruel. Someone should've called the RSPCA.

The back door banged. I looked out my bedroom window and I could see Edward had gone out into the garden. He was smoking, even though he didn't smoke, so he must've taken one of Millie's. He walked round the garden for a while, his lips moving as though he was talking to himself.

I opened my bedroom door and tiptoed out along the corridor, hoping to overhear Hugh and Millie. My mother was sitting at the top of the stairs, in front of the bathroom. She was wearing her work clothes still, the ones she'd had on for the tribunal, but her feet were bare and she'd wiped off all her make up. She'd been wearing a lot of kohl liner that day, though, like Princess Di, so her eyes were still blurred.

'What are you doing here?' she asked.

'I just want to use the bathroom,' I said. 'I do live here. You have an ensuite. You never have to share with anybody.'

'You only share a bathroom with Edward.'

'But that's after years of never sharing, so it's worse for me, specially sharing with a man. He leaves little hairs round the sink like ants. And when he gets out of the shower, he doesn't tread on the mat. He leaves these big wet footprints all over the place.'

She gave a laugh, not a nice one. 'Yeah. You've really suffered.'

'So can I used the shower, then? Or are you using my bathroom as well, now?'

'I was just collecting my thoughts.'

This was a very strange sentence coming from my mother.

She didn't collect anything, except vouchers for free stuff and, ages ago, Green Shield stamps, which she used to buy a garden swing that didn't go in the ground properly.

'What thoughts?'

'Things are complicated, Freya. I don't want you coming to the tribunal tomorrow.'

'But you said I could come.'

'That was wrong. I've rung Jessica's mother. She says you can spend some time over with them, until they go away on holiday.'

'I want to come to the trial.'

'It's a tribunal, not a trial. You should never've come. It wasn't appropriate.'

Typically, the one interesting thing my family had ever done, being taken to court, and I was banned for no reason, when I'd done nothing wrong. 'Why're you sitting on the stairs?'

'I'm thinking, Freya. I'm not ready to sleep yet.'

'You spending the night in the huffy bed?'

'Yeah. Perhaps.'

'And why's Edward smoking your cigarettes?'

'Was he? Naughty boy. Expect he's upset. Must've calmed him down.' She stretched her hand out towards me. 'I'm moving to the huffy bed, darling. Just for a while. You're father and I…We're having a….readjustment.'

'You're not going away?'

'Just to another room. Just for a while. We're very much a family, Freya. Always will be. Remember that.'

'Does our family include Edward?'

'What you getting at?' She narrowed her eyes.

'I just wanted to know if I can talk to him about the bathroom. I mean, if he's going soon, there's no point. But if he's family...'

Millie was silent for a moment. Then she said, 'Yeah. If you like. But politely, Frey. You know how sometimes you can be....'

I gave my mother a kiss on the cheek. 'Yeah. I know.'

On the third day of the tribunal I'd been at Jessica's so long I thought I'd scream. I was dying to be in my lovely empty house so I could spend some time on my own. But when I got back, all the cars were parked out front. The BMW, the Audi and the Mazda luxuriated in the sunlight, pleased with themselves, like they'd won an award.

I walked in the front door and smelled something strange – chemically and sour, like the half a rat we watched the teacher dissect at school. Even though the stereo was playing Sade – the only album my parents had bought that year – Millie heard me come in. She shouted to me through the open sitting room door. 'In here, darling. Come join the party.'

Hugh was on the sofa nearest the window, asleep. Millie sat on the other sofa, while Edward was crouched down on the floor, holding my mother's left foot as he painted her toenails letterbox red.

My mother's feet were not her best feature, because her big toes bent inwards. Plus today her soles were grubby where she must've been walking around in the garden with no shoes on. Her feet probably didn't smell, but you wouldn't catch me touching them. I didn't know how Edward could bear it.

She wriggled her toes. 'No need to look so horrified, darling. He did offer. He's done it millions of times before.'

He grinned. 'My stepmother had a bad back so she could never reach.'

She kicked him lightly on the head with her other foot. 'Oi! You saying I'm like your stepmother?'

'Not at all. Her feet are much daintier than yours.'

Millie put on an expression of pretend outrage and kicked him again, a bit harder this time. Hugh shifted his position on the sofa, but he didn't wake up.

'Why aren't you at work, anyhow?' I asked.

'Good news, darling. Case adjourned. That nasty little piece of Hugh's just couldn't go through with it. Not fit to bear witness.'

'So she's dropping the whole thing?'

Edward had finished his pedicure. My mother inspected the results. 'Hmm. Not bad. Don't expect any tips, though.'

They both giggled.

'Mum!'

Millie turned back to me. 'Sorry, sweetheart. I got distracted….So where was I…? Ah yes. Well, Jackie either looks mad or bad at this point so we're hoping she'll take an offer. Either which way, the present crisis is averted.'

'So we don't have to worry about money any more?'

'God, no. We're still poor as church mice. Or at least, we will be until himself pulls his finger out.' Millie glanced in Hugh's direction. 'Oh. And by the way, your little chums the Glinkas have invited us round next Saturday. They mumbled something about it when I saw them in the freezer aisle and I was noncommittal as I could possibly be, but now she's rung and confirmed, so what could I do? Now don't sulk, Freya. It's not OK for you to have friends I don't know.'

'We aren't really going to go, are we?'

'That's grown-up life. Obligation before fun. I invited them to Hugh's, so they have to have us for dinner. And so it goes on. Dear God. What have I started?'

'Freya?' Edward's knees clacked as he stood up. He had premature osteoarthritis, he'd told me. 'D'you want a cup of tea or something? Or a biscuit, just to tide you over? I've a nice bit of steak for our supper.'

I frowned at him just then, partly because he was trying too hard to be nice, which made me embarrassed, and partly because I was annoyed with him, though I didn't know why. 'I'll have some toast. I'll make it myself,' I said.

The toast took ages. I was so hungry, I kept pulling it out of the machine and nibbling bits off of the edges. I thought about going to the Glinkas for dinner and how awful it'd be. Hugh and Millie pissed, Mrs Glinka feeling sorry for me, and Mr Glinka saying nothing, because he expressed everything he felt through poetry, not through being alive. And Sasha… I couldn't think about that. One thing I did know was that Millie had said yes to going on the Saturday like it was just any ordinary day and nothing special. Which could only mean one thing: for the second year running, she'd forgotten my birthday.

✳ eight ✳

It was a trick day, the August morning my mother took me shopping. The sky might have been spotless when I woke up, but as soon as we got in the car, darkness rolled overhead like a dirty tablecloth.

We went shopping in the Grafton Centre, which was like the centre of town, but tackier, without any colleges in it. Millie liked it because there weren't so many people there and it was cheaper to park. We drove over the bridge where the graffiti read JACK THE BISCUIT IS SKINHEAD OK.

'What about a little black dress?' she asked.

I shuddered. 'No way. I won't need one of those until I'm thirty at least. I was thinking more new jeans. And baseball boots, perhaps.'

She pretended to gag. 'You do realise that most mums with teenage daughters are threatened by their emerging sexuality. I'm scared of yours, all right, but for all the wrong reasons. You have to stop dressing like a Vietnamese rent boy.'

In the end I got pink shiny trousers and a stretchy blouse that'd be see-through unless I wore a vest underneath.

My mother wasn't completely happy. 'Too casual and

149

summery, that get-up. You should never really buy summer clothes. Just wear winter clothes, but less of them.'

She took me for a cream tea in Debenhams, although she just had tea, no scones. Then she sent me off to the toilets to change into my new clothes. I had to wait for ages before I found a free cubicle. I never understood why women took so long to go to the loo. There was no biological reason for it, far as I could work out.

When I came out, she looked almost pleased with me. 'Better. Now, what about hair and make-up?'

'I'm not getting my eyebrows done.'

She laughed. 'That's fine. The two ferrets facing off look might eventually catch on.'

She'd been in a strangely good mood since Hugh's trial stopped. Hugh and Edward were back to work as normal. They spent the evenings planning how to start making money again.

My father said he was now sanguine about the whole thing. 'We could always go bankrupt, then start up again under a different name.'

Millie looked the daggers at him. Everything we had was on tick – the cars and the house and the kitchen appliances – so if my father went bankrupt, then maybe they could take all our stuff off us.

'It'd only be for a while,' he said. 'And just think – the market will rally. Now's the time to buy, not sell. That's what we should be doing. Don't you think, Edward?'

Edward nodded, slowly and sarcastically. He and Millie had a laugh.

'Edward's shouldering the burden,' my mother told me in private. 'Hugh's thinking of making him a partner, even.'

'I thought there was nothing left to be a partner of.'

'Not true. Who told you that?'

'No one.'

'That's business, Freya. Risk. Capitalism. Boom and bust. You don't want your dad becoming a wage slave like me.'

I let her take me to the hairdresser's, where a Spanish woman called Belen gave me layers I wasn't sure about, because it'd be hard to tie them back for games. When we got home, Hugh and Edward didn't say anything about my hair, it couldn't have been too bad.

A bit rich, I thought, my mother saying she was a slave. She got to do whatever she wanted. If she hated her job that much, she could go out and get another one. I, though, had no choice in anything. Millie went on often enough about how horrible childbirth was and how she'd suffered thirty-seven hours of labour and an episiotomy to produce me. But in the end, it clearly hadn't been as memorable as she made out.

On the morning of my birthday my mother pretended she'd never forgotten at all, and it was deliberate that she'd planned the night at the Glinkas' to coincide with my special day. She handed me my present, a satin cocktail frock I'd tried on in the shop with her, but which I didn't want and would never have occasion to wear.

She smiled when I tried it on. 'I only said we'd go to the Glinkas' tonight because you never want to go anywhere special. You can have a treat with your friends if you like.'

I didn't want a treat with my friends. I didn't know who I'd invite, except Jessica and Connie and I wasn't really sure I'd want to invite Connie. I couldn't leave her out, though, because then there'd be a row. Luckily, they'd both gone on holiday, so I was spared the dilemma.

'We can just go out as a family,' I said.

I decided to wait and see if family meant Edward. Also, I realised there was another reason why we were going to the Glinkas' on my birthday: a night round theirs was way cheaper than any other option.

The sight of Edward's special Saturday morning breakfast – pancakes and waffles – made my stomach heave.

My mother didn't like it when I skipped a meal. 'God! Don't tell me you're joining the ranks of the anorexic. Every time I see your chunky little calves I thank my lucky stars.'

I waited for my father or Edward to say something nice about my legs, but they pretended not to have heard.

When I rang Jessica, she thought it was awful that Hugh and Millie were having dinner with the Glinkas. She said it better not be the beginning of a trend. Her parents had tried to be friends with Connie's parents, but she'd put a stop to that.

'I have my life and they have theirs. Your parents don't really have your best interests at heart.'

'Why not?'

'Because human beings are selfish. Bound to be. Even my

parents, who are much more human than yours. My mother apologised about the thing with Connie's parents and then she got a bit weepy and said how she'd forgotten how nearly grown up I was. From now on, she's going to accept my boundaries.'

'What does boundaries mean?'

'Not coming in my bedroom without knocking. And that maybe I can get my own phone line.'

Jessica was only slightly less indulged than Connie was: this, surely, was no preparation for adult life. I didn't have much power over my boundaries where Millie was concerned. She was peeved that I'd got myself a mother substitute in Mrs Glinka. As far as she was concerned, I was one child with two parents – three if you counted Edward – which should've been more than enough. We both knew I'd been disloyal and now was time for me to pay the price.

My mother wore high heels and a little black dress and too much make up. She'd also recently started wearing this perfume that came in a flamboyant twisty bottle and smelled of exotic hamster. I coughed when she strolled downstairs.

She scolded me. 'Don't do that, darling. It's terribly rude. One day you'll learn to get more sophisticated.'

My father wore a cravat, which embarrassed me, because it made him look like he was trying to be posh. Cravats were like bow ties – not normal things worn by men. He thought it gave him personality. Millie said on most people cravats were disgusting, but on Hugh they were OK. His accent, which was a mixture of public school posh and Brighton spiv, allowed him to carry it off, she said.

Edward was the only one who looked normal. He was in jeans and stripy shirt he hadn't ironed. Millie tutted when she saw him. 'Take that off and let me press it, at least. I'm begging you.'

But he shook his head. 'Can't start ironing stuff at the week-end. That's where the rot starts.'

He caught my eye and I couldn't help laughing. Edward, I'd started thinking the last week or so, might be the partner in crime I'd always been denied. First he'd been Hugh's, then Millie and Hugh's, but now, potentially, he was mine.

Mrs Glinka had told us 7.30 for 8, but we got there too early, so we sat in the car, staring at the house. The earth around was churned up, buckled with heat, the lawn scuffed as if space-ships had used it as a landing site.

'What a funny house,' said Millie. 'Teeny weeny. What's the point in living in the middle of some bloody field if you end up without any space?'

'It's not so small,' I said.

She sighed. 'Ah! Your devotion. It's so touching.'

When Mrs Glinka opened the door, I could see my mother was wildly overdressed. Mrs Glinka wore one of her everyday outfits, a full skirt and a shiny blouse with a pussy cat bow at the front. She flashed her gold-encrusted teeth.

'You look very nice,' she said to Millie. 'Beautiful dress. And what a figure! You won't be able to eat anything tonight,

I'm afraid. None of it's any good for someone on diet.'

She led us through into the dining room. Even though the sun still drooped in the sky, the room was dark, all shiny wood, heavy curtains. On the sideboard stood Russian bowls and spoons, decorated with berries and flowers in the Rasta colours – red, gold, green and black.

'What's this stuff called?' asked Hugh.

'Chochloma.' Mrs Glinka rasped the hard 'chs' from the back of her throat. 'Roman hates it. But his mother keeps sending it to us, so we have to keep it.'

'Your husband has a mother?' I asked. Mr Glinka didn't seem like he'd ever been somebody's son.

Mrs Glinka looked at me strangely. 'Oh yes. Everybody has a mother.'

Hugh handed her a couple of bottles of wine in a plastic bag. They were nice ones, although it was cheating really, because Millie had bought them at discount.

Mrs Glinka looked pleased. 'Marvellous. Marvellous! But I never really drink any more. Not since I started the change.'

She poured Hungarian wine into goblets made of Bohemian crystal. I only got half a glass. Millie held her wine up to the light. She was either valuating the crystal or marvelling at how small a measure she'd been given.

'Excuse me.' Our hostess hurried out towards the kitchen.

We didn't dare sit at the table, which was laid out with a cloth white as a shroud.

Edward took in the dark wood and white doilies. 'Rustic. Unpretentious. Must be lovely to have a culture.'

'Bigger inside than out,' said Millie.

Hugh said nothing. I knew he wouldn't like it. He found it physically painful to be around antiques. If we ever went to a museum, he stayed in the coffee shop.

Mrs Glinka came in carrying bowls of hot red soup on a tray.

'Sit! Sit!' she said.

We stood for a while, not sure of where to place ourselves, because where would Sasha and Mr Glinka go?

Just as we had dithered to the limit of social tolerability, the men of the house appeared, as if summoned by a whistle only they could hear.

'Hi,' said Sasha. He hadn't dressed up, not like us. He was in jeans and a T-shirt, which made me really cross I'd been made to wear my new trousers and wispy top.

'Welcome, my friends!' Mr Glinka strode into the room like he was appropriating it for an invading army. He hugged my father and Edward in turn, then gave them a firm peck on each cheek. Social hugging and kissing between two men was not the done thing back then. Edward responded to Mr Glinka's embrace as if it was the most natural thing in the world. My father would clearly have much preferred a firm handshake, but sportingly submitted. Mr Glinka turned to me and kissed my hand. His bristly mouth scratched my skin but I didn't flinch. I hadn't much experience in having my hand kissed, but I guessed that recoiling wouldn't be polite. He saved my mother for last. He gave her a look of wondering admiration, like he was seeing the Taj Mahal for the first time. He gave her the same kiss on the hand he gave me, but as he bent his head, he murmured, 'Enchanted.'

I looked at my mother, waiting for her to roll her eyes to show what a ludicrous rigmarole this all was. But instead she gave her girlish laugh – not the deep phlegmy one she used at home. She gazed Mr Glinka with mock shyness. She parted her lips, about to say something, then didn't speak. It wasn't often I'd seen my mother at a loss for words.

Silently, we spooned sour cream into our soup. I'd watched Mrs Glinka make borsch before now, so I knew it was more cabbage than beetroot and that she cooked it for about three days. Small wonder it looked better than it tasted. Sasha mixed his sour cream in, turning the liquid dark pink and globuled – bloody, like a liquid salami.

'Delicious,' said Hugh, although I knew he hated beetroot. But my father was brought up during rationing, so he could eat anything. 'Lovely house you have.'

Mrs Glinka laughed. 'Except we don't really have it. A house and no land. The university let us live here when Roman first came, when they thought he was another Tsvetayeva or Mandelstam. Now we can't move. Who in this market buys a house with no land?'

'Still – a marvellous little billet. Bijou.'

'We wouldn't mind if the university gave us a house at a knock-down price,' said Millie. 'Not that that's ever going to happen. No geniuses in our family.'

I thought this was a bit mean, because I hadn't been given the chance to be a genius yet.

'Roman works hard at a job which demeans him. We have no reason to feel guilty,' said Mrs Glinka.

'Nothing demeaning about selling big clothes. Growth market, as far as I can see,' said Edward.

Since no one else obliged, he gave his own joke a hearty laugh. I joined in a bit, too. Then Sasha laughed and couldn't stop. He giggled for ages, even after Edward and I had stopped. His mother glowered at him.

Mr Glinka mumbled something.

'Catalogue,' Mrs Glinka explained. 'Fat people don't want to go out and shop. They do home shopping.'

'When I was younger,' Edward said, 'I never understood why flies were so short. You know, the flies in trousers. But then some old chap in a gentleman's outfitters explained it to me, how waists aren't supposed to go round your middle – not at all. Trousers are designed to be zipped up under your bulging stomach. So after all those years of cursing short zips, now I'm grateful.'

Mrs Glinka waved her hand dismissively. 'You are still a young man.'

Edward dipped some bread in his borshch and mopped it up. 'Oh, no. Once you're over twenty-five, you're just like everybody else. No real difference, is there, between thirty and sixty? Just a working stiff.'

Mrs Glinka narrowed her eyes. 'Marriage and children, though? Easy at thirty. Not so easy at sixty.'

Edward blushed. 'Ah, yes. Quite. But there's plenty of time for that.'

'Men, I suppose, they don't worry so much about getting left on the shelf.'

'Except they should.' Millie set down her soup spoon. She'd only eaten half. She didn't believe in soup because it wasn't proper food. If ever they offered her soup of the day as a starter in a restaurant, she wrinkled her nose and refused even to listen when they told her what kind it was. 'Men get worse than women do, on their own. Fussy. Set in their ways. Maybe they can reproduce at eighty, but who on earth'd want them?'

'I expect, Edward, that you play the field. Love 'em and leave 'em,' said Mrs Glinka.

Edward stared down into his soup.

Millie spoke for him. 'Edward's just coming out of a rather traumatic break-up, actually. Hugh and I are offering him support. And of course, he's a tremendous asset to us. Isn't he, Hugh?'

My father gave a strange smile. 'Oh, yes. Very handy about the house. In all kinds of ways.'

Then there was silence.

'Finished?' said Mrs Glinka.

Everybody nodded. We'd all eaten up our soup, more or less, apart from Millie.

'What?' said Mrs Glinka. 'Did you not like it?'

Sasha laughed, but no one else did.

Millie and Mr Glinka said they'd go out for a fag.

'You can smoke in the house, at the table, even,' said Mrs Glinka.

But Millie waved the ashtray away. 'The night is so refreshing. It's no bother.'

My mother and Mr Glinka went outside together. I didn't envy her having to make conversation with him, but as she often said, 'Smokers always have something to talk about. Like mothers. Or motorcyclists.'

The next course was beef stroganoff, greasy rice, and tiny onions in a béchamel sauce. Sasha scoffed down big portions of everything and stayed quiet, like his father. Millie asked for a little helping and I could tell Mrs Glinka didn't like that. Mrs Glinka didn't approve of fat people, even though she was fat, but she didn't like thin ones, like my mother, either.

'Traffic's a nightmare over the railway bridge,' said my father.

Mrs Glinka shrugged. 'I never go over there. And Roman likes to take the bus into town. Parking is such nonsense.'

Road routes, my father's failsafe conversational topic, had failed.

Mrs Glinka spooned more stroganoff onto my plate, even though I put out my hand and said I'd had enough.

She said, 'The longer I live, the more I realise how silly it is to go out. I have everything here. Kitchen, garden, bed. What more does one require?'

Millie's face was getting a little pink now. 'Yeah. Stay home, play house. Chance'd be a fine thing.'

'Two cars, private schools... None of this is necessary. Just look at Roman's sister. She has a dacha outside Leningrad. Just a hut, but exquisite. You swim in the lake. Eat the biggest, juiciest tomatoes you have ever seen.'

'Big 'cos they come from Chernobyl,' said Sasha.

Millie smiled. 'We're terrible, aren't we? What can I say? A little bit of security. Not such a bad thing when you've grown up poor.'

Mrs Glinka refused to agree, even a little. 'The only life is the spiritual life. That's how I was brought up. But I see it's not for everyone.'

'Suum cuique,' said Hugh. He paused, then added, 'Each to his own.' It was always socially acceptable, far as I could make out, to say something banal – so long as it was in Latin.

Mrs Glinka kept staring at Millie. 'The only thing more important than that which we offer up to God is what we give to our children. They are everything. The sun and the moon. Day and night.'

My mother shook her head. 'For God's sakes! This one's spoilt enough as it is. Thinks the world revolves around her. Needs to learn sooner rather than later that life's not quite like that.'

Mrs Glinka's face kept changing just then, the way the sun goes hot then cold on a windy day. She was amazed, then furious, then outraged, then sad.

My mother giggled. 'Oh God! Your face! You should see yourself! You are just priceless!'

Mrs Glinka's face settled on a lemony regret. 'You yourself – you were ignored as a child, I expect.'

My mother opened her mouth, like she was about to speak. Her red lipstick had rubbed off onto her teeth, like she'd just chewed angrily on a crayon. Then she closed her lips. She didn't find anything to say and neither did anybody else. The silence continued for a few seconds, then another few seconds. It went on so long, I wondered whether anybody would ever speak again.

Mrs Glinka didn't so much break the tension, as ratchet it up. 'I would have given my right hand for a daughter half as good as yours. Where is your love going, if not to her?'

My mother gulped. When she spoke, her words came out small and scratchy. 'Freya is, of course, the joy of all our lives. She is a very special young woman. And obviously, I appreciate you for recognising that.'

I couldn't help grinning, because Mrs Glinka had stood up for me against Millie and Mrs Glinka had won. I'd never seen anyone do that before. And then I remembered, as my mother had told me often enough, that everyone sometimes wishes they were adopted. I'd wished that quite a lot.

Mrs Glinka fixed her gaze on Edward. 'And you, how do you fit into all this? First here, then there. No fixed abode. No real roof over your head.'

Edward smiled, but nervously. 'Oh, it's really not like that.'

He glanced about him, to Hugh, then to Millie, searching for rescue, but we all ignored the SOS. By this point, it was every man for himself.

Mrs Glinka pressed on. She leaned forward, resting her bosom on the table. 'But you have a girl, yes? One you keep hanging around? Seeing but not seeing?'

Edward's mouth fell open. He gave me a glance which said he knew I'd been gossiping. Then he looked back into Mrs Glinka's relentless ink black eyes. 'Um. If you're talking about Penelope, then no. We're not together any more. So my current arrangements are quite…they're working out fine, actually. For the foreseeable. Thank you for asking.'

Mrs Glinka seemed pensive, like she'd discovered something shameful.

After she'd cleared the plates, all the grown-ups went outside together for a cigarette, even Hugh and Edward.

I followed Sasha into the kitchen, where he was washing the dishes by hand, because his family didn't even have a washing-up machine. 'Shall I dry?'

He glanced at me over his shoulder. 'Poor little rich girl. You don't know how.'

'Do so. But I don't have to help, because I'm a guest. Suit yourself.'

'It'll drain on the rack.' Patiently, he soaped the stroganoff pan, raising mounds of soft white foam. His movements were deliberate, dextrous − a ballet for hands. 'Know why mum invited your lot tonight?'

'No.'

'Because of the party round yours. Mum feels she should go, but she can't. She doesn't like strangers.'

'She likes me.'

'You're young. Not scary. She was thinking if she knew

your parents a bit, she might be able to face it.

I studyied the vulnerable nape of his neck, newly clipped, where the sun had burned the skin and bleached the hair. 'I thought she invited us because she wanted Millie to trust her. So I could keep coming round.'

'That's a very solipsistic view.'

'What does that mean?'

'Go look it up.'

'You're not very nice.'

Sasha turned round. He left the dishes in the sink, then sat down at the kitchen table and pointed towards the chair beside him. Obediently, I sat down.

'I am quite nice, actually,' he said. 'But you're a kid, so I treat you like one. D'you get me?'

I nodded, even though I didn't get it.

He breathed out, like he was tired. 'There's a thing on next week, if you want to come. Some mates of mine are doing this Death of Summer ball out at the rugby club. Twenty quid a ticket.'

'Is summer dead already?'

'Near as dammit. If you can sell ten tickets to your mates, you get to go free.'

'I don't think I have ten mates.'

'Doesn't matter. Just bring the ones you were with the other day. They're quite fit. It's just an offer. If you don't want to go, it's no biggie. Just thought I'd mention it, that's all.'

'Even though I'm a kid?'

He grinned. 'The ball will not be an appropriate venue for

164

a young lady, if that's what you're asking. But that's OK once in a while.'

For a minute, I'd thought Sasha was asking me out. But then he'd made it pretty obvious he was just selling tickets as a favour for a friend.

'I'll ask Millie,' I said.

He patted my hand. 'You do that.'

'You are going to be there, aren't you?'

He chuckled – and not in a nice way.

Outside, their faces illuminated by light from the kitchen window, I saw my mother chatting to Mr Glinka.

'Why's your dad so quiet all the time?' I asked.

Sasha said, 'He's a pretty amazing guy actually. But I think being amazing exhausts him, so most of the time he conserves his energy.'

Mr Glinka was telling my mother some story, waving his hands around and doing sound effects, even. That was the response Millie got from men: she could get chat out of a Trappist monk, I expect. She laughed uproariously, as if he'd just told the most hilarious joke in the world. I wondered where she'd learned how to bring out the amazingness in men and whether, if I asked her, she'd be able to teach me, too.

The grown-ups came back, cold from the outside and Mrs Glinka served coffee – real stuff from a cafetière, not instant like we had at home. Then she nipped back to the kitchen. Mr Glinka turned off the lights and everybody giggled. Of course, I guessed what was coming next.

Mrs Glinka glided in carrying a birthday cake with fifteen candles. As they sang Happy Birthday I pretended to be embarrassed, when actually I was thinking – about bloody time, too.

'Chocolate sponge with raspberries,' said Mrs Glinka. 'I wanted to make one, but your mother got it from Fitzbillies.'

'Make a wish,' said Millie, when I leaned forward to blow out the candles.

Mr Glinka turned on the lights. 'What did you wish for?' He leaned over me and his breath against my neck was hot and drunk.

'Nothing,' I said. 'Everything is just perfect.'

My mother gave a satisfied snort that said I told you so.

'Maybe we should walk?' I suggested, before we got in the car to go back.

But Millie took the car keys off Hugh and unlocked the driver's door. 'Don't be stupid. It's only half a mile or so.'

'But you've been drinking!' I looked at Edward, hoping he'd overrule my mother. My father would never dare, but Edward, from what little I knew of him, seemed more sensible than either of my parents.

He shrugged. 'One sniff of the barmaid's apron, and I'm anybody's. How much did you have, Millie?'

'Two glasses, tops. Just get in.' She turned the key in the ignition.

I climbed in the back, but I was cross no one had listened to me. However good my mother was at driving while pissed and wearing high heels, she still shouldn't do it. All the journey back, I longed for her to crash the car or get stopped so the police could breathalyse her, but of course, neither of these things happened. That was typical. My mother always got away with everything.

As we pulled up outside our house, Hugh turned to her. 'Decent people, the Glinkas, though I'm not so sure I'd like to be trapped in a lift with either of them.'

'Oh, I don't know,' she said. 'The way she yaks on means she does all the work. And he's no bother. Quite nice, really – the way he sits there like a big sullen cactus.'

Hugh shook his head in disbelief, like they must have been at two different dinner parties entirely.

I couldn't sleep that night because I didn't feel happy like I had earlier, when I cut my cake. My heart was being squeezed by a giant hand. When I went downstairs to make a hot chocolate, I saw the sitting room door a little bit open. One of the lights was on – not the main one, but even so – and the telly too, so no wonder I couldn't sleep. It was still officially my birthday, so maybe it'd be OK to walk in. I hesitated outside the door. But then I heard this sound, slurpy and needy, like suckling kittens.

I listened harder and realised it was a mixture of noises – squeaking and whispering. I edged towards the crack in the door until I could see the back of Millie's head. She was sitting on the sofa, but the wrong way round, her legs splayed out to either side, jagged and white, like she'd broken them in an accident.

Then I realised it wasn't so much a case of what she was sitting on, as who. Her hands were clasped around Edward's head as she kissed him – that was the horrible slurping noise. She was a sow at the trough while Edward was grotesque – a vile pudgy man chair.

Holding my breath, I backed away from the door, tiptoed upstairs then got back into bed. I lay there, waiting for the anger to flame through me. Edward, after all, was shaming my father, his boss, in his own house. There was no excuse, even if Hugh had probably done it with Jackie.

I tried, but after the initial shock, I didn't feel so cross. Hugh, after all, didn't pay my mother enough attention. She complained that since I was born, all my father's love went to me, not her, so it wasn't surprising she wanted more. I suppose I must've known that something was going on. I'd try not to think about it. I closed my eyes and thought of Sasha, our limbs meshed together, the knottiness of his forearms.

I slept until dawn, when I was yanked from sleep. I was breathless, sweat-slicked, my whole body twitchy and tender. My belly spasmed as if I was going to vomit, but I didn't feel sick – just scared and excited at the same time. Maybe it was the cake, or the heat, or the wine I shouldn't have drunk the night before.

Whatever was wrong with me, it sent me straight to sleep. By the time the alarm went, I was good as new, like if nothing'd happened.

✳ nine ✳

My mother had already gone to work but it wasn't like she hadn't thought of me before she left. Outside my bedroom door, on the back of a flyer advertising the benefits of double glazing, lay one of her lists.

Do not under any circumstances stay in bed
Don't you have some holiday project to do?
Make a new friend
Sandwich for lunch – cheese in fridge only one day
out of date
No complaining – you are on holiday and have
nothing to complain about.

The list didn't even make sense because if I'd stayed in bed all day, I'd never have got round to reading it. I'd no intention of following any of her instructions. She knew nothing about my holiday project, so she'd never find out whether I'd done it or not and there was no way I was prepared to eat cheese that was off or make friends like I was a six-year-old. Plus how could I complain when I was on my own? I put the list with the rest, in the dossier I was compiling on the disturbed balance of my mother's mind.

Downstairs, I picked the paper up off the mat. On the front page was a picture of two dragonflies mating, while the caption said this was a sign summer had really arrived. The beautiful male one, covered with turquoise spots, had hold of the female's neck. The female wasn't so pretty – all brown and yellow like a long wasp. If that was what they were putting on the front of The Times, then clearly nothing was happening in the world.

The corpulent air promised rain. The clouds were slices of puffy white bread, sandwiching the atmosphere to the earth.

'Storm brewing,' said my father.

'Best bring the milk in.' Edward darted outside to salvage the bottles from their plastic caddies. 'Thunder makes the milk go sour.'

The milk bottle holders were crusted green with algae. When we had a cleaning lady, she used to empty them out, but now no one bothered, so the milkman had to leave stuff we drank in what was basically a stagnant pond. Sometimes, grown-ups could be very lazy.

Hugh and Edward drove into the office together. They asked if I wanted a lift to go see Jessica but I lied and said no because Connie's mother was going to pick me up on the way back from Sainsbury's. Of course, I wasn't going to Connie's at all: I'd made newer, better plans. I was going to get Edward away from my mother. He was going to pay.

*

First I thought about doing something to his car, so I took his keys off of the hook in the kitchen.

The Mazda roosted smugly in the driveway, which was totally wrong, for a start, since my father had to park his on the street. I climbed into the driver's seat and stretched my feet towards the pedals. I could've moved the seat forward, but I was scared I wouldn't be able to get it back again. The plastic bit in the door was full of sweet wrappers: Edward seemed to like Marathons and KitKats and Twixes pretty much equally. The mileometer read 84,000, which explained why the Mazda made that tired farty sound when it drove along.

Even though the car was pretty old and rubbish, I could still do something to make it more horrible. I'd read about it in the paper – how angry ex-wives did in their husbands' motors. I could put sugar in the petrol tank or a kipper under the bonnet, but then it'd be obvious who'd done it. If I'd been able to drive, I'd have just zoomed away and plunged the banger into a ditch and even if my fingerprints were on it, that kind of evidence was purely circumstantial. I banged my fists against the steering wheel and the horn went off, just a little, which made me scared in case the neighbours heard. What if I got caught when I hadn't even done anything? I was no good at being bad: my parents had always outnumbered me, like in a high-security prison where there were always more guards than murderers.

Then it came to me – how to get my own back on everybody, not by being evil, but the reverse, by being really really good, like a heroine in Bunty. I realised then that I must be properly clever – not just at schoolwork, but at life.

I hadn't been in the spare room since it became Edward's. I'd wanted to looky-see, but it seemed rude. Plus I knew it'd be different, which I wouldn't like. His toothbrush and shaving things in the bathroom were bad enough.

When I first walked in, it was like no one lived there. Maybe Edward was like me, and didn't understand why people had posters and pictures. If you saw them every day, you stopped noticing them, even, so what was the point? There was a book on the bedside table about how to get people to do what you wanted. On the front it had a quote – 'Success is getting what you want. Happiness is wanting what you get.' Some self-help guide for business, I suppose it was, but he'd obviously bought it to use on my family instead.

He'd only filled half the wardrobe, which meant either he didn't have much to wear, or he'd left lots of stuff round Penelope's. He had jeans, chinos, suits I'd never seen him in, and a dozen shirts, all decent brands, though poorly treated, with missing buttons and manky cuffs. Edward's clothes, although vaguely interesting, weren't strictly relevant. It was information I was after.

At the office, Hugh and Edward had this big Rolodex full of names and addresses which they guarded with their life, because in their game, contacts were everything. Hugh had started it long before Edward. When I was little, I'd loved listening to the thwack of card against card – the sound sumo wrestlers made when they slapped their haunches. But the Rolodex wouldn't have the address I wanted. Edward would have it stashed somewhere at home.

A little chest of drawers stood by the bed, the top of it scarred by coffee cups – not our coffee cups, obviously, because we always used coasters – but by the cups of whoever had owned the chest of drawers before. We'd had the chest for years, since before I was born. Hugh had bought it from a junk shop to furnish his first flat, then never thrown it out. He kept it, I think, as a reminder of how far he'd come.

Edward didn't have a Filofax, even though they were the best and latest thing, so you could show everyone how busy you were. He didn't like anything that looked too grown up, like suits and briefcases and proper cars, because he preferred, he said, a smart casual personal style. Clearly he'd be a rubbish spy, because he'd made no effort to hide his secrets. Soon as I opened the top drawer of the little chest, I found it – a brown leather book embossed with Edward's name. On the front page it said 'Property of Mr Edward Albany.' I didn't like to think it, but Albany was a really lovely name – much nicer than my family one. Freya Albany would sound way better than Freya Baines.

I turned the page, and there, under owner's contact details, inscribed in his happy rounded handwriting, was the address of our house. It made me feel a bit sick when I saw that. He really thought he lived with us. On top of our address was another one – crossed out, but not so I couldn't read it. I smiled when I saw how near it was – further than I'd normally go on a bike, but not so far as Sainsbury's. I imagined the look of surprise when I arrived at the door – the confusion, then the pleasure. I was about to do a very good thing indeed.

I knew she'd be in because that was one of the things Edward complained about. He went out in the world all day, making phone calls and having meetings and driving about in the Mazda, while she sat in her room, mostly.

Sometimes she went to the library, where she was a member of the Cheese Scone Society. The society met for tea and cheese scones and that was their idea of fun, which just went to show that being a grown-up was nowhere near as enjoyable as it looked. Other times, according to Edward, she drove round to the university computer department to type up her thesis. All her friends were the same – they'd used up their grants and now they relied on part-time teaching or overdrafts or boyfriends or parents to keep them going. They were miserable because there weren't any jobs, so it wasn't even like they had the option of selling out. That's how I knew Penelope would most likely be home, because only really poor or really rich people were always in.

She lived to the north of town, not far from Connie. If anyone asked me where I'd gone, I could say I went to Connie's, which I'd do later, as an alibi. Her house was close to Midsummer Common, where they had the Strawberry Fair, and I once came third in the under 12s T-shirt designing competition, except that actually, Hugh had done the design, so I hadn't really won. Winning still felt good, though, even when I hadn't deserved it. Hugh especially didn't like that bit of town. The muesli belt, he called it. Full of hippies who though trees were just as important as people. But I quite liked the ruddy-faced terraces cosying up to each other. I didn't see that living in a detached house was the only human way of being civilised.

Penelope's was a lower ground floor flat in a converted Victorian terrace. Poor Penelope – conversions were never as good as purpose-built. Plus a lower ground flat, I knew from my father, equalled basement, which equalled total crap. I was surprised that Edward lived somewhere so rubbish when he was in the property game, but then probably they'd been renting, which was the greatest crime of all, since rent was dead money. Edward must either have been really skint or insufficiently committed.

Commitment was a problem all men suffered from. We'd done that in On Becoming a Young Woman. It was biological, apparently, because they wanted to give their sperm the best possible chance. The job of society was to stop men putting their sperm wherever they wanted. In this case, society was me.

I pressed my finger to the buzzer. I knew Penelope was in because her handbag-on-wheels car stood outside. There'd be no escaping.

When she came to the door, her red hair wasn't curly any more in a tumbly-down-her-back sort of way, but more frizzy, like sofa fabric scratched fluffy by a cat. She wasn't wearing make-up, so she had no eye lashes whatsoever and her dungarees didn't help her look remotely like a girl. I was worried then, because I could see why Edward had lost interest.

From her blank expression, she neither knew nor cared who I was. I dare say I was an unpleasant reminder that she was old already, because she was twenty-five and still hadn't thought what to do when she grew up. I was her before she made silly decisions – like getting a tattoo and writing a PhD that no one would ever read.

'I'm Freya!' I spoke in a perky voice, then held out my hand for Penelope to shake.

She looked at my hand like she thought it was dirty, then touched it very lightly. Millie said that some women didn't shake hands because it was unladylike, but I couldn't very well lean forward and kiss Penelope – that'd be just weird.

I presented her with the invitation. 'Hugh's fiftieth. It's going to be a really great party. Free wine. You don't even have to bring a bottle.'

She opened up the envelope. The invites weren't posh, not really, not engraved or anything, but Edward had designed them on the computer with a little champagne glass drawn in the corner. You could hardly tell they were home-made at all.

As she read it, I got a feeling round my neck like I was wearing a scarf that was pulled too tight. I reminded myself that I'd been told to invite whoever I wanted. Penelope was the guest I'd chosen.

She ran her white blue fingers over the edge of the card. There was something about redheads that was different from other people. I'd never picked on a ginger, because I wasn't the kind of girl who picked on people – I was too well brought-up for that – but I still couldn't help looking at them. It wasn't just the hair, but their skin and the way you could see their blood flow.

Penelope held the invite like it was radioactive.

'Edward really really wants you to come,' I said.

What if Edward had invited Penelope already, without my knowing? Even if he had, that was easily explained away. I concentrated on breathing slowly. It was like Mrs Rally had said in our Self-Actualisation session, 'You can do whatever you want in life, cope with any situation. All you have to do is breathe deeply and concentrate.'

'You sure he asked me?' Penelope screwed up her face.

'We wrote a list. Your name was on it.'

'Then why didn't he deliver it himself?'

'Cos I'm visiting a friend who lives round the corner from you. It's my holidays. My friend's name is Connie.'

It was always best to include details if you were lying. I wasn't a good liar – not at all – but I was banking on the fact that Penelope would want to believe me. Also, I was assuming that she wouldn't ring Edward, that they weren't in contact and that she was still fancied him enough to come see him. My plan relied on lots of assumptions: that was its major flaw.

She was trying not to appear excited, but her eyes had the same poignant look as a rabbit round feeding time. 'You can tell Edward I'll think about it.'

'Great!' I gave her the sort of smile she'd expect from a nice fifteen-year-old girl. 'And wear something pretty. You know. Glam.'

It was a bit embarrassing telling a grown-up woman what to wear, but I couldn't risk her turning up her dungarees, even if she did think they were fashionable. I was doing her a favour.

As I pedalled up the road towards Connie's, the wind swooped in from the canal, fanning the sweat on my collar bone. When I thought of Penelope and her happy Edward-expectant face, the awfulness of the night before grew fuzzy. I might have just been dreaming when I saw Millie with Edward. I'd a new dream now – of Edward and Penelope back together.

'See a vision of the world, and that vision will come true,' Mrs Rally said.

Now the first part of my vision was up and running, the rest should be easy.

We lay under Connie's duvet, eating chocolate digestives. Connie had a double bed all to herself, so if friends came to stay, they could bunk up with her. Then, when she was old enough to have boyfriends, they'd be able to sleep there as well. I didn't think I approved of that.

Connie claimed it was the only way to live. 'My parents think it's barbarous to sleep in a single bed, even if you're single. I've had this one since I was seven.'

Jessica stuffed a biscuit into her gob. 'You know, Connie. Your house really is brilliant. I never thought I'd like one better than mine, but I do. You're so lucky.'

I couldn't bring myself to agree. The walls were decorated with bobbly wall-hangings and collages made of recycled waste – the sort of thing that'd never be an investment. The kitchen was full of beans in jars and icky brown sauces that had weird names, like tamari. Her family used apple juice instead of sugar: that just wasn't natural.

I asked Connie how come she was allowed to eat shop-bought biscuits.

'Contraband,' she whispered. Her and Jessica had a good laugh.

That morning was the first time I'd seen them since they'd been on holiday – Jessica to Florence and Connie to a yoga retreat in Greece – and already I wished I hadn't come. They compared tans and related their exploits in bum-numbing detail. For Millie, being boring was the greatest crime of all. 'There's nothing duller than other people's holidays or other people's dreams. Never mention yours to anybody.' I told Jessica and Connie I'd been pleased to stay in Britain. 'After all, it has been the hottest summer since 1976,' I said. They looked at me like I was speaking in tongues.

Jessica and Connie had come back different from their trips abroad. Before, Connie had been a dark-haired, breastless beanpole, while Jessica was a fair, porky milkmaid type. But since they'd been away, they'd grown more alike. Connie had filled out a bit and her hair had turned a strange burnt orange colour. 'Sun-In and henna,' she said. 'Hope it grows out before start of school.' Jessica now had bigger breasts and something that could be described as a waist. They'd both got the same new haircut, a bob with a long fringe which they kept away from their eyes with pink sparkly hair clips. When had that happened?

'I don't know about this thing, Freya.' Connie took the biscuits off of Jessica, before she scoffed the lot. 'Death of Summer Ball. I mean. It's a bit pseud, isn't it?'

'I think it's more Sloane than pseud,' said Jessica. 'I mean, pseuds and goths and stuff, they don't do balls, do they?'

'Sasha's not a goth or a Sloane or a pseud,' I said.

Connie and Jessica looked at each other, then burst out laughing.

'What?' I could feel myself scowling.

Jessica sang. 'Freya and Sasha, sitting in a tree, K.I S.S.I.N…'

My face grew hot. 'Stop it! I need to know whether you're coming or not. Before I ask Millie.'

We'd only had two discos so far, one at the boys' school and one at ours, which had both been chronic but acceptable to parents. Sasha's friend's ball promised older boys and booze and it wasn't in a school or anything. I was a bit scared thinking about it.

'I'll go,' said Jessica. 'It's just a disco, really. Mummy and Daddy won't mind. Come on, Connie. I can't go without you. And you've got that dress, you know, the blue one. You've got to wear it.'

Connie looked outraged. 'No way, José. It's a bridesmaid's dress, and you can totally tell. I'm not going looking like a total dill. I don't know if I can go anyway. I'll bring it up at the next family meeting. '

When Connie had an issue, her and her parents and her sister all sat round the table and took in turns to listen to each other. Then they voted and everyone's votes counted equally. The upshot of it all was that the parents always ended up doing stuff they didn't want to, like taking ballroom dancing lessons and stopping smoking.

'Will your parents say yes?' I asked.

Connie winked. 'I'd say my chances are excellent. When we were on Crete, they let me go out all night on my own with Spiro three times.'

'So he's really your boyfriend now?' Jessica sounded wistful. She wasn't interested in boys yet, though it was high time. Could be she was underdeveloped, or one of those people who weren't even gay or straight, but more like a dog that'd been done.

Connie showed us a photo of a bloke with a tan and a mullet, which I dare say was still trendy on remote Greek islands. 'He's only sort of my boyfriend. He's eighteen and he's supposed to marry this girl. He doesn't love her, but her dad owns the restaurant with his dad, so he can't get out of it.'

'Can't he just go to university and get a job and come to England and you can marry him instead?' I asked.

Connie regarded me with pity in her eyes. 'Not everyone, you know, has our advantages.'

I'd already heard from Jessica that Connie and Spiro had done it and I'd only really come round because I was hoping for details. But it didn't look like Connie was going to dish. Her bottom lip trembled.

'Are you missing him?' Jessica reached out her hand. Connie burst into tears and her and Jessica hugged like I wasn't even in the room. When Connie was around, what would I have to do to be the centre of attention? Set fire to myself, I expect.

Connie dried her splotchy face on Jessica's T-shirt, so it looked like Jessica had been lactating.

I got out of Connie's bed. 'I'm going home.'

'Bye,' said Jessica.

Connie was sorting out her make-up. She was too busy to say goodbye.

There was no point asking Hugh about the ball because he'd just say, 'Ask your mother.' If he had his own way, he'd let me do whatever I wanted. When he was young he didn't have very good parents, only a mother who was out of it and Grandpa Eric who didn't really understand the world at all. Because Hugh hadn't been brought up properly, Millie was the judge, and I had no right of appeal. Millie said fathers were useless, 'And that's no offence to your dad. But they're either so strict or too soft.'

It wasn't easy to get an appointment with Judge Millie. Now there were more people in the house, I had to choose my moment. Then Hugh went away on a business in Manchester. I wanted to go too, like a holiday, but my father said a holiday in Manchester was an oxymoron. So even though I wasn't allowed to come with, I was half pleased, because Edward would be busy and I'd have some time with my mother on my own.

I wasted the first day of my father's absence, worrying about whether to ask her. Then, when she came home the night he was due back, I heard the rustle of shopping bags. This was my chance.

'Freya!' She shouted up the stairs. I waited a bit before I came down to help unload, because I knew that'd make her appreciate it more.

She stood in the kitchen, holding a pack of Eccles cakes. 'I don't even like these. I got them because my mother always used to. Stupid, isn't it? Leave the sodding shopping. I can't be bothered. Edward can do it later.' She mixed herself a vodka tonic. 'Want one?'

Vodka was the only spirit she really liked because she thought people couldn't smell it on her breath. She poured me out a glass, but only a single.

She shucked off her high heels and exchanged them for clogs and then I followed her clunking feet into the sitting room. No one had tidied up since the night before. My mother plonked herself down on the sofa with the best view of the telly and switched on the news.

I decided to wait a bit, until her cocktail hit home. I had about three minutes before the regional news came on and she closed her eyes.

'Can I go to the Death of Summer Ball?' I asked.

She narrowed her eyes. 'The what?'

'It's out in the country somewhere, so I'll need a lift. And it costs twenty quid for a ticket. Jessica and Connie are going.'

'That's funny.' Her voice just then was small and squashed. 'The school doesn't normally organise discos out of term time. Who's going to supervise?'

My mother, although not intellectual woman, had psychic powers.

'Nobody, really.' It sounded awful, put like that. 'I think it must be some private company. Sasha's selling tickets to people he knows.'

'Sasha?'

I shouldn't have mentioned Sasha.

She smiled. 'I see.'

'No, you don't. There'll be hundreds of people going.'

She shook her head. 'Listen, Freya. I know you're fifteen now and all grown-up, or so you think, which I dare say is partly my fault. I've tried to treat you as an adult and that could've been a mistake. If it was a boy your own age...'

I sipped my vodka tonic. 'It's not a date. He didn't ask me as a date. He gets commission from the tickets, or he gets to go free or something.'

'Freya, if it's Sasha and his friends, then they're over eighteen. Which means booze and drugs and God knows what else. If it was down to me, I might give you the nod, provided you came home at a reasonable hour. But you know what fathers are like with their daughters. He'd never stand for it.'

I'd hardly eaten all day, so the vodka curdled my saliva. Much as I'd worried about asking her, when I'd rehearsed this conversation in my mind, she'd always said yes. I'd done nothing to earn her mistrust. Well – almost nothing.

'Please!' I begged.

She glugged back the rest of her drink. 'Now, come on, Freya. If you do things that are too grown-up, it'll spoil your childhood.'

'Childhood?' I gasped. 'You think I'm still a child?'

She stared at me for a moment. Then she laughed. 'Oh, God. Sorry, darling. But you're so funny when you're angry.'

I stood up and turned towards the door.

'Now don't be like that.' Her words were slurring a little, even with half a drink. After the first sip she became instantly fuzzy, but ten glasses later, she was no worse for wear. That was one of her many talents.

She gestured for me to sit back down. 'I know you're not a little girl any more, but until you've a job and a husband and a great whacking mortgage, you just don't understand how the world works.'

'And how does it work?'

'There's lots of worlds, sweetheart – lots of workings.'

'You make up the rules as you go along.'

She laughed again. 'You sound just like my mother, God rest her soul.'

'Thought Grandma was still alive.'

'Christ only knows. Take a stake through the heart to kill that one.' She knocked back the rest of her drink. 'Come on. Let's get another.'

On the kitchen floor, bulging white shopping bags lay in a heap like a dismantled snowman. My mother emptied one of the bags out onto the counter. She'd bought an iceberg lettuce, AA batteries, malt loaf and a tin of asparagus. I must have been starving before we got Edward.

'I thought I'd a lemon. I hate drinks without lemon. Something barbaric about it.' She leaned against the kitchen counter, vodka bottle in hand. Her painted nails were OK – two coats of unchipped vermillion, hair dryer set. She always bought quality varnish, which paid for itself in the end, she said. But she'd been biting her cuticles, because all down the sides of each nail, the skin was raw and tasselled. She glowered at the bags as if she was attempting to trigger X-ray vision. 'Can't even think what I was looking for.... Ah well. Maybe I'll have an Eccles cake after all.'

I hated her pretending to be a nice normal housewife when it was all a lie. 'I know,' I said.

'Know what?' She bit open the Eccles cakes, took one, then offered me the packet.

'You've no right to tell me what to do. I'm going to tell Dad. Tell him everything. Then you'll see.'

She bit deep into the pastry. Fragments of sugar broke off and stuck to her upper lip, giving her a tiny glittering moustache. She licked her lips 'Dear God! These are fantastic! I'd forgotten just how good. It's the currants, Mum always said. Vostizza, they're called.'

'Jesus!' I took a family-sized tub of cheap strawberry yoghurt and hurled it to the floor. As the plastic cracked, pink guck splatted over the tiles.

'That was very selfish, Freya. Just because you're annoyed

with me, there's no need to spoil other people's things. That was Edward's breakfast.'

'Oh, yeah. Edward.'

She set down her cake, half eaten. 'Edward? That what this is about?'

'What d'you think?' I shouted. 'What d'you think it's like for me? Whatever Dad's done with Jackie, he doesn't deserve this. Not in his own house.'

Finally she was listening, but she didn't act surprised or guilty. She stepped towards me, avoiding the yoghurt. 'Oh Freya. I'd no idea you'd take it so badly.'

I pushed her away. 'How else am I supposed to take it?'

'I know it looks funny, darling, but one day, believe me, you'll understand.'

'Edward is leaving, though? He has to — now that I know. The longer he stays, the more likely it is that Dad'll find out.'

My mother gave me a look I'd never seen before.

'Shall we have another drink, darling?' she said.

Before I think of something else to say, we were back in the sitting room, and I knew by smell alone that my second drink was much stronger than the first. It felt like we were people on the television — not real at all.

'Sometimes,' she said, 'telling the truth is a very selfish thing to do.'

'That's not what they said at school. They said if things were out in the open and honest then that'd be best all round.'

She frowned. 'That's half right, I expect. Listen. You've had

187

a shock. But it's not the way it seems. Your father and I – just because we were comfortable, that didn't mean we were happy.'

'You shouldn't tell me that.' My glass was chill in my hand.

'If you didn't want to know, then you weren't to bring anything up. Least said, soonest mended. That's what my mother used to say.'

'You set a lot of store by your mother. Given that you hate her.'

'Hate's a strong word, darling. She's not Hitler or Satan, you know.' She flung her long white legs over the arm of the sofa and lay back, slantwise, against the leather.

'Your mother said you could do what you liked, so long as you didn't get caught?'

'I'm just exercising a consumer preference.'

'Comparison shopping? Between Edward and my father? The man you're supposed to love?'

'You want me to be bad and Hugh to be good, but we're all in a grey area, darling. You, too. There's no point explaining. Not now.'

'That's a cop-out.' I couldn't look at my mother just then, so I stared at the ashtray. Long white cigarette ends lay huddled together, worms seeking mutual heat in their thin burnt-out bed.

She sighed. 'Not my fault, Freya. This is how the world just is. Women need more than men do. Your father'd be quite happy seeing me once a week for high tea with kippers and five minutes of handholding. It's like we're singers but I've got two more octaves than he does, which he can't even hear.'

'So it's Daddy's fault?'

'We've all made mistakes. But no. It's not fault – it's need. The way I see it, in terms of love, one man equals half a woman.'

'That's stupid!' I thought about what Mrs Rally had told us about her and her husband, how they were two halves of the same soul.

'What about Plato?' I said. 'How d'you explain that?'

She pursed her lips. Her lipstick had bled, fraying the edges of her crimson mouth. 'I've no idea what you're talking about. Plato was some old poof who lived two thousand years ago. You're telling me he understood women?'

I hadn't expected her to even know who Plato was, but she went to pub quiz sometimes with the men from work, which meant that she had quite good general knowledge, even if she didn't understand anything in depth.

I struggled for breath. 'I just want to be normal.'

'If you accept my equation, which I think you should, Freya, you see that one woman is too much for one man. He's constantly trying to run away. That's why men invented pubs, chess, sheds at the bottom of the garden. And women – we try to get that extra half the man won't bloody give us. We try and please him with cooking or frilly knickers. When I first started going out with your father, I even memorised the football results, just so's I'd have something to talk to him about.'

'They tell you to do that in Just 17.'

'See! And when we've done all that malarkey and still can't

get what we want, then we look elsewhere – yoga and manicures, sun beds and Egyptian folk dancing. Just to be looked
after. Noticed. Loved.'

It was like I was being told the rules of some cult I'd been
living in, but no one'd ever talked about. Grandma Lily, Hugh
once told me, got this chat on the eve of her wedding, when
her mother told her the facts of life, and what would be
expected. My grandmother cried when she found out.

The drooping sun had turned our pale room amber. I
thought about everything in the world all at once and tried
to fit it in with what my mother was saying.

She stretched out her legs, sunbathing indoors. 'The last
few months with Edward – think how much happier we've
been.'

'He's all right. I don't want you thinking I hate him. Or at
least, if I do, it's nothing personal.'

She stood, lurched from her sofa to mine, then slouched
down next to me. She laid her hot hand against my cold arm.
'Thank you, sweetheart. For understanding us. Or trying to,
at least. The three grown-ups in this house are way happier
than they've been in a very long time. You too, I'm hoping. It
works, doesn't it? Maybe one day all families'll be like ours.
Best thing all round as far as money goes, not to mention love.
There's more love for you, Freya. Really, ultimately, I'm doing
this for you.'

I'd this feeling, and I don't know where it came from, that
she was going to leave me. I couldn't feel angry any more, so
I hugged her, even though I knew she wouldn't want it,

because she never wanted it. She didn't exactly hug me back, but she let me squash her tight as I could.

When I let go, I said, 'You're just greedy.'

She laughed, baring her strong creamy teeth. 'I dare say you're right, darling.' She stroked my hair. 'And just to show you I trust you…' She stood up, did a pirouette, and touched my head with an imaginary wand. 'Cinderella, you shall go to the ball!'

'As long as I don't say anything to my father? About you, I mean?'

'You don't want to hurt him, Freya. He's happy. He'll be coming back late and he won't want trouble. You'll just have to believe me when I say I know what's best.'

'Thank you, Mummy.'

I'd won, then, on paper, though I never really won, not where my mother was concerned. At least she'd given me permission for the ball. I wondered what else she'd let me do.

✳ ten ✳

Next morning, Edward sat alone at the breakfast table. He sipped coffee and stared towards the back door, as if he was expecting someone to walk through it. He was wearing a dressing gown and pyjamas, even though it was almost nine. I'd never seen him in nightwear before. He should've thought twice before not being dressed in front of an impressionable teenage girl who wasn't a relation.

'Why aren't you at work?' I asked.

'Why do children die of cancer? Why does democracy and capitalism not lead to a stable monetary system?'

Clearly, he was in no mood for chat.

When I looked out front, I saw my parents' cars still parked outside. I wasn't very happy that none out of Hugh and Millie and Edward was at work. If they didn't take work seriously, how were they going to pay for my school fees and university education and gap year in Florence studying Italian and History of Art? Even if it was a Friday, that was no excuse for standards slipping.

From the floor above, I heard a thud and the ghost of my mother's laugh. Edward winced.

Upstairs, the door to Millie's room was open, so at least she was up. But when I went to get her, she wasn't there, and her bed had that clean unmussed smell like it hadn't been slept in. Up on the next landing, the door to my parents' old room remained firmly closed. My parents were having a lie-in. Together. On a Friday, even. That could only mean one thing: my mother loved my father again.

I went back to my own room and waited for the day to pass.

That was when I saw it, lying on my dressing table by the mirror, a few scrawly lines etched onto the back of an old envelope in a ballpoint pen that was running out of ink.

FREYA, Re Ball
No more than 2 units of alcohol (2 small glasses of wine)
No smoking
No snogging boys. You are far too young to handle them. They are only after one thing.

I found it quite touching, just then, that my mother was concerned for my safety. It wasn't like her advice wasn't well-founded. If anyone knew what boys were after, it was her.

'Jesus fuck!' Connie screamed when she saw her eyeshadow. 'I look like bloody Judy Garland. And I'm not talking about the Wizard of Oz. I mean the booze and barbiturate years.'

'Sorry.' Jessica seemed quite put-out. She'd been copying a photo in 19 magazine, which was like Just 17, except it had articles about how to dress for the job you want, not the job you have. The smoky evening style looked OK on the page, but in real life Connie's eyes stared out, punched and black.

'Jesus, Jessica!' Connie wiped the worst of the guk away with a moistened wipe. 'You were obviously a drag queen in your last life.' The colours bled down her face like she'd been caught out in the rain.

Since Millie was going to drive us to the ball, we were meeting at my house to get ready. My bedroom, which I'd always found quite large for my purposes, was now overstuffed with girl. Connie filled the place all on her own, while Jessica had brought so much make-up, she needed a suitcase to carry it.

'Don't boys prefer the natural look?' I asked. That's what it said on the Just 17 problem page. But then later in the magazine, it had a thing about 'sultry eyes for autumn', so it was a bit difficult to decide was actually the truth.

Once, the publications I'd read hadn't told me how to act or what to look like. I used to read Bunty, which always had a picture story about a girl in an orphanage who'd been diagnosed with a terminal illness. Instead of telling the other orphans she was sick, she turned them against her, one by one, so they wouldn't be sad when she died. Then, in the last instalment of the story, she suddenly found out she wasn't dying and she could tell the other orphans that she wasn't a horrible person after all. I wasn't quite sure what the point of these stories was, except that maybe it was OK to lie, as long as you had your reasons.

Millie had made me put on my birthday dress, even though

I wanted to take it back. She said I should wear it while I still could, before my boobs got too big and ruined the line. Shocking pink, she described the colour, which made me embarrassed. The satin was tight, but I could still move because it was had five per cent lycra. Lycra was new or newish that season, but I wasn't sure about it because I'd had to get special knickers with no side seams, which were nylon, not cotton, and gave me a hot crotch.

I didn't understand why we needed three hours to get ready. 'It's the main part of the fun!' Jessica insisted. I didn't find it fun. I stopped being nervous and got bored instead.

'I wonder,' said Connie. 'Is it actually a rave? I got invited to one earlier this summer but I didn't dare go. I mean, you've got to take E, because if you don't, you can't have a good time. But it's supposed to do your brain in. What if I ended up too thick to do my GCSEs?'

'It's not a rave!' Jessica stood in her Mr Man bra and pants and unzipped her ball dress. Green silk, strapless, with frills round the hem, her frock was something Miss Piggy might wear for a Muppets Christmas Spectacular. She stepped in, then wrestled to squeeze herself into the corsetry.

'Colour's nice on you,' I said.

'Thanks!' Jessica grinned. 'You know how I went on that Colour Me Beautiful course? Well, I'm an autumn, and this is on my palette. Will you zip me up?'

Connie appraised the dress with a critical eye. 'That's the trouble with strapless. Unless it's tight, the whole thing'll fall off. Just don't dance with your arms above your head. And don't drink anything fizzy, or your stomach will get bloated and you'll burst your seams.'

Ever since the fashion and beauty talk we'd got off the Mrs Marks, the needlework teacher, Connie thought she was some kind of style expert. Mrs Marks' talk had mainly been about how we should never try and dress too old for our age. 'Lamb dressed as mutton – you'll only get yourselves into trouble.' Her wisdom was suspect, because Millie had spent her teens doing the whole mutton thing and it'd never done here any harm. But Mrs Marks did give us some useful tips as well. 'In an emergency, repair a ladder in your tights with nail varnish.' Only if we were wearing tights and nail varnish, we'd be looking old for age. That was the trouble with advice – somewhere along the line, it always contradicted itself.

When we trooped downstairs the grown-ups were in the sitting room. The TV was on, but no one was watching.

Edward gave us a mock wolf whistle which I considered to be rather inappropriate. 'Well, well, Charlie's Angels.'

Millie laughed. 'Lovely, darling. But I do think the blusher is a bit de trop.' She spat onto a tissue, stood up, then bore down on me. Before I could protest, she'd wiped away half my face. She scrubbed at my cheek till it burned.

'I must take a photo,' said my father.

He lined us all up in front of the sofa. As he snapped the picture, the flash gun went off, leaving little white fractures in my field of vision. I was worried that I'd blinked at the critical moment, but when I looked at the print the other day, my eyes were wide open, staring into the lens. My grin wasn't quite as large as Connie's or Jessica's – I'm more like a dog baring its teeth. Dogs in the wild only bare their teeth when they're up for a fight, but pet dogs, apparently, learn to grin when it's expected. That's what my smile looks like in the picture.

'What about you three?' I gestured for my father to hand me the camera.

Edward leapt up. 'Where d'you want us?'

Millie didn't look happy. 'Come on, darling. I haven't brushed my hair.'

'For God's sakes, woman. Hair's hair. Don't worry about that.' Hugh gathered them all together.

In the picture, Edward and Hugh are sitting on either side of my mother, snuggled up to her. The men have the same cheery, camera-ready smile. My mother is squashed in between looking grumpy and put-upon.

'Now you, Freya.' Jessica took the camera off of me. 'Just fit in with the rest of them.'

I sat down on the floor, my back against the sofa.

'Don't do that, darling,' said my mother. 'You'll snag your tights.'

I nuzzled between Millie's legs and my father's. Now that I'd skewed the family portrait, Edward was a little to one side. Even though the composition of this picture wasn't quite as good as the last one – the one without me – it was a better photo. Everyone is that bit more relaxed and, better still, all of the grown-ups are looking at me, like I'm really quite something.

Of course, at the time, I couldn't see their expressions, but I must have felt the warmth of the adults in my life, even Millie, because I left for the ball feeling candyfloss fluffy inside. My anger – that'd been sitting crouched in my brain, ready to pounce – dissipated. Nothing mattered any more – not exams or school or whether Jessica had managed to cover up my acne with her oil-free foundation. Tonight I'd have proper fun, like I'd been wanting.

Millie scooped up her car keys off of the coffee table then jangled them in her hand. 'Taxi at your service.' She said it half like a joke and half like she was being put upon. But my mother was in no position to make me feel guilty – not ever again for as long as she lived.

The Death of Summer Ball was being held at a rugby club in some village with a silly name. I'd never been to a rugby club before, so I imagined it to be macho and tasteless, but I was hoping, even so, for a whiff of magic. I wanted banners and streamers and multicoloured helium balloons, like in an American high school prom.

We knew we'd arrived when we saw boys in black tie and girls in satin ra-ra skirts hanging around smoking outside what looked like an oversized public toilet. Connie glowered at me. 'You'd better start praying, Freya.'

My mother pulled up to let us out. 'It'll be lovely, I'm sure. Don't do anything I wouldn't do!' She laughed as she waved goodbye.

As she reversed out of the rugby club gates she can't have

been looking in the right direction, because she didn't quite make it. As she hit the gate post, the car made a spangly crunching sound. She got out to survey the damage. 'Rear bloody light smashed to buggery. Freya, come here! What about the bodywork? Can you see any dents?'

When I went round the back, I saw how the back right corner of the car was squished up like it'd been punched. The boys and girls outside the club were pointing and laughing. It's supposed to be typically British, to laugh when people have accidents or get hurt, though I've never understood it myself. I didn't know who to be most cross with, the laughers for being mean or my mother for being too pissed to drive properly and showing me up as a consequence.

My mother lit a cigarette and inhaled in sharp hungry gasps. 'You could have bloody warned me about the post, Freya.'

'Can't you just claim on the insurance?'

'And lose my no claims? Yeah. That's all we need.'

I didn't get why she bothered having insurance when she could never claim on it.

She threw her cigarette in the direction of the rugby pitch then got back in the car. Rolling down the window, she said, 'Expensive little night this turned out to be.' With a wild revving of the engine she drove off into the darkness.

When we walked inside, the so-called ball promised to be even more pathetic than the disco we'd been to in The Cedars' assembly hall. The rugby club function room was low-ceilinged, sweaty and stupidly dark, probably so that people could snog. I gave a dazzling smile – not at anyone in particular, but that was what it said in Just 17 – make sure you've brushed your teeth, then smile when you walk in, so you look confident. But no one in that light could possibly have seen my freshly-brushed teeth. Even Connie seemed nervy. We were the youngest there by at least two years. Some sixth formers from St Joan's were dancing in a huddle on the far side of the room.

'If they see us, they'll be annoyed, I said. 'They might tell on us.'

Connie rolled her eyes. 'Don't be stupid. You only ever recognise the girls in the years above. To them, we're invisible.' She pushed her way to the bar and returned with gin and tonics she'd purchased effortlessly in spite of being way underage.

We squished our plastic glasses together. Jessica proposed a toast. 'To us! The Three Musketeers!'

Connie wasn't impressed with the music. 'Crowd-pleasers and floor fillers. Nothing outside the top 20. Pump Up the Volume? Please!'

Jessica giggled like Connie had said something really clever. She wasn't used to boozing at home like I was, so her G and T had her three sheets to the wind in five minutes flat. She twirled round and her dress flew out at the sides and the whole room saw her Mr Man knickers.

We'd only just arrived but it felt like I'd been there for hours and that all those older cooler girls and boys were staring at us and thinking what babies we were. In my fantasies, Sasha had been there from the moment I came in the door, and this evening was going to be all about him and me. Now he wasn't there and maybe he'd never even show up. My father was coming to pick us up at midnight, so if anything was going to happen, it'd better be soon.

Connie took in the crowd. 'They're all a bit goth or a bit Sloane. No casuals, thank God. I can't see any horny blokes.'

Jessica stared at her. 'Doesn't horny mean "up for it"? I mean, how can you tell if they're horny or not?'

Connie gave her an exasperated glance. 'Horny now means good-looking. Or tasty. That you fancy someone. For God's sakes, girl. Get with the programme.'

It was only that year that horny had started meaning sexy. Connie knew all the up-to-date stuff way before Jessica or me because she was in The Woodcraft Folk, which was like the Guides, except run by hippies. Instead of sausage sizzles they had tofu sausage sizzles and practised handicrafts which were friendly to the environment.

A bloke came up to Connie. He was ginger like Penelope and his skin looked raw and painful – even in the dark.

'Dance?' he mouthed at her.

She nodded, then followed him into the mass of dark bodies.

Jessica looked on forlornly on as Connie disappeared from view. 'It's a cattle market. You and me, we're the cows nobody wants.'

I could have slapped her round the face just then for being

so ungrateful. Just getting to the ball, bargaining for permission, wheedling the twenty quid for the ticket plus spending money, persuading Jessica and Connie, tarting myself up – all that had taken so much energy that now I was exhausted. All this had been for Sasha and he'd let me down and Jessica just wasn't my real friend right then, because if she was, she'd have understood my pain.

'No one else is wearing green,' she said. 'I told Mummy it wasn't in fashion, but she wouldn't listen. Everyone's black and white and pastels.'

'I'm in a colour. Besides, I thought you didn't suit black or white or pastels. You're an autumn. That's why you went for green.'

'That's not the point! I told Mummy and she wouldn't listen. Now look!' Tears threatened the edges of her eyes.

'For God's sakes, Jessica.' I wished Connie would come back, because she'd make no bones about giving Jessica what for. Connie, I had to remind myself, had her uses. Maybe more alcohol would calm Jessica down. It always worked for my mother. 'Fancy a bevvie?' I said.

When I came back from the bar, Jessica was talking with boys – my boys. Sasha stood leaning against the wall, his undone bow tie dangling round his neck. His friend, the tall one with the long hair, was talking to Jessica's breasts. Sasha and his friend could only have seen Jessica once before, in the Berlucci's, and now they were chatting her up like she was a supermodel or something – Jessica, a girl who'd never even snogged anyone – who wasn't supposed to be interested in boys at all. I knew we were good enough friends that she'd never turn me over, but her looking as if she might, that felt rubbish.

Sasha was the first one to notice me. 'Hi, Freya.' He bent down and kissed me on the cheek. His mouth was rough where he hadn't shaved properly.

He pointed to the drinks I was carrying. 'Those for us?'

His friend gave me a wave. 'I'm Dezzer.'

Dezzer, now I got closer to him, was obviously completely pissed. He had a silly smile on his face and he was trying to smell Jessica's hair. There was nothing I liked about him from a superficial point of view, except that he was a boy. Even his name was silly. Since he was Sasha's best friend, though, I'd have to like him. What if Sasha and Dezzer had decided to divvy us up between them – only I got Dezzer, while Sasha got Jessica? I thought about asking Sasha to dance, but I couldn't do that. Girls didn't ask boys to dance, and even if they did, I was rubbish at it and I'd only show myself up. Where did people learn how to dance at discos? Perhaps there were secret classes and I hadn't been invited.

'You girls want a top-up?' Sasha asked.

'No,' I said.

'Yes!' Jessica drained her plastic cup then held it out to show she wanted more. 'We only just got here, Freya. We've hardly even started.'

The sight of two actual boys going to buy us proper alcoholic drinks had her squealing with excitement. 'They're getting us drinks! Spiro, Connie's boyfriend, that's how it started with them.'

'And Spiro and Connie are true love?'

I downed my tepid gin and tonic. I wanted to give off that I was above it all, but seeing Sasha made me feel like crying. I'd been preparing for tonight not just for weeks, but for years.

Over at the bar, Sasha was talking to a girl who, by the fact she was wearing a mini-dress and fishnets, I could tell was a bit cheap. He handed her something and then she mouthed him a thank you and slipped out into the crowd.

Jessica gazed around her anxiously. 'Oh God. And now I have to pee. I always pee when I'm nervous. Come with?'

'No way! We're waiting for them to come back.'

'I'm going anyway. I never feel like I've visited a place until I've been to the loo. All women do that.'

'I don't.'

'No wonder. You're not a woman.'

I wasn't sure what she meant. 'I'm staying. We can't run out on them. That'd be rude.'

'It's what's called being mysterious.'

She handed me her bag and flounced towards the toilets.

When the boys came back, Sasha nodded in the direction of a table on the other side of the room.

'What about Jessica? She'll freak out if she can't find me.'

He strolled away and I followed. Jessica, I decided, would understand.

When I sipped my drink, it was all wrong. 'It's water.'

'I'm not made of money, honey.' He pulled a mock sorry-for-himself face.

'Sorry. It's just that…' He'd got one over on me, as per, but what could I do about it?

Leaning forward, he placed his hand in mine. 'Here. Take this.' He snatched his hand away.

When I looked down, in my palm lay an aspirin wrapped in clingfilm.

'They're normally a tenner,' he said. 'But you can have a freebie.'

'Have what?'

'It's an E. For God's sakes. I thought you knew.'

I massaged the pill in my hand. 'Aren't they dangerous?'

'Less than drinking – and it's way better than blow. It's up to you. You don't take booze with them, so you save money, if you think about it. Just thought you needed a bit of cheering up.'

The campaign on the telly was all about 'Just say no.' But wasn't that more about heroin? They never said. But what about the idea of only having one life? Anything once except incest and folk-dancing? I hadn't even stuck to that, because I'd done folk-dancing quite a few times – skipping round the maypole at primary school, and international dances of peace at the Strawberry Fair.

'Aren't they bad for you?' I asked.

Sasha shook his head. 'Only afterwards. Suicide Tuesday and all that. But it's worth it. Just take half – an Aristotelian mean – then see how it goes.'

Put like that, it seemed quite reasonable. Half a pizza or half a piece of cake – that didn't really count, although the whole thing'd be really bad for you. But I didn't much like the sound of Suicide Tuesday.

Connie's advice was that in a sticky situation, the trick was to play What Would Madonna Do? But I wasn't sure I wanted to be Madonna. Whenever she came on the telly, Millie sighed and said, 'That woman's trying far too hard.'

I shook my head. 'I can't.'

'Freya. Have you ever experienced total pleasure? Total happiness? Freedom from all worry?'

'Course not.'

'Well…' He gazed into my eyes. 'Take this and find out. Uncle Sash'll be holding your hand, every step of the way.'

That was a very appealing thought indeed. 'How do I…?'

'Don't tell the whole world about it. Go the bogs and do it in there. Just bite it. Save the other half for later. Or give it to your little mate.'

There was no going back.

As I passed Jessica coming back from the toilets, I handed over her bag.

'I can't believe you!' she said.

'Sorry. I need to go now. By the way, did you know that Sasha's got some…?'

'I know! What a low life, Freya. Dezzer doesn't deal, though. I think you can tell when someone's a kind person, just by looking at their face. D'you think he's good looking?'

The toilets had the same clear loo roll we used to have at primary school, the kind like greaseproof paper that just slides off of you. I didn't think it existed in the real world. A girl in the next cubicle was chucking up. In the light, I saw the pill had a little picture of a pound sign on it. When I bit into it, I realised I hadn't any water, so I dry swallowed and gagged at the gritty, alkaline taste. I stashed the other half in my bag then flushed the toilet to pretend I'd been. At the sink, I scooped cold water from the tap so I could swig the pill. A goth in stilettos and studs was standing at the next sink painting a dark black line round her mouth.

'Jesus! That's disgusting!' She looked at me like I'd just crawled out of the toilet. 'That's not drinking water, you know. You could catch rat syphilis.'

I didn't contradict her, even though I knew you only got rat syphilis from falling in The Cam. I'd been in the river once, on my last birthday, when Jessica and Connie pushed me in the river. That was pretty much compulsory if you had a birthday in the summer. If absolutely loads of people got hold of your arms and legs and flung you in, then you were really popular. Getting shoved in, that was nearly as good.

The pill didn't do anything. People on the telly said drugs weren't all they were cracked up to be and now I had proof. Alcohol wasn't that good, for a start. It was just something you had. Didn't make you feel better or worse – just got you through the night.

*

When I got back to the table, I realised that in Sasha's company, I didn't mind my grim surroundings – the noise and the dark, the sticky carpets and pine-clad walls. For a few minutes, I smiled silently at Sasha and he smiled back. Hard to believe I'd spent so many months yearning for this boy who hadn't even got A-levels. He really wasn't so very unattainable.

'Well?' he said.

'Yeah. Nice party.'

'Not that. The other. You know. The disco biscuit.'

'Don't think it's doing much for me.'

'So why you smiling?'

'I'm not.'

'Bloody are. Come into the light.'

He led me away into the entrance hall where the lighting was corporate strength.

'Look at my eyes,' he said.

His pupils were weirdly huge and black, like he was possessed.

'That normal?' I asked.

'Yours are the same, silly.'

'Don't believe you.'

'Take a look.'

I had a compact in my bag that Millie had insisted on me taking, for getting the shine off of my nose. I clicked open the cold lacquered metal and cleared the powder from the glass. My blown pupils stared deadly back at me.

'You're all right?' He brushed his hand against my shoulder.

'Yeah. Like nothing matters.'

'Keep having this.' He handed me his cup of water. 'Now come outside with me while I have some snout.'

I followed him out into the car park, where we leaned against a red brick wall and looked out onto the grim infinity of the pitch. The hair follicles on my arms went rigid with the cold.

'Chilly?' He pulled on his cigarette.

'Bit. Yeah. Lots, actually.'

'Feel the back of my neck.'

His skin glided against my fingers, chamois leather soft. 'Wow. That's the wonderfulest thing I've ever felt.'

I ran my hand across his bare arm and found he wasn't cold at all. We were so close right then, just like I'd always known we could be. We were joy – better than the end of exams and Christmas put together.

'You're such a funny little thing,' he said.

'I think I'm serious. No one ever finds me even remotely amusing.'

He threw his cigarette end into the blackness. 'I meant funny strange, not funny ha-ha. A rare bird. Black swan. That kind of thing.'

'You're rude.' I tried to feel angry, but I couldn't. I was in a cloud – a cloud that might make me sick. I wasn't even sure that I was alive at all. Why was no one else out in the car park having a fag? It was like they'd all been stolen.

'Don't be annoyed. You're great. You know that?'

'You, too.' I wanted to tell him I loved him then, but that'd be going a bit too far.

He bent down and kissed me. I could barely notice what it was like. All I knew was that his tongue was in my mouth, feeling my teeth, and that this was my first proper French kiss with someone I liked. I'd had one before, obviously, because I wasn't a total dill, whatever Connie thought, at the fourth year disco with Martin somebody. But he wasn't very good-looking and he never asked for my phone number, so that didn't count. Also Connie told me he'd only done it for a dare, which I didn't believe, not really.

Sasha's hands ran over the back of my dress, skimming along the outline of my bra at the back, around the waistband of my pants. I was glad I'd worn matching underwear – not that anyone would be seeing it.

It was him who stopped kissing me first, which I knew was a bad sign. It was always supposed to be the boy who started the kissing and the girl who decided when was enough.

'We can't start anything,' he said. 'I'm going away.'

'What? Like prison?'

'Don't be stupid. Away away. You know what Mum's like. She doesn't understand what I'm really into.'

'What's that?'

'My music.'

'Oh. I didn't know you played anything.'

'I don't. Well – not any more. When I was little I did violin and stuff, but that's not relevant. Got to Grade 8 by the time I was ten then packed it in. Couldn't hack the six hours scraping away each day to get to concert standard.'

'So you don't do anything unless you can get to concert

standard?'

He looked at me like I'd said something wrong. 'I'm going to make money, that's all. Not like mum and dad. I want to manage bands. Do nights like this.'

'Wow! You organised all this? I didn't realise.'

'Not just me, but I helped, obviously. Mum doesn't think that's a proper career, so she's sending me to France so I can have another language and then she wants me to go into tourism.'

He said the word tourism like he was saying Barry Manilow or Brussel sprouts.

'Tourism would be fun,' I lied. It wasn't a good job like being an MP or a vet, but men weren't like women. They had fragile egos – that's what Mrs Glinka said.

'Only said I'd go to France because it'll be good to have French when the band goes touring. Russian's no use. I don't want to be a spy or create world peace. Dad's got some cousin who lives in Toulouse. Runs a bar.'

'I'd love to work in a bar!'

Sasha shook his head. 'Bollocks you would. But it's better than sitting home pulling my chod, I suppose.'

I snuggled my head against his chest. Through the starched whiteness of his shirt, his breastbone pressed hard on my cheek. I should have felt sad, but all I could think of was the glory of this moment. Sasha was mine now and his leaving made it all the more perfect. We were destined for each other, like Scott and Charlene off of Neighbours, or Jason and Kylie in real life.

He nuzzled his chin against the top of my head. I could feel his stubble picking up scraps of my hair.

'You can brush my hair with your face!' I looked up at him, smiling. 'D'you think that's what they used before they invented combs and stuff?'

He kissed me again. It wasn't quite as good as the time before, because I was sort of expecting it. He didn't stick his tongue in so much, which was better, but I noticed how he smelled of cigarettes and that my neck hurt craning up to reach him. He stroked his big hand across my left breast. I knew I should stop him, but I didn't want to. I didn't feel cold any more. Now I knew why this night was special.

'Sasha?' I broke free first this time, which was another good sign.

'Mmm?'

'You do like me, don't you? You will miss me?'

'Yeah, course. But we better go back in. I mean, Dezzer and that. They'll be asking after us.' He stopped touching my breast. That was not a good sign.

Mrs Rally had told us we shouldn't even kiss a boy unless we really really liked him and we felt safe and we wouldn't hurt anyone and we were preferably over sixteen, or even more preferably after our A-levels, because who knew where it would lead. And we shouldn't let it go any further until we were twenty at least. But that wasn't how Millie lived. She did whatever she wanted and everyone let her. She seemed more than happy – and it wasn't like they warned us at school. When she slept with a man, he didn't think he'd got one over on her or dump her because he was only after one thing. The more she gave, the more they wanted.

'Let's do it.' Thrilled at my own power, I ground my body against his.

Sasha stepped back a little. He shifted his weight gingerly from foot to foot.

'Shall we go in?' he said.

'No!' He hadn't understood me. 'Let's do it.' It was like Mrs Rally said about soulmates – that Sasha and me had once been one person. Now we had our chance, maybe our only chance, to be together again. All my aloneness would disappear.

'Are you suggesting what I think you're suggesting?' For a minute, he looked excited, tempted. Then he wrinkled his brow and pushed me away.

'Please!' I tried not to sound desperate. 'You're going away and I might never see you again.'

'It's the drugs. Plus you're my mother's best friend. Believe me, that is one love triangle that just ain't gonna fly.'

'You make it sound nasty.' My joy was frazzling. Splinters were falling from the glassy sky, stabbing into the earth below.

'Fuck me sideways. Freya. Just go inside and find your little mates…'

'Jessica and Connie.'

'Whatever. The fat one and the bitchy one. Then ring your daddy and go home. You might not sleep too well, but you'll be fine. And another thing. Throw away that other half an E and never ever drop one again. You hear me?'

I checked my watch and realised my father would be coming soon. The hours had stretched and squashed until I'd no idea when I was in time.

'But you're the only person in the world who's ever really understood me!'

He shook his head. 'I'm not. Nobody ever understands anybody else. D'you not get that?'

'Why, then, Sasha? Why invite me? Give me drinks and pills and touch me and kiss me and…'

'All right, all right! I'm sorry. Just didn't think that it'd…. Sorry, Freya.'

He strode back towards the club. I ran after him, not wanting to follow him, but I had no choice. There was nowhere else to go.

As we walked back in, the guys on the door smirked – like they knew. Sasha had promised me total happiness and now look. Everyone was staring and judging me and I'd never even done anything. It wasn't fair. Fear sliced into the ether of my brain. Cleary I'd just done something dreadful and since I never got away with anything, it was only a matter of time before I received my punishment.

* eleven *

'Honestly, darling. You're supposed to be in the prime of your life. You must've slept for a week. From now on, you don't go out past eleven. You just get too tired.'

Now it was going to be Hugh's party on Saturday, then back to school the Thursday after that and the summer had seeped away. I hadn't even my usual surveillance on the neighbours, recording times of cars in and out. The steamy August air infiltrated my blood, deadening my curiosity, my drive, my hope.

Five days after the Death of Summer Ball, I was still catching up after my sleepless night, while the world folded in on me, making me the filling in a giant calzone. Millie was getting me go shopping as a form of deliberate torture, I was sure. Sasha had left for France without even saying goodbye. I was too scared to go see Mrs Glinka in case Sasha had said something about me. Mrs Glinka said there were two kinds of girls – nice ones and not-so-nice ones – and we were both clear which kind I was. But if you were really really in love with someone, then whatever happened between you was OK, wasn't it?

Since we never had parties, Hugh's bash had to be extra

extra special to make up. Millie was hiring glasses and buying fine wines – champagne, even – on a deal from work. She thought about getting waiters to hand round drinks and stuff, but that might look like she was trying to hard.

'It'd be a bit much, don't you think?' As we waited at the supermarket check-out, she rubbed cuticle softener into the beds of her fingernails. 'Besides, that's what you and Edward are for.'

She stopped to use a payphone while I stowed the bags in the boot of the car. At home, people were ringing up the whole time. We'd only invited fifty or so, but they all had to call and confirm, then call again to find out what to bring. Edward told my mother she needed a car phone, but she said she wasn't important enough. My parents didn't actually have fifty friends, so the guests were mainly work colleagues or acquaintances and that was why they kept ringing. They didn't know anything about us – how to get to our house, or what to bring, or what to wear.

We were going to clean the house from top to bottom, but on the day before the party, the cleaning day, my mother disappeared off into town and left us holding the hoover. Since Edward had a deal to clinch, it was down to me to pick up bits of fluff off of the floor, because my father couldn't stoop.

'Knees not up to it,' he said. 'Not since I fell victim to a dodgy tackle.'

We blitzed the kitchen, my father stashing stuff in high cupboards and me wiping down the work surfaces. A bit rich,

I thought – my father clearing up for his own party while Millie swanned around being the big I Am, but he said he didn't mind. 'It's like your mother's Maggie Thatcher and I'm her Dennis. I've had my turn in the sun – now it's hers.

'Can't you both have your turn at once?'

He looked thoughtful. 'Nice idea. But that'd bring its own problems, don't you think?'

I knew my father was trying to reassure me but he had this knack of inspiring the opposite effect. 'Daddy, are you happy?'

'God, Freya! Why do you obsess about happiness like it's some toy that everyone's got for Christmas except you?'

'Mummy's so busy all the time. Now she's got Edward to look after as well, what about your time together?' I watched for the tiniest reaction, for a sign telling me to say more. It was wrong for my father to have his birthday and for all the fun to be pretend.

He was holding a tin of baked beans and scanning the shelves for its rightful place. 'Edward's no bother. Lovely chap all round, don't you think?'

I screwed up my eyes. 'I suppose... Mummy says you like him here. But do you really?'

'Is there something the matter, sweetheart? Apart from all your usual teenage stuff?'

I paused, then made my decision. 'I'm happy if you're happy.'

He stretched his hand and ruffled my hair. 'I'm the happi-est man alive,' he said.

If what he said was true, then I hadn't any business spoiling it, not the day before his birthday.

I attacked the kitchen floor with the squeegee, painting long white streaks in the greyness. The slosh of dirty water in the bucket, the pristine wetness of the lino, they lifted my heart, and for the first time since the ball, I was a bit less miserable. I wasn't like my mother. I liked doing women's things.

The night before the party I must've slept half the night with my mouth open, because when I woke, my tongue was heavy as a dead snake. I felt all right after I had a drink of water, but then the dread started up again.

I was allowed to invite friends to the party, but I wasn't sure that Connie and Jessica were speaking to me. Connie said that if I'd just been snogging Sasha, then I would've done it inside.

'Only the slags go outside with boys,' said Connie, as we waited outside for Hugh to pick us up. 'Everybody knows that.'

I protested. 'No, they don't! So not everybody knows that.'

She gave me a disdainful glance. 'Well, now you do.'

Part of me was quite pleased to be a thought a slag. Before that ball, it'd been unimaginable that I could be anything except straight and boring. A spod – that's what they called people like me. But I wasn't sure I could carry off having a bad reputation. I didn't think the other slags would want me as a friend.

*

That morning, when I heard that Jessica was on the phone, I

couldn't help smiling.

'Oh, hi! Freya!' She sounded excited. 'I'm really sorry, but I can't come tonight. Daddy's taking us off to London. We're going to Harrods and to see Starlight Express.'

'Oh. Sounds great.'

'I feel really really bad. I mean, there you are, and you haven't even had a holiday yet, and here I am, having my second.'

'Don't worry about me. We're going away at half-term.' That was the lie I'd prepared for school.

She spoke in a rush. 'Thing is…I'm allowed to bring a friend to London, and I'd have chosen you, obviously, but then I knew it was your dad's birthday.'

I felt sick. 'So you invited Connie.'

'That OK? I mean, she doesn't have as much money as you do, so she's never even been to Harrods or anything. Her family don't believe in it so this could be her only chance.'

'Course. I can see that.'

Neither of us said anything for a while.

'Are you crying?' She virtually shouted at me.

'No! We're going to have a great night. Champagne. Loads of really interesting people. I'm looking forward to it.'

'You sure?'

'Yeah. I've been to London tonnes of times. It's a very sweet thing you're doing for Connie.'

'Oh. OK. See you when I get back then.'

She hung up. I supposed it was OK. She wouldn't enjoy the party, and if she came, Connie would come. But if Jessica was really going to ask me to London, then she could have said so before, so I'd get to decide whether to go or not.

She hadn't sent me a birthday card or given me a present that year, like she usually did, though people often forgot, it being in the holidays. It was my fault, probably, for not dropping any hints. I pictured her and Connie sauntering round Harrods – talking about me and not in a nice way. I hadn't exactly been popular when I was a spod but now I went out and kissed boys, I was even more of a social leper than I was before. I couldn't win.

By seven thirty, we were ready. Some of the scoff was shop bought, but it was all quality. Instead of peanuts, we had macadamias, which were the most expensive nut you could buy, though actually, they weren't as nice as peanuts, because they didn't taste of anything. Edward's unwieldy fingers had managed to craft extra special sandwiches – tiny crustless triangles filled with asparagus, cream cheese and smoked salmon.

'Smoked salmon used to be posh,' said Millie. 'But now it's got cheap, I'm embarrassed to put it out.'

Edward looked affronted. 'Just because it's cheap, doesn't mean it's not nice. It's not like we're dishing up fish paste.'

My mother had no right to complain, because Edward had cooked more that day than she'd done in the last year. He'd done four different kinds of continental tartlette, blue cheese dip that he claimed was ironic, and guacamole – never before seen in Cambridge, he said. He taught me that it was made out of avocados and how you had to watch it in case it went brown and woofy, even in the fridge.

He surveyed his creations. 'I could have done hot as well. Barbecue, perhaps. Everyone loves barbecue. Or mini Yorkshire puddings with rare roast beef and horseradish sauce. I had those earlier this year at a wedding.'

'We wouldn't want you stuck in the kitchen all night,' said my mother.

I think Edward, when he was younger, was a bit like me and kept himself to himself. That was why he liked being ordered around by Millie.

'Men may run the world but when they get home at night, they want a bit of discipline. Remember that, Freya.' That was one of my mother's favourite insights.

Edward gave her a soppy smile. I wanted to punch him in the stomach then shove my mother's face into the guacamole. But soon Edward would get a surprise and Millie would realise that she was old and not really very attractive at all, and then everything could go back to normal.

Hugh wasn't allowed to have a say in what got eaten or drunk, because it was his party.

'You know your father,' said Millie. 'He's a big picture man. It's the details that've rather done for him, haven't they?'

Half an hour before the guests arrived, she poured us all a glass of champagne. We had a couple of bottles of the real stuff, so only us and the early arrivals would get any.

'Always best to have a glug or two before your guests

221

arrive,' said Millie. 'That way you're relaxed when you greet people. It's only politeness really.'

Edward offered me one of his little pastry tarts. 'Cheese and tomato. I made them for you specially.'

'No, thank you.' I was sure to say no quite pointedly. 'I had spaghetti on toast for lunch. I'm still full.'

I wasn't full at all, but Edward wasn't going to get round me by cooking. No one had ever cooked much in our family, so it wasn't like it meant anything to me. He didn't really love me – just himself and maybe Millie.

We raised our glasses, which were smart ones – not bowls, but flutes – because they made the bubbles last longer.

'To my lovely wife!' said my father. 'Who is the pride of Cambridge. Even if she does, on occasion, have one too many, thereby causing her car to have fights with garden gates.'

'Least the gate came off worst,' said Edward.

'You're a right pair of so-and-sos.' My mother smiled. She gazed deep into my father's eyes. 'To the best husband a girl could have!'

Though I hadn't wanted any, the champagne did make me feel better. The day was starting to look a bit more like it should, because at last my father was the centre of attention.

My father wasn't easy to please, gift-wise. The Christmas before, I'd given him some detective stories I knew he hadn't read. All he said was, 'Lovely, Freya.'

'What's wrong?' I asked.

'I do have to read an awful lot for work, you know.'

Once I gave him bubble bath, but it turned out he was allergic. Then I'd tried joke presents, like the flowers which danced by the stereo, but they didn't really make him laugh, so the joke was spoiled. That birthday, though, he greeted his presents – the tie, the pen, the crossword solver – as if they were the objects on earth he most coveted. 'Marvellous. Marvellous!' he said. Millie had been clever to get him drinking before he opened his swag.

He topped up our glasses and my mother put on a Michael Jackson record. She was far too old to be listening to pop music, but she said she didn't care – he was fun and she liked him. My father held up his glass. He didn't look anything like fifty. He was too handsome to ever get old. 'Another toast. Freya and Millie, you've been here for many birthdays, but Edward, you've helped make this one…'

Then the doorbell rang, and it had to be the Harmisteads, because they were always on time owing to Dr Harmistead's tight schedule. Being fashionably late wasn't an option when you worked shifts, and you couldn't be pissed when you went into the operating theatre.

My father gave a rueful smile. 'Oh Christ. I've no idea what to say anyhow. Let's just get the bloody door.'

We all laughed. Then Millie kissed Hugh on the lips – for a lot longer than she usually did. I rolled my eyes at Edward, expecting him to respond in kind, but he didn't even notice me. He stood watching until they'd finished kissing. Then silently, he went to answer the door.

*

Interesting, to find out after years of social desolation,

whether my parents could muster a houseful. But people kept arriving, virtually everyone, we'd invited and even some we hadn't.

I walked round offering nibbles so I wouldn't have to make conversation. People I didn't recognise – men in jeans that had once fitted but were now too tight, and women in Laura Ashley sundresses – kept telling me how grown-up and pretty I was. I didn't believe them.

We kept answering the door till it got to be more trouble than it was worth, so we just left it on the latch. Our guests gulped down their first glass of wine, then the second one almost as fast, but after that, they slowed down. Their cheeks grew pink and their lips droopy.

Mrs Harmistead looked enchanted when I passed her a mini quiche lorraine. 'How adorable! Did you make them, Freya? All by yourself? Or did Mother help you?'

'Edward's done all the catering,' I replied. Mrs Harmistead frowned at this. She believed in sexual role reversal in principle, but not in practice. She'd been very scathing when Mr and Mrs Greening from up the road started childminding as a couple. 'I'd never allow a man to care for a child of mine,' she said.

She took the mini quiche but didn't eat it. 'Your family never do anything the conventional way, Freya. I'll give you that.'

She didn't mean that as a compliment. Her mouth was sad so she was probably thinking about the rabbits. If I'd been better brought up, her babies would never've been killed.

Because of the open door, I hadn't even noticed the Glinkas' entrance. Mr Glinka was in the sitting room chatting to Millie, waving his hands up and down. He stood very straight, very confident, face animated, eyes luminous. It was like all the atmosphere in the room emanated from him alone. I could see how when he was younger, he could've been as gorgeous as Sasha. How, I wondered, had Mrs Glinka managed to nab him?

Mrs Glinka spun round and looked me straight in the eye. For a moment, she was stern, like she'd caught me out. Then she ploughed across the sitting room towards me, arms outstretched.

'Dushenka!' She kissed me twice on each cheek and hugged me hard. 'Why don't you come to see me any more? What? Are you bored of us?'

'Just busy getting ready for the party. Doing my summer project for school.'

It was a lie about the summer project. I did have one, an RE assignment about A Famous Person Who Has Influenced My Life, but I hadn't even started yet. The project was supposed to be an expression of our creativity, but that was pretty much impossible when we had to choose the famous person from a list of dead Christians we'd never even heard of.

She pinched my cheek. 'I have no chicks in the nest. Now my ryebyonok has gone to France. May the Lord preserve the people of Toulouse.'

'Is he gone long?' It was good Sasha hadn't lied to me about going to France. That meant there was hope. But he'd never rung me before he went, and he hadn't left an address. If you got off with a boy and he didn't ring you within a week, that meant he wasn't interested – everyone knew that. Perhaps it was just as well. If we got married, I wouldn't want to change my name to Glinka, and I didn't think I'd like Mrs Glinka being my mother-in-law. It'd be nice, I supposed to be properly related to her. But now, when she bossed me about, I could always go home and do the opposite. If I was married to her son, then when she came round to tell me how to bath the baby and stuff, she'd find out I'd been ignoring her all along and we'd have a row. I didn't think I could bear that.

Mrs Glinka popped a tartlette into her mouth. 'He's in Toulouse as long as it takes. England has corrupted him.'

'Corrupted?'

She brushed a crumb from her upper lip. 'His cousin in Leningrad came fourth in the Maths Olympiad. Fourth out of all the children in the Soviet Union. He could have come first, if only he wasn't also playing the viola to near concert standard. Five hours a day he practises. But my Sashenka, he hardly reads a book.'

'Not everyone's academic.'

She sighed. 'A few years ago, we sent him everywhere. Educational psychologist. Adolescent specialist. Hearing test. Eye test. There is nothing wrong with him, they said. Growing pains.'

'He seems quite normal to me.'

'And what do you know of how a normal boy is? There's things I could tell you...' She paused, and her face looked sad.

'But no. You mustn't trouble yourself.'

'When's he back from France?'

'If it was up to me, I'd keep him here. Hold him fast.' She clutched her arms around herself. 'But fathers... My Roman comes from a different culture. No unemployment. Every citizen is productive. Under Andropov, they'd stop you in the street during the day time, ask you why you weren't at work. Imagine that.'

I noticed, with relief, that she was talking to me about Sasha just like normal, no catch in her voice or anything. That meant that he hadn't told her anything about what'd happened at the rugby club – or hadn't happened, rather. I'd spent so much time fantasising about Sasha, I was hazy about what was real. The things I remembered saying were so unlike me. There were two Freyas right then – the normal me and the other one, who lived hidden behind the door in my head.

I mumbled some excuse and shoved off to the kitchen, where Millie was stabbing mini candles into a vast cake. She'd let Edward bake it and she was less than satisfied with the results. 'I said carrot cake but he's only gone and put raisins in it. Your father doesn't agree with raisins. They give him the wind.'

The cake sat on the work surface, a gooey lopsided bungalow. Edward had baked four small square cakes then welded them together with cream cheese icing. On top, in loopy orange handwriting, he'd piped HUGH and FIFTY.

My mother was having trouble with the candles. 'They just don't stick in cream cheese properly. That's why people use icing. Normal bloody icing.'

Mrs Harmistead was leaning against the sink, gazing out onto the garden, where in the late August twilight, the cat from two doors down was peeing against our fence. 'This must be his mousing ground,' she said. 'No wonder he looks so pleased with himself. Can I help with the cake?'

'Nope.' Millie drove in the final candle spike. 'We're done. Do the honours, Freya?'

By the time I lit the last candle, the first one was dripping wax all over the icing.

'Dammit to buggery!' Millie picked up the cake and strode across the kitchen floor. 'Open the door. Quick! Why do I have to do everything in this house?'

I followed her into sitting room, where Edward had already dimmed the lights. My mother strolled up to Hugh and started singing Happy Birthday. Everyone else joined in, awkwardly, like they'd forgotten the words. My father's face in the candle-light was soft, unwrinkled. He smiled like he was a little boy again, the one who had things to hope for, before his mother killed herself and his father went bust. He took a deep breath and blew out the candles. There were so many, he didn't manage it the first time, and everybody laughed.

Seeing him like that made me think that maybe getting old wasn't as bad as everybody said. I decided that from then on, I'd have proper birthdays and proper parties. I'd make more friends at school and I wouldn't care if they were slags or dim or wore blue eyeliner. Hugh wasn't that friendly with most of his guests, but even if they were just making up the numbers, it was good to be able to muster a roomful of anybody.

When Edward turned up the lights, there she was, standing next to my father. Twenty years odd years younger than most of the guests, she wore a full-length sequined evening gown which revealed quite a lot of her round white breasts. The transformation was quite astonishing. Only the peacock tattoo on her shoulder identified her indisputably. Penelope had come to save me. She hadn't let me down.

Some of our guests noticed her, but out of the corner of their eye, because they were still watching Hugh as he cut the cake.

Edward was standing next to Hugh, so he saw Penelope right away. Edward always looked pleased to see everybody, even the postman, but he wasn't pleased to see Penelope just then. That made me cross because after all, they'd lived together so they should still love each other – just a bit. Hopefully his surprise would wear off in a few minutes and then he'd remember how young and pretty and clever she was. Penelope had two post graduate degrees while Millie hadn't even stayed on for sixth form. He'd wept half the night when first she kicked him out. That must've meant something.

He tried to kiss Penelope on the cheek, but she wouldn't offer it, so he puckered his lips against nothing.

'Drink?' he said.

'Yes, I would like a refreshing beverage, please.' She pointed at Millie. 'Whatever she's having.'

Edward hesitated for a moment, then walked away.

Millie and Hugh were divvying up the cake.

'Would you like a slice, Penelope?' I asked.

She stared at me like I was mad. 'God, no!'

'Edward made it.'

'Yeah. I'll bet he did.'

Edward came back with her drink.

'Nice do,' she said.

He chewed his lip. 'Didn't expect to see you. Not that it's not great to… It's just I thought you wouldn't…'

Her tattoo and her tarty dress were getting enough attention as it was, but then she barked out a laugh that made people stare. The music had got switched off while we sang Happy Birthday but not switched on again, so there wasn't the background noise to soak her up.

'Got invited, didn't I?' she said.

Edward flicked an imaginary speck of fluff from his sleeve. 'Gosh. Mmm. Everything changes.'

'But how much, Edward? You were giving me some space to finish my thesis, so's I could get my head together, decide where the future lay. And meanwhile, you were going to help your boss out with the rent.'

'That's what happened.'

'No, darling. Because you were supposed to be patiently waiting for me. Not having it off with the boss's wife.'

She said the last bit quite loudly and I think people might have overheard, because they'd stopped pretending not to listen. Now my parents had noticed her, too. I didn't understand how Penelope could know about Edward and my mother. She'd looked really pleased to get the invitation. Why bother dressing up if she was just going to be horrible? Why was it that when people were supposed to be on their best behaviour, they were actually on their worst? I'd thought she was the injured party and an intellectual and therefore nice. I'd been very wrong to invite her.

Edward's eyes were pleading. 'Penelope. Please. Can't we talk about this another…Now's hardly the…'

She slouched her sequined hips against the wall. 'Know what? I've just spent the last three months writing about the hedonic calculus of the new millennium. In that time, I haven't had a drink, a shag or watched a minute of telly before ten thirty. My only pleasure has been watching Newsnight, which in summer is pretty bloody boring, I can tell you. So no, I will not go outside. I plan to stay and enjoy myself.' She raised her glass in my mother's direction. 'Cheers.'

My mother grabbed Penelope by the wrist and dragged her out of the room. For a slim woman, Millie had a surprisingly strong grip. She hauled Edward's ex through the corridor and into the kitchen beyond. Edward followed them, and then Hugh, so it seemed natural for me to go, too. Penelope thrashed in my mother's grasp, a silver fish on a hook.

'Get this bitch off me!' Penelope screamed at Edward.

Mrs Harmistead was still hanging about in the kitchen, picking at the last few cocktail sausages left on a place. As my mother dragged Penelope into the room, Mrs H recoiled, mouth open in horror, the sausage on its stick suspended in midair, never to be eaten.

My mother opened the backdoor and shoved Penelope out,

but the younger woman hung onto the door handle and wouldn't let go. 'How can you live like this?' she shouted. 'It's disgusting. And you have a child. Social Services'll hear about you.'

My mother laughed. 'When I was a kid they used to come round the house. Check for bruises or what have you, and then they're off. Believe whatever you tell 'em.'

Penelope lunged back towards the kitchen. 'He's weak. That's why this has happened. Line of least resistance. Doesn't have to have a real relationship – just be the third wheel in some tedious suburban ménage. Is he gay now as well? Do he and your hubbie go at it while you watch?'

Millie shook her head. 'No, darling. Hugh's most definitely not that way inclined. And as for Edward, well… You're the one with the MA in gender politics. Shouldn't you be able to tell?'

'That's cheap. Just what I expect of you. I'll just tell you one thing. I know him. He's got no spine. No idea who he is or what he wants. And when he's had enough of sleeping with mummy, he'll be moving on. You'll see.'

She was crying, but not properly. She cried the girls at school did when they got a B instead of the A they'd wanted.

My mother put her hand on Penelope's arm. 'You poor sweetheart. I know how this must look to you, but honestly, none of us could've planned it. It's something very real and beautiful.'

'That's a lie!' She was crying more properly now, with huge great sobs. She doubled up like she was getting punched in the stomach. My mother, who never hugged anyone, not even cats or dogs, took Penelope in her arms. Penelope resisted for a moment, then relented.

My mother stroked her back as she wailed. 'I know this is going to be hard news to hear, but Edward and I, it's more than a passing thing.'

'Don't believe it.' Penelope looked up, her face zebra-mottled with mascara and tears.

Millie stroked her hand through Penelope's hair. She lowered her voice to a whisper. 'We find our happiness where we can, love. Don't we?'

Hugh was standing almost next to them. He must have heard everything. No one was trying to protect him. No one was hiding any of the terrible things they were saying.

Finally, I got it. This great power I was wielding over my mother – threatening to reveal all and make my father realise he'd married a tart – it was nothing. Whatever arrangement Millie had with Edward, that didn't matter – whether it was kissing, mainly, or whether she snuck into his room at night and only pretended to sleep in the huffy bed, whether they were in love or it was just a bit of tit for tat, because of Jackie or my father being a failure at work. Whatever was going on, my father must know all about it. Everybody – Hugh, Millie, Edward, Penelope, even – everybody knew except me.

✳ twelve ✳

Overnight rain had turned the grass so jungle dewy, earth-worms had catapulted out of the ground, throwing themselves in front of waiting predators in some invertebrate kamikaze mission. Their mucus trails formed a glistening tube map on our front lawn. Inside, our home was filled with grubby silence. I decided to stay in bed until somebody fixed things.

No one was sure what'd happened after Penelope left the party. Since it was going home time anyway, people just melted out of the house and onto the pavement. Most of them hadn't witnessed the scene between my mother and Edward's ex because they'd been too drunk, too deaf, too far away. I'm sure they took it with a pinch of salt, because apparently that's what grown-up parties are like – instead of snogging and being sick, adults shout at each other and say things they don't mean. At least, that's what Hugh told me afterwards.

I was up in my room trying to read one of our set texts, which was all about trying to be a good Catholic. The book was fat and the heroine was tortured – not literally – just in her head. If she'd just stopped trying to be a good Catholic, everything, it seemed to me, would have been fine.

My father knocked on my door then came straight in without waiting for me to answer. Heavily, he sat himself down on
my bed.

'There's nothing to explain,' I said. 'I understand.'

'You can't possibly.' He looked tired, sad as the saggy old
tiger we'd seen in Linton Zoo, the one that was going to die in
a too-small cage and never go out and hunt.

'You all think I'm stupid,' I said.

My father's breath, when he drew near, told me he'd eaten
birthday cake for breakfast.

'Listen. I won't make this long and drawn out. Just to say…
It's not anything like as vulgar as it seems.'

'I never thought the word vulgar.'

'It's not about sex, Freya. Not where I'm concerned. We're
all going to have separate bedrooms, so you won't be confused.

'Yeah. Like that helps.'

He winced. 'Believe it or not, Millie and Ed are no longer
involved. The three of us are more like friends – living in the
same house, sharing our lives. We've all had hard times
recently and somehow this makes it better.'

'If I had a husband, I wouldn't want another woman
moving in.'

'But what if it was your best friend? Someone to laugh with,
chat with, rely on, confide in? No one planned this.'

'Like that makes it any different.' I held the book, using a
finger as a bookmark. I hated the book for having so many
pages, for the time it was going to steal.

'I can see you're peeved, Freya.'

'No, I'm not. I don't care. It doesn't matter.'

He drew together his eyebrows in pain. 'Having Edward here, it's probably kept us together. Not that you aren't a reason, Freya. But when you're a grown-up, you'll understand. In the last few months, it's like I've fallen in love with your mother all over again. I appreciate her generosity, warmth, her companionship on life's journey.'

'I'm your companion.'

'But one day, you'll up and go and that's as it should be. But we three, we'll have each other. We'll all be waiting for you whenever you decide to toddle on home. Give up jealousy and anything's possible.'

'So monogamy's just a societal construct?'

He laughed. 'Where d'you get that idea?'

'Off Miss Gillis at school.' I hadn't entirely understood what she meant, because if swans mated for life, then why should-n't humans?

'Miss Gillis has some interesting ideas.' He looked round at my bedroom walls, which were bare except for a painting of a windmill I'd bought at a jumble sale when I was nine.

'Edward being here – it's not some summer thing. I get that. He's not a lodger or just a colleague or just a shag. You're far more handsome than he is, Dad.'

My father winced. 'Please don't say shag, Freya. But I do like it when you call me Dad.'

My parents, I realised, had brought me up without think-ing the process through. They sent me to a school where if, like us, you ate fish and chips once a week instead of something Mummy had cooked out of Elizabeth David, other girls were horrified. Hugh and Millie had me call them by their first names, so we'd relate to each other as human beings, not just as family. How could the other girls understand that? My parents wanted me to fit in and be normal, but I never had done and now I never would.

'Freya? You look a little less than tickety-boo.'

'Do I?' I knelt up so I could see myself in the mirror. Lit only by my reading lamp, I was ghoulish, with sunken eyes, bleached out mouth, floppy hair.

'Do'you want Edward to leave? He only stays at your say-so. Not everyone will understand what he's doing here. We might have other... bother, even though we're not hurting anybody, even though we're just...living generously.'

I was being asked if I'd prefer a pet camel or a pet elephant. How could I decide? What information did I have? 'But are you really happy, Daddy? What about the black dog?'

'The black dog is dead. He is most definitely an ex-dog.'

I pressed my face into my father's chest, and he hugged me, like Millie had hugged Penelope. He smelled of the aftershave my mother got him for Christmas but he never wore. At that moment, he belonged utterly to me. I was so grateful then my parents weren't splitting up. Everyone was doing it, like Princess Anne and her husband, even though they had loads of houses and could avoid each other no problem. What if some judge gave me away to Millie? Were they allowed to do that? Mothers were better parents than fathers, that was what everyone thought, so a judge wouldn't decide any different, not unless my mother was a murderer or a heroin addict.

'Daddy? It's quite clear to me that the present situation is not moral. We've been learning about it at school, how if you really really love someone and you want to live with them, then you have to get married. Living in sin is simply not OK.'

My father looked at me like I was an alien being. 'That's a very sweet sentiment, Freya, but there's laws and the suchlike. Marriage, in this case, just isn't on the menu.'

'Isn't it?' I smiled. 'I've always wanted to be a bridesmaid.'

Wandlebury was magic wood which embraced a magic circle, a centre of ancient power, straddling a ley line. In the midst of the circle stood a hill where there used to be a fort and if you stood at the apex of the hill, some said, you could see all the way to Ely Cathedral. That was a lie, I think, because Ely was miles away. Nearby in the Gog Magog Hills, giants were buried. Even I, who didn't believe in that stuff, found the place spooky. Sophie Kennedy in the Lower Sixth was a white witch and she went to Wicca Sabbaths at Wandlebury that nobody was supposed to know about. She was only a junior witch, but when she left school she was going to move up through the ranks.

When I was little, Hugh used to bring me to the wood so I could run around until my legs got tired. Nowhere else could I see fire cones and acorns and rabbits and centipedes. I might be older now, but this was still absolutely my favourite place. That was why I'd chosen it.

Wandlebury was empty that afternoon, so the only sound we heard were the beech leaves and pine needles beneath our feet, crunchy as dead cockroaches.

We ambled beyond the Ring through a skeletal black metal gate, which you had to step into then out of again, like an iron maiden. Through the gate lay a luscious stretch of green which led to an orchard and a vast plane tree, whose branches reached out and begged us to come closer. Fronds of raggedy grass gnashed at my bare ankles.

Millie and I stood by the plane tree, shoulder to shoulder, with her a little taller than me, even in her flat sandals. We wore garlands of pinky-purple flowers in our hair and matching white dresses we'd bought on sale in Laura Ashley. I'd picked the outfits specially. The dress looked better on me than it did on my mother, but that was only right and proper. I was only going to be a bridesmaid once in my life, so I might as well enjoy it.

I'd wanted a bigger wedding, but it ended up being just the four of us because, like Millie said, if we had other people, there'd be lots of explaining to do. Grandpa Eric was too old and sick to come, even if he'd been invited.

No one had said anything about what Edward was bringing to the table, family-wise. He was always going on about his parents, but only historically, about when he was little. It was like when he got to be a teenager, they'd disappeared. They never called the house and he never called them. Maybe he had brothers or sisters, who could be my new uncles and aunties. I wanted to ask him about it, but Hugh said not to.

'We'll get into all that jazz at some later stage. Until then, we'd best observe a sleeping dog protocol.'

We stood in a circle and linked hands, so it was hard to avoid looking at each other. I'd made Millie do a speech because I'd read in the paper about how people wrote their own vows. She hadn't made a very good job of it, though. She talked about oneness and unity and altruism – words that sounded silly in her mouth since she never used them in real life.

Hugh gave Edward a wink. I'd let them wear whatever they wanted, so they'd chosen white shirts and cream trousers. It was hard to think of two men more physically unalike: where my father was pale and slim, with high cheekbones I'd semi-inherited, Edward was tanned, healthy, robust. Dressed the same, though, and sharing a joke I didn't get, I could see their likeness. In ten, twenty years, they might become a co-ordinating set, plumpened by Edward's cooking, dressed according to a mutual taste.

Tiny green apples lay scattered on the grass, an abandoned epic game of marbles. We'd had an eating apple tree at our old house – not the dream one. The apples were supposed to be a treat, but they weren't, not really, because it was so hard to find a perfect one. When I picked them up, even the ones that looked all right were pecked or rotting or had maggots in them. I was never tall enough to pick the fruit off of the branches. Only grown-ups could reach the best apples.

When they'd all done talking, Hugh cracked open a bottle of champagne, while Edward stuck a tape on his ghetto blaster and played It's a Wonderful World. 'It's a waltz. Did you know that? Listen to the beat. 1-2-3. 1-2-3.' He conducted the music with his forefinger. 'Do you waltz, Millie?'

'Bugger off, you,' My mother leaned forward and gave him a big kiss. She didn't smudge her lipstick, though, because of a trick she'd taught me. You apply one coat, blot, then another coat, blot, then dust with translucent powder. The method didn't work on me because my skin was too greasy, but it was info I was storing for later use.

Hugh gave an exaggerated sigh. 'Millie doesn't dance. She didn't dance even at our wedding.'

My mother threw wide her hands. 'It's true. Never even shuffled from one foot to the other.'

My parents had never talked much about their wedding. It was nothing flashy, but that was normal in the Seventies. No family came, because they either didn't care or didn't approve. My parents brought a witness each, a man and a woman, who were their best friends at the time, but they'd hardly seen since. They all went out to a restaurant afterwards and had steak and chips and champagne and there was no dancing. The day was entirely unmemorable, according to them, except for the fact that Hugh had ordered mulligatawny soup and the waiter dropped it all over the couple at the next table, who were getting married as well. They laughed when they told that story, but I always found it a bit sad.

Millie shoved me towards Edward. 'Dance with Freya. She was never any cop at ballet, but she did a bit of the other stuff at school. Didn't you, Frey?'

I shook my head. 'We did rain dances and ceilidhs. When we tried waltzing, I was one of the tall ones so I had to be the man.'

'It's OK.' Edward held out his arms, so I danced with him while Hugh chatted to my mother. Edward guided me, his hand pressed to the small of my back. Over his shoulder, I saw my mother leaning sulkily against an apple tree. She hadn't enjoyed getting married the first time and the second time round, she didn't look any more keen. But her being pissed off was just part of the fun.

Then we swapped, so Edward stood holding my mother's hand while I danced with Hugh. Everything was a bit the wrong way round, I suppose, but what would be the right way? The wedding of my three parents was never going to appear, with a colour photo, on the announcements page of the Cambridge Evening News.

The day after the wedding I went to see Mrs Glinka. Obviously, I wanted to know about Sasha, but I still loved her, too, only not in a romantic way. I was missing our chats. Everyone in my house talked the whole time, so I fought to get a word in and then they complained I was secretive. But the Glinka house was dead air, waiting for the sound of my voice.

As I cycled up the driveway, even from a distance something wasn't right. As I drew near, it wasn't a tiny fault in the picture, but more an enormous blemish. First I saw the fuzz of colour, then the shape of the car, then, up close, the number plate and the ding on the bumper. My mother's car was parked outside the Glinkas'.

I laid my bike on the front lawn and pressed the doorbell hard.

It was Mr Glinka who answered. In the daylight he looked more Russian than usual, with his hewn cheekbones and gently slanting eyes. He wore a rumpled shirt, baggy jeans and no shoes. His bare feet were high-arched, tanned, with neatly trimmed toenails. I wondered whether Sasha had feet like that.

'I came to see your wife,' I said.

He grinned. 'Of course, of course.' He gave me a kiss on each cheek.

'Why's my mother here?' I hadn't meant to sound accusing, but that was how it came out.

He didn't seem bothered by my tone. Him being foreign meant he was used to emotions, I expect. He stood back from the door. 'Come in.'

My mother was sitting at the Glinkas' kitchen table, in my chair, drinking vodka from a glass shaped like an upside-down bell. 'Sweetheart! Fancy a snifter?'

Mr Glinka took a glass down from the shelf and held it out to me.

I shook my head. 'I came to see Mrs Glinka. And in the afternoons I only drink tea.'

My mother laughed. 'Course, darling. I forget. Roman here said he knew the name of a reasonably-priced garage. Thought I'd drop by and get the number.'

He showed me a businesscard. 'This man, he is the Yehudi Menhuin of the carburettor.' He poured himself and Millie a shot of vodka. 'My wife, I'm afraid, is visiting her sister in Lowestoft.'

'I'm come back another time,' I said. 'We can go now, please?' I glared at my mother.

She downed her vodka in a single glug. 'At your service, milady.' She gave Mr Glinka a fake martyred look as I took her by the hand and tugged her gently towards the door.

I cycled home while she drove, because by the time we got the bike in the car we could have been half way home anyway. All the way back, I tried to work out why I was cross. Getting a number to fix her car, that was reasonable, and the Glinkas were poor, so they were bound to know someone cheap. My mother could always produce some rationale for her actions, however outrageous they might be.

When I arrived back at the house, she was already in the kitchen, taking down one of her old lists from the fridge door.

'Cup of tea?' I asked.

'Not for me, Freya darling.'

'Are we really that skint, still?' I'd thought things were better, but then why was she going to some Russian garage?

'Oh, it's not so bad.' She hoisted herself up to sit on the kitchen work surface, kicking her heels against the cupboard down below. 'Little job like that – no point shelling out the big bucks.'

'It's OK, if we're poor. There's this ski trip you can go on in the Upper Fifth and I wasn't even going to ask you about it. I know we can't afford it.'

'You can ski if you want, darling. Edward's diversified the business. Repossessions, don't you know. Buy at rock bottom, tart them up – all tax deductible, mind – then rent them out or flip them.'

'Isn't that a bit cynical?'

'If you think making money is cynical, Freya, you won't be doing much skiing in your life.'

'But if people can't afford these houses, then how are other people managing to buy them?'

'That's the world, darl. Always need somewhere to live, don't you? See how our domestic economy is on the upturn! A man with two wives, it makes no sense. Too many kids and not enough money. Plus the women would get bored. No one to give them attention.'

'Don't women in harems look after each other? Isn't that how it works?'

'That's what they'd have us believe. I think the eunuchs must've not been done, not properly.'

'Mother!'

'You won't always find the thought of sex repulsive, you know. I never had a multiple orgasm till I was thirty.'

I made for the door. Truly, my mother grew more appalling by the day.

She caught me before I could go, grabbing my elbow. 'Sorry, sweetheart. Only sometimes you look so grown up... Why don't we go shopping later? That's what you should get a career in – make-up. It's recession-proof. Women always buy lipstick, even when there's a war on.'

I wrenched my arm away. 'Thanks for the advice.'

From now on, my mother had no right to tell me what to do or who to be. Parents were supposed to be better than children. If they weren't, they lost their rights. Every time my mother did something I wanted, she ruined it by doing something I didn't. She'd obviously been trying to see Mrs Glinka to stir up trouble for me. I decided I was going to be nice to Edward, but I wasn't going to eat his food any more. That way he'd know that however hard he tried, I'd never really like him – not after what he'd done to my family. If people did wrong, they had to expect a come-back. He and Millie should know that by now.

The day before I went back to school, a woman from Social Services came round. I was playing with the functions on the new scientific calculator I'd got for quadratic equations, so I was really too busy to open the door. Everyone else, though, was either upstairs or in the garden, which meant I had no choice.

'Freya Baines?' she said. She wore a black trouser suit one size too small and a wrap-around top that showed loads of cleavage. Her hair shone blonde and glossy against her tanned face. She plonked herself down in our sitting room, quite relaxed, like she'd been in lots of strange sitting rooms. 'Are your parents home?'

My mother was outside on the lawn having her sundowner, so she wasn't going to like being interrupted.

'There's someone from the council here to see you,' I said.

Then I went upstairs and packed my schoolbag for the first day of term.

The lady from Social Services must've talked to Hugh as well, because it was past dinner time and she hadn't gone away yet. When it was my turn, Millie came to get me.

She stood in my doorway. 'Freya…You need to come speak to the lady.'

I'd only ever seen her that nervy once before, the morning of her root canal.

'What d'you want me to tell her?'

That annoyed her, I think.

'I can't possibly dictate to you, Freya. You know that.'

'What d'you think foster care's like, Mummy? Would I get my own room or would I have to share? I'm not sure I'd like sharing. Or perhaps it'd be a children's home. Orphanages seemed such fun when they had them in Bunty.'

Her nostrils flared. 'You won't be going anywhere.'

'But they could take me away, in theory. What if they decide you're not a suitable parent?'

My mother was only ever able to be polite for so long. 'Just get down there! No one's ever a suitable parent. Whoever said motherhood was the most important job in the world? Most poorly paid, most difficult, most thankless, more like.'

I laughed. 'True to form, then.'

She stretched out her hand towards my face. 'Freya, I didn't mean…'

I brushed away her hand. 'It's all right.' I zipped up my

schoolbag. I was all ready – nice and neat. 'I know what to say.'

The social worker looked sad not to find the dirt she'd been promised. Even if I'd broken down and confessed that the three adults slept in three bedrooms, but not always alone, what could she have done? It wasn't like I was deprived or abused. I always did my homework and I never ate crisps. I rolled up my sleeve and showed her my arm. 'Would you like to examine me for bruises?' I asked.

I shouldn't have said the last bit, because she didn't think it was funny or clever. She gave a look like she was sorry for me. She said, 'You may not believe this, but you are not necessarily the best judge of your own welfare.' She handed me her card. 'Give a ring if you change your mind.'

Then she picked up her handbag and left. I could tell she hadn't much liked my parents and she didn't much like me either, I dare say. No doubt she thought we deserved each other.

✳ thirteen ✳

I hadn't time to see Jessica before school started, but she'd be dying, I knew, to hear about Sasha. In my pocket lay my secret weapon – a letter. It wasn't a real letter, actually, just a post-card in an envelope, but Sasha had sent it all the way from abroad.

> Don't bother with France. OK grub, but music,
> clothes and haircuts somewhat below par. Luckily,
> there's an Irish boozer in town which soothes my
> angst of deracination. Sash.

The postcard might be short, but he'd made a real effort with it. He'd managed to be casual and witty at the same time, proving he was lots more amusing than he first appeared and possibly the funniest person I'd ever met. He'd even included his return address so I could write back. Obviously, I could-n't write too soon, because that'd look desperate and whatever I put, it had to be exactly right. I'd ask Jessica and Connie to help me – that would put me back in their good books. I didn't even know for certain if I was in their bad books, but I'd rung

Jessica the night before school and she hadn't rung me back.

I'd fallen out with her once before, when I'd gone 83% in our Geography end of year exam and she'd only got 48%. She cried and wanted to go and tell the teacher how upset she was, except I told her she was being a baby and she should just work harder next time. When I said that, she cried even more. But that was in the days before Connie, so Jessica had no choice but to make up with me. This time, though, I hadn't done anything. I'd organised us going to the ball, with lifts there and back, and her and Connie both said they had a nice time. I was being paranoid, I expect. Things were always different after the summer holidays, and most times they were different, but better.

The bell rang, launching us into another year. When I walked into my new form room, Jessica and Connie had already bagged a couple of desks together at the back. The lesson was starting, so I had to sit near the front next to Davina Wylam. No one ever wanted to be next to her because she had eczema and when she scratched her face, skin snowed on the desk in front of her. She'd tried everything and her parents had sent her to half of Harley Street. It was worse if you had to share a book with her, because then you and it got covered in face dandruff. Sitting next to her, though, was a kind thing to do.

We had a double lesson for meeting our new form teacher, Mrs Rally, except that we already knew her from RE. She gave out timetables and told us how we were allowed in the garden at break times now. We'd be doing proper exams that year.

Everyone was scared, but I wasn't, because exams meant school was nearly over. Eleven years down, only three to go: I was up for parole. With Sasha's postcard in my bag, finally I was starting to imagine a future me who had a nice life – one that'd compensate me for all those boring wasted years of childhood.

The second bell went and Jessica and Connie bolted out of the door. When I tried to talk to them, Jessica pointed out of the window, meaning she'd meet me outside. Even though it was autumn, Jessica was still wearing her gingham summer dress and long white socks. Being well-covered, she didn't feel the cold.

The lawn, scuffed during term time by a hundred pairs of sensible shoes, had grown fluffier during the holidays. September meant the world was restored to its healthier, more ordered self.

I found Jessica and Connie sitting on a low wall by the tree that Hugh had leaned against when he'd come to the summer fête. I thought about that Rubik's cube solution he'd bought, and how he'd never used it, or even bought a Rubik's cube. My father was like that. He got more fun from thinking about things than actually doing them.

'Hello,' I said. 'What you up to?'

Connie opened her bag, took out a Chemistry textbook and pretended to read.

'Hello.' Jessica was sort of looking at me, sort of not, like I had a spot on my chin.

'Did you have a good time in London?' I asked. 'Hugh's

birthday was great. Sorry you couldn't make it.'

Connie sniggered.

I wanted to ask what the matter was, but I didn't. 'We had real champagne Millie got on discount from her work. She says that Californian Cuvée Napa is just as good, if not better – but for special occasions, only the real stuff will do.'

Connie closed her Chemistry textbook and turned to Jessica. 'Millie. Calling your mother that – bit weird, don't you think?'

'What's weird about my mother's name?' I asked.

'You call your mother Mummy. Or Mum if you're common.' Connie curled her upper lip. She didn't look very pretty. 'No one calls their mother by her first name.'

'She likes it like that. It's more normal.'

Now Jessica laughed. 'Normal? Jesus, Freya! What's normal about you and your family?'

They knew.

I could feel the other girls looking at me. They knew too, or soon would: nothing stayed secret at St Joan's. I wished aliens would land and teleport me away to somewhere better, where I was a stranger and nobody knew my shame.

Connie flicked her hair over her shoulder. 'Well, Freya, though it's none of your beeswax, you know Paulette Davenport from the Lower Sixth? Her mother was there. At your house. As someone's date, would you believe? She's some tragic divorcée, apparently. She's going out with some doctor friend of that anaesthetist bloke who lives next door to you. And Paulette's mother works with my mother as a volunteer in the Oxfam shop in Tuesdays. My mother was very upset, actually. She said you were a right lying little madam because you must be in on it, too. She's really disgusted I've been round your house, where anything could've happened. I could've been molested – or worse. And she's told me that I can still be friends with you if I want, out of sympathy…but she thinks it best if I keep away.'

I wanted to hug Jessica or maybe slap her round the face. She'd always accepted me, even if other people hadn't. She didn't think it was strange I kept my mother's lists. Even when Connie first laid claim to her, Jessica had still made an extra special effort so that I'd never feel left out. Before she met Connie and I'd met Mrs Glinka and Sasha, we'd survived a year of our lives just by having each other. That must mean something.

Jessica didn't look at me as she spoke. 'When Connie told me, I had to say something to my mother. Sorry, Freya, but I mean, I could've slept over at your house when we went to that ball. So I told her all about that man you've got living with you and it all sort of added up with what Connie had said. My parents, they want my friends to come from nice families. That's why they send me to St Joan's.'

'So that's it?' I asked.

I wanted to say something better – more aggrieved and more profound. A year at school without my Jessica flashed forward in my mind. I could spend break times in the library, doing homework, but what about lunchtimes? Who would I go into town with on Saturdays? Talk to on the coach on school trips? Even if I'd shared Jessica with Connie and got the smaller half of affections, I still wanted her. I couldn't go back to being alone.

Jessica frowned. 'Sorry, Freya. But you did a wrong thing. You lied about your family. You misled us.'

'I never lied,' I said.

'So you won't lie now?' Connie smiled. 'You won't deny that your mother – sorry – Millie – is a total and utter slag.'

'She is not!' I stepped towards her. I wanted to lean forward and take her hairclip off her bleached fringe and stuff it down her throat. But I couldn't do that. I couldn't do anything. I stepped back again. Triumph flickered in Connie's eyes.

Jessica looked a bit sad. 'I'm afraid, Freya, that that's what everyone's saying your mother is. A slag , I mean.'

Connie giggled. 'Runs in the family.'

Jessica shrugged. 'Makes things difficult. You must understand that.'

'I don't understand,' I said.

And really, I didn't. If you were in love, everything was always OK. That's what they'd told us at school. Don't be guilty, just be careful. Or was it Millie who'd said that? My mother, I supposed, hadn't been careful enough.

I should have walked away, left the garden, left the school, but a smidgeon of hope kept me standing there, waiting for Jessica to realise that Connie was just a horror who'd never deserved her, while I had seen into the heart of my ex best friend and not found it wanting. I was sorry I'd silently criticised her for being overweight when really she was lovely.

Why hadn't I ever told her how lovely she was?

Connie sighed. 'Just fuck off, Freya.'

No one had ever said those words to me before. No one at St Joan's ever said the word 'fuck', or at least, not until sixth form. I could feel my lower lip trembling, something I'd thought people only did in cartoons. I waited for Jessica to change her mind, but she stared downwards and fiddled with her socks.

With the sounding of the bell, the school year began again.

I zombie-walked the rest of the day. I could have killed someone and not even realised it. I never once raised my hand in class, not even when we were discussing our new Class Civ text, Oedipus the King. Miss Gillis was so excited, she could barely contain herself. 'Listen! Best sentence in world literature. You know not how you live, nor what you do, nor who you are. The human condition encapsulated.'

Every play we read encapsulated the human condition, supposedly, but all the plays were different, which didn't make sense.

'You're very quiet today, Freya.' Miss Gillis leaned over my desk so that I could see a shred of marmalade stuck to her chest.

'Summer cold.' I got a Kleenex from my bag and blew into it. She backed away.

I kept expecting to be called in to the headmistress's office, or at the very least to see my head of year, but nothing happened. Everyone was quiet with me, like if the nit nurse had been and told everyone I had headlice. The next day, I'd be lucky if even Davina Wylam would sit next to me. I'd be begging her to scratch eczema onto my jumper.

As I was leaving for day, pelting down the corridor towards the school's back door, Mrs Rally held out her hand and stopped me.

'No running, Freya! If everybody ran, then we'd all end up in sick bay with broken arms and broken legs.'

As usual, she was overstating the case. I had a teacher like her in primary school who told us that one little boy hadn't washed his hands after he'd been to the toilet and then everyone in the whole school had died. When I told Millie about this, she said the teacher was lying, because virtually no men ever washed their hands after they took a piss, and if that was such a problem, then we'd all be dead by now.

'Sorry,' I said.

Mrs Rally tilted her head gently, giving me that look that said she was onto me and that God was on her side. 'Are you really sorry, Freya? You don't look it.'

She was giving me special attention but I didn't want it. I was sick of her education. The more she taught me, the stupider I became. I was right up close to her and I could see how the muscle beneath her right eye was pulsing, keeping time to unheard music.

'You don't know it all,' I said.

'Freya!' Her twitch upped its tempo.

At St Joan's, we weren't allowed to talk back. Our thoughts, theoretically, were our own, but even that was dicey. I felt my temperature rise. 'I've tried to be good. I've tried to be the best I can. I tried what you said in the classes and it hasn't worked. You don't know anything.'

She was going to go red and angry, I thought, or she'd threaten to tell my form teacher or my head of year or my parents. Like I cared, anyhow.

But her eyes filled with tears. 'Sorry, Freya. I tried my best. So very sorry.'

I wanted to reply, but I couldn't think what. I brushed past her and walked, not ran, through the back door and out of the school.

When I got home Millie's car stood in the drive way. She'd had the light fixed, but the back bumper was still miserable and battered. Someone had written West Ham FC in the dirt on the hood. Beside it a purple Fiat Panda stood parked at a silly angle, with the front end poking out into the street. Ours was one of the widest streets in Cambridge, which meant it was always full of learner drivers practising their three-point turns. Learner drivers, though, didn't drive Pandas.

Inside, my mother sat on the sofa, a glass in her hand and a slender bottle of Alsace-Lorraine Riesling, frosted from the fridge, by her side. The carpet in front of her was still littered with crumbs left over from Hugh's party. Edward had whizzed round with a hoover the next day, but he hadn't exactly made a decent fist of the job.

Jackie, Hugh's ex-secretary was sitting on the sofa opposite my mother. When I walked in, Jackie flinched, but she didn't say hello. She'd lost even more weight since the tribunal. Her neck was haggard with sticky-outy tendons, so just looking at it was real nails-down-the-blackboard territory.

'Best be off,' said Jackie. She stood, adjusted her weight from foot to foot for a moment, then marched past me out of the room. She banged the front door behind her.

I turned to my mother. 'What's she doing here? I thought she was Satan in a dress, or whatever you call her.'

'Never said she wasn't. Stupid grasping bloody cow. I told her we were both victims. Think she liked that.' She drained her glass.

'Victims?'

'Male bloody oppression. You never win, Freya. Mark my words.' She poured herself the remains of the bottle.

'How d'you mean?'

'Bloody lawyer's made her an offer and now she wants a bump. It'll cost more money to pay the solicitor to negotiate her down than it will to cough up. Well, sorry, Freya. Bang goes your ski trip. You got any complaints, kindly take them up with the management. By which I mean – your father.'

'It's his fault?'

'Ultimately, yes. Pretty much, I think you'll find. Today, at any rate.'

'But no one's calling him a slag.'

'You what?' She sat up a little straighter.

'You any idea what it's like going to school? Now I'm more of a freak than ever. Worse than a freak. A monster. Only this time, it's not my fault. It's you.' I wanted to rail against her in righteous outrage, but my words came out mewling, self-pitying.

My mother raised her glass to me. 'Well, Freya. Let's face it. It's not like you've ever been very popular.'

'I had friends.'

'Really? That's not what I heard. The way your teachers go on about you, anyone'd think you were Myra bloody Hindley in the making.' She smirked like she'd just told a really brilliant joke. At that moment, I found her quite horrible. Her eyes were bloodshot, tights laddered and nail varnish chipped.

'You're selfish,' I said. 'My life, Hugh's, Edward's – it's all about accommodating you, whatever the cost.'

'For God's sakes. We're all selfish. Born selfish. Darwin and all that. Don't tell me that Mother bloody Theresa doesn't want to be the best nun on the planet – screw the poor old sodding lepers.'

'You've ruined my life.' I stared right at her, letting her know I was serious.

'Everyone thinks that about their dear old mum sometime or another. Even Jesus. He probably thought Mary was a right cow.'

'Everybody else I know, their mothers care about them first. More than anything else in the world. Like Mrs Glinka… I wish she was my mother.'

Millie snorted. 'Her? Christ! Well, I suppose the grass is always greener. You don't know the half of it.'

'How d'you mean?'

'She's crackers, her. Completely off her chump.'

'You don't know anything about her.'

'She never goes out. Can't go into town. When Sasha was at school, never went to the concerts, parents' evenings, sports days. Won't get help.'

'You're lying. She came here, didn't she? Round ours.'

'For ten minutes. Course, she leaves the house sometimes. Goes the supermarket once in a while. But it takes her a week to gee herself up for it, then a fortnight to recover. Why d'you think we had your birthday round hers?'

'She goes to her sister's in Lowestoft.'

'Once every five years.'

I thought about the fact that Mrs Glinka was always at home. Her coming to Hugh's birthday was almost the only time I'd ever seen her outside of her own house, and she'd seemed uncomfortable, constantly looking towards the door. But then, that was how I felt at parties. 'I met her in a cinema. You forgot about that.'

She rolled her eyes. 'Saturday morning with subtitles? How many in the audience? Two? Three? She goes once a year. Big fucking deal. Her kid gets sent to an educational psychologist and she never takes him so he never goes. And now look at him.'

'You're just jealous of her.'

She sighed. 'Dear God. Why d'you think she doesn't go out to work?'

'Because she thinks you can have marriage and children or a career – not both at the same time.'

'She can't cope with work – with people. The Glinkas are poor as church mice, and there's her, lounging around all day. She's a disgrace. All his family, all his mates, all of them back in Russia but he's stuck here. Can't even visit.'

'They don't go to Russia because Roman Glinka is a political dissident.'

'He's been pardoned. Did you hear? Rehabilitated. Glasnost and perewhatsit.'

'Perestroika.'

'Whatever.' She took a deep angry drag on her cigarette. 'It's her, Freya. That family have no life because it all revolves around that one mad sorry cow.'

I shook my head. 'Why d'you have to be so mean about everybody? Even if what you're saying's true, how d'you even know about it?'

She poured the last of the bottle into her glass. 'Everybody knows. That's what this town is like.'

'Like everybody knows about you?'

'Yeah. Dare say so.'

I'd put my schoolbag down on the floor, but now I picked it up again and slung it over my shoulder. 'Maybe she is mad, but nobody despises her. No one hates Sasha because of her.' I stood in the doorway, making it clear that I was going to leave.

'You off to see her?' She took one last puff on her cigarette, even though she'd burned it down to the filter.

'Maybe.'

'It's not like you've anywhere else to go.'

'Thanks to you.'

'Thanks to yourself and all. Jesus, Freya. Stay in for bloody once. I'm here, aren't I? Isn't that what you wanted? Quality time? Everything'll sort itself out – you'll see.'

I hesitated. I didn't really want to have to ask Mrs Glinka if she was mad. Then I thought of the day I'd had at school and all the horrible days to come. 'I'm going.'

'I can come after you, you know.' Millie picked up her car keys, which were lying on the table beside the ashtray, and jangled them.

'No, you can't,' I said. 'You are, as usual, way too pissed. You're disgusting.'

I slammed out of the house.

Soon as I was pedalling down the road, all the things I wished I'd said screamed through my brain. I'd wanted to tell her that she never loved me enough. If only she could tell me that I was the most important thing in her life, just for a day, or an hour, maybe, then everything'd be all right. I wouldn't mind however else our world turned. How come I hadn't said any of that? As ever with my mother, she got the better of me. She always made me behave like a worse person than I actually was.

When I got to Mrs Glinka's, she let me in without saying hello or how are you. I followed her into the dining room, where she knelt down on the floor. She was going through papers, which was something that my parents did quite often, only not with passion.

Her hands rummaged furiously. 'One moment, Freya. Then we can have tea and somesuch. Cake or dinner. But first, I have to find something.'

Letters, bills, receipts, pages of handwritten manuscript in English and Russian – they were strewn all over the place, carpeting the floor.

'I get in such a muddle.' She shuffled through one pile, then moved on to the next. 'Roman will never let me touch. Not a thing. So we live in this midden and year on year, worse and worse.'

'Can I help?'

She recoiled. 'No! Now he wants to publish a new book. New Russians, old Russians. With Gorbachov, there is interest again. His time has come.'

'Thought he didn't write much any more.'

'Not for years. He got depressed. Saw no point. But the last month or so, he's back. He says he's a mighty river – damned up, now broken free. So now I'm finding the rest – the bits of this and that he's done over the years. People will look to him. How do we build the bridge between East and West? Who knows better than my Roman?'

Mrs Glinka did look a bit mad just then, sifting through mounds of rubbish. Her hair was usually bound tight in a bun, but that day she hadn't pinned it up. Two long plaits, yellow at the tips but fairer towards the crown of her head, hung down limply on either side of her face, so she looked half schoolgirl, half witch. 'He stays late at the shop to write. Doesn't even know what he writes about. They're the scribblings of an alien hand. Did you know that's an actual illness? People try to strangle themselves.'

I'd heard of having an alien hand, but only the strangling kind. I was a bit disappointed in Mrs Glinka. I'd hardly seen her the whole summer and I was expecting a warmer reception, or a sandwich, at least. She'd made me my first ever egg and cress sandwich, which I only ate because I was in someone else's house, even though I didn't like cress. But when I tried it, it was actually quite good. There were other things that Mrs Glinka got me to eat as well, which Millie and Hugh never did. They spent their whole childhoods being made to eat revolting stuff, so they wouldn't do that to any child of theirs.

My stomach rumbled, but she ignored it.

'Will you get a job now that Sasha's left home?' I asked.

She looked up. 'This is my job. A great man, he needs constant support. He can do nothing for himself. When you marry, Freya, don't choose a great man. Chose an average one. That way, you can be great.'

Sasha, while he wasn't great yet, could become great in the future. He might not have any qualifications, but he did have an IQ of 168. Surely somewhere people cared about stuff like that. America, perhaps.

I wanted to ask why Mrs Glinka didn't work in the clothes shop while her husband stayed home writing poetry. Then he could be great all day, not just for a few hours after closing time.

'When he publishes the book,' I asked, 'will you go to

Russia to do publicity and stuff?'

She slammed down a wad of papers on the carpet. 'There's so little money… And other factors. A problematic situation.'

'What about Sasha? Are you going to see him in Toulouse? Wouldn't it be nice to go on holiday? Specially seeing as how you speak all those languages and things?'

She gave me a scary look, like she could see through my skin and into my soul. Then her hands went back to the papers. The room had become gloomy but she didn't turn on the light. She wasn't actually sorting, I realised: she was more like a detective, searching for evidence.

'I better go,' I said. I hadn't brought my bike lights, so if I left it much longer, I'd have to walk back.

She stood, held out her arms, then hugged me tight. It must have been strange, always to be cuddling somebody else's daughter. She smelled older than my mother did – but beautiful, a scent that made me want to weep.

'You're a good girl,' she mumbled, as she set me free. 'Never mind what anyone says.'

I wanted to tell her about Jessica and Connie, how horrific the party'd been, the bit with Penelope she hadn't noticed, how I didn't understand anything any more and that her and Sasha were my only hope now. But she never asked me what was wrong, so I never told her.

She stroked my hair. 'Come tomorrow. We'll make gingerbread together. Or we could flavour vodka with berries. Would you like that?'

*

265

Back home, my mother had gone out, so my agony was prolonged. I knew she'd be angry and that I'd have to apologise for calling her a disgusting slag and for not believing her about Mrs Glinka. Hugh would be upset and I couldn't see Edward siding with me rather than my mother, not after I'd been being nasty to him. Whatever tiny victories might be scored in battles along the way, my mother always won the war: that was one of her talents.

Edward made lasagne for dinner which was maybe my favourite thing in the world, but when we sat at the table, I said I wasn't hungry and I'd have a toastie instead.

Millie said that if I kept eating toasties, I was destined for piles. I didn't really understand what piles were. Teachers always told us we'd get them if we sat on the radiator, but everybody sat on the radiator and nobody ever got sick. Piles were something you got when you were pregnant, Mrs Rally said, when someone asked her. But nobody ever talked about that because then it'd spoil the joy of motherhood.

While I was in the kitchen, I heard Hugh talking to Edward. 'They all have food fads at that age. It's a girl thing.'

I sat down at the table and munched at my sandwich. 'I don't understand where she's gone without her car,' I said.

I watched Edward and Hugh carefully for the way reacted when I mentioned my mother. If they went a bit funny, that'd mean she'd told them what I'd said. But they didn't flicer.

'There's always the bus.' Edward set his cutlery down neatly in the centre of his plate.

'Millie doesn't take the bus. She doesn't like it because it's full of poor people,' I said.

Hugh helped himself to seconds. 'She's got a couple of evening meetings this week. She did tell me but I forget which. Importers wanting to sell the Christmas specials – port, sherry, champagne and whatnot.'

'It's not Christmas for months,' I said.

'A tradesman's lot.' My father gave a comedy shrug. 'I'm rather looking forward to Christmas this year.'

'Already, Dad?'

Hugh could be funny. Each year was a trial to be completed: that was the fault of Millie's lists. The mini-lists that ruled each day were bad enough, but January's mega-lists were the worst. Number three on my list for that year was Competence in Public Speaking, which I'd done nothing about whatsoever. My father's tasks were even worse. He'd to earn more, sleep less, spend less time watching television. He longed for December when, completed or not, his tasks could finally be forgotten. Since Edward's arrival, however, our lists had been greatly reduced. No wonder my father wanted to keep him.

I've no idea what was on telly that night. Hugh and Edward weren't really watching either, because they were talking about work. Whatever they were trying, it was getting them out of the shit, or so they said.

When Millie came home, after I'd said sorry for calling her names, I'd ask her how to deal with Jessica and Connie. No one was ever horrible to my mother, because they were terrified of her. I'd get her to teach me how to be the same. She was brilliant at finding ways to get back at people. When she was at school, a girl in her class had tried to go out with her boyfriend, so she put a dead mouse in the girl's pocket. My mother wasn't a creative person, not in any conventional sense, but she knew how to get people feeling what she wanted them to feel.

At ten o'clock, when she still hadn't rung, Hugh started glancing at his watch.

Edward lounged out along the sofa. 'Chill, my friend. You know what she's like when she's on a roll.'

By eleven my father was staring at the phone and Edward wasn't telling him to chill any more. The fact it was only Thursday made my father more worried. On school nights, Millie liked to get sloshed early, zonk out on the sofa, then stagger up to bed no later than ten.

Edward had been trying to stop smoking, or so he said, but he took a pack of Millie's from the carton she'd bought, then smoked a couple of fags, one after the other. It didn't calm him down, though. He got up off the sofa and went to do the washing up. When he was upset he washed up by hand, even though we had a washing up machine to do it for us.

He was still elbow deep in bubbly water when I went in the kitchen to fetch myself a glass of milk.

He turned to me and spoke, his voice reproachful. 'You don't eat my food, Freya. Not any more.'

I'd been waiting for this. In my fantasies, I was honest. I rounded on him and poured out my outrage and my disdain.

But now I had my chance, I couldn't bring myself to be mean.

'It's just not what I'm used to, Edward. When you usually eat stuff from packets, real food tastes funny. And it's been the holidays. In the holidays, I get to eat what I want.'

The last bit was a lie. But since my mother had acquired a second husband, I didn't see why I couldn't forge some domestic innovations of my own.

'I started cooking for me and my dad,' he said. 'He'd never learned and didn't want to, so I thought I'd give it a go.'

'What about your mother? She didn't cook?'

'God, yes. She was amazing. Best pastry ever. Used a mixture of self-raising flour and plain. Never wrote down the recipes, though. It's all lost now.'

'She's dead?'

He nodded. He stared down at his scuffed Oxford brogues which, according to him, were the most expensive thing he owned, apart from his car. The bottoms of his chinos were frayed where they'd scraped along the ground. He didn't have the feet and ankles of a man who was being taken care of. That sort of thing wasn't included in Millie's job description.

He kicked against a bubble in the lino, flattening it down. Hugh, I knew, wasn't happy about the flooring and wanted quarry tiles instead, but the money had run out before he got the kitchen floor of his dreams.

'My mother died of breast cancer when I was twelve. She was sick for years before that, though.'

'Sorry.'

'I hated people being sorry. I was embarrassed. Lied.

Started saying she'd moved away. Almost believed it myself sometimes.'

'But you've still got your father, though.'

He shrugged. 'Men can't really cope without women. That's what he says. Not unless they're gay, and then they usually have their mums or something. So he found someone else. She's nice enough. Naturally, she found me a bit de trop.'

Though I hated myself a bit for it, I loved the sound of Edward's voice. My parents had the strange nothing-like accents of people who'd moved around. The vowels were all jumbled up, the haitches sometimes dropped and sometimes not. But all of Edward's vowels and consonants and phrases sounded like they came from the same place. He sounded a bit like me.

'How did you know your stepmother didn't like you? Perhaps you imagined it.'

'She'd send out Christmas cards from the family and she'd forget to put my name on. Stuff like that. The only time I ever really belonged was when I was a little boy and now. Here. With you.'

I supposed the no mother thing was why him and Hugh got on. Except Hugh's mother was pretty crap even when she was alive. Maybe that was why he had a black dog and Edward didn't.

'You don't really live here because of me,' I said. 'Be honest. No one wants to live with a teenager. It's not like I'm sweet or anything. I've never been sweet.'

He laughed, which made me laugh.

He pinched me on the cheek like Mrs Glinka did. 'You are sweet, actually. You're part of the package, Freya. If I couldn't love you, I wouldn't be here. You not see that?'

I let him hug me. His heart beat next to mine, but slower and stronger. When he let me go, I missed my mother.

'I don't like her not being back,' I said. Through the kitchen window, the sky was slick and grey as polished slate.

He lifted the tray of leftover lasagne from inside the oven and placed it on top of the stove. 'I told her to get a car phone and she wouldn't.'

'But she didn't take her car.'

'That makes it worse.'

Miss Rally said it was good to talk about things, but I preferred Millie's solution – put up or shut up. Stuff was better kept in its cage, because once it was out, you could never get it back in.

'Millie always comes home,' I said. 'Worse luck.'

We smiled at each other – not big smiles, but more a brave tightening of the face. I didn't smile enough – I knew that from Millie's lists, but only TV presenters and morons smiled all the time.

I hadn't wanted to say anything, especially not to Edward, but I couldn't hold back any more. 'I was horrible to Mummy. I told her things I shouldn't have and now she'll be cross with me.' I felt tears at the back of my nose.

He patted my hand. 'Knowing your mother, she was no angel herself. She'll be home soon and then you can make up and it'll be like nothing ever happened.'

'D'you mind if I have some lasagne now? I just wasn't that hungry before.'

He handed me a fork still warm from the heat of the washing-up water. 'Just eat from the tin. There's only a bit left, anyhow. Millie won't be wanting it.'

I gulped down the food, barely tasting it. All I experienced was the texture – the fusing together of softness and burntness between my teeth. As I ate, Edward smiled – not in a fake way, like the royal family did when they were bored. He was trying to pour his happiness into my heart, I think. I wondered if I'd ever learn to smile like that.

I was thinking about brushing my teeth and going to bed when an unfamiliar car pulled up outside the house. I heard a car door slam, then another car door. Feet clomped up our path, but there were too many of them for it to be just Millie.

The footsteps stopped. I listened for the pause as she fumbled in her handbag, then the metallic swivel as she placed her key in the lock, but our visitors had no key. They banged at the door. They didn't even use the bell like they were supposed to. Maybe they couldn't see it in the dark.

The open front door sucked in cold air from the outside. Two police people, one man, one woman, stood on the doorstep. The man was very tall with a flat nose, like it'd been broken. The woman was trying to seem kind, but she just looked nervous.

'Mr Hugh Baines?' said the policeman.

My father nodded.

'Husband of Mrs Millicent Baines?'

He nodded again.

'May we come inside?'

✳ fourteen ✳

Even though we sat there for hours with nothing to say, read or watch, I remember nothing about that family room except the overbright tubular lighting and the cut glass pub ashtray they gave to Edward. I wondered where they got it from, since it wasn't allowed to smoke in hospital. He sat puffing one Marlboro Light after another. The nurses gave me hot chocolate which I knew I shouldn't have so near to bedtime because it was bad for my teeth. It was bitty and oversweet, but I drank it anyway. The nurses fussed round us for a while, then left us alone. Clearly, they'd put us in the family room so we wouldn't upset the people outside, the relatives and friends who had something to hope for.

After a couple of hours a policeman, but not the one who'd been to our house, came and sat with us. He looked at Edward smoking and wrinkled his nose. Then he spoke to my father like he'd done something wrong. 'How many units of alcohol did your wife consume this evening?'

Hugh didn't know, because he hadn't seen her, not since morning. But I had, obviously. 'A bottle of wine, pretty much,' I said.

The policeman wrote that down, then pointed at me. 'Is there a relative or a family friend who could take her home?'

'I'm staying,' I said.

The policeman looked like he wasn't happy.

We still didn't understand how the accident had happened. Millie had been driving a Volvo, they thought, but who did she know who drove a Volvo?

'Who was the other passenger?' Hugh asked.

The policeman looked down at the ground. 'I'm afraid we can't tell you until his next of kin have been informed.'

'His? So it's a man? And the man is dead?'

The policeman shrugged. 'That's all the information I have at this stage.'

I thought my mother was dead and I was only half wrong. She was not quite dead, not quite alive, but somewhere in between. They'd know more after surgery, then more in twenty-four hours, and then they'd get to the stage where there was nothing new. The doctor came in and told us that she was alive, but not as though that was good news.

'Death,' she said, 'is sometimes the preferable option.'

We kept drinking cups of hot things, then leaving them, then going to the loo, then coming back. My father's face was grey. Edward got up, lumbered about the room, then sat down again. He seemed quite young to me just then.

It'd be strange to have Millie die before Grandpa Eric. There was only one girl in my year who had less than two parents –

Emmie Unsbrook whose father was in the Faulklands and got shot in combat. Although it was ages ago, people were still really nice to her, because not only was she half an orphan, but her father was a hero. Even the girls who believed in passive resistance instead of war, they never slagged her off. I wondered if Jessica and Connie and all the rest of them would feel guilty towards me when they heard. They'd come up to me and apologise, get me a present, maybe, and a condolences card. But then, in their eyes, Millie wouldn't be a dead hero: she'd be a dead whore.

Hugh went out to go to the loo and as he was coming back, the not very nice policeman stopped him. I got worried that my father really had done something wrong, until I remembered what Millie said about the police. 'They treat everyone like scumbags. That's their job. Must be terribly difficult for them.'

Hugh came back in and said, 'She's in Recovery. But don't get hopeful.'

We gathered up our things and followed my father down a long squeaky corridor. Now I was feeling excited. My mother wasn't going to die, after all. The awfulness was over. 'Doctors always tell you to expect the worst,' that's what Millie used to say. 'That way, if you get better, you think they're bloody Jesus.'

Just as we were about to get into the lift, I saw Mrs Glinka coming into the hospital. Or at least, I thought it was Mrs Glinka. She was a long way off and when I waved at her, she didn't wave back. Then she disappeared. If it was her, she hadn't seen me.

'Did you ring Mrs Glinka?' I asked as the lift doors closed. Hugh shook his head.

'But that was her, wasn't it? Did you see her? Did you? That proves she's not an agoraphobic.' I turned my father, then to Edward. They both looked blank.

We got up to Recovery, where you were only allowed one visitor at a time and family only, but they let all three of us go up. They were bending the rules for us, which was not a good thing.

My mother was lying in bed, her head covered in white bandages, like Humpty Dumpty after his fall. The illustration in my nursery rhyme book made out that Humpty was OK, but if you believed the poem, they couldn't put him together again. When it was my turn to talk to her, I held her hand. 'I love you, Mummy,' I said. I wanted to kiss her on the cheek, but the bandages and the tubes put me off. 'I'm sorry, Mummy,' I whispered, but she didn't move or flicker her eyes or do anything to show she'd heard me. I kept thinking this was a scene in a film and that any second I'd snap out of it. I closed my eyes for a moment, so the nasty dream would stop. But when I looked again, my mother was still there but not there, still teasing me with her impending death.

Hugh and Edward each gave her a kiss. Then they made us leave.

A doctor – a woman this time, not the man we'd seen down stairs – led us back out into the corridor. Hugh turned to her.

'No private room? In her condition?'

The doctor, I think, had heard this lots of times before. 'She is receiving the best possible care. There's nothing more we can do. With a severe head injury, in a deep coma…'

'What now?' I asked.

Edward put his arm around me. 'Let's go home, Freya. Get some rest. Come back in the morning. Maybe she'll have woken up by then.'

'Yeah,' said my father. 'Home. I'll stay a while, then I'll see you back at the house.'

I tugged at my father's sleeve. 'Can we go find Mrs Glinka? I'm sure it was her. I mean, who else do you know who wears their hair in a bun? No one does.'

Hugh opened his mouth, then closed it again.

'What is it?' I asked.

Hugh and Edward looked at each other, then at me. 'That was Mrs Glinka,' said my father.

'I thought so! If you saw her, why didn't you say?'

He bit his lip. 'You're not really old enough for all this, Freya. Maybe I'm not either. But that was Roman Glinka's car your mother was driving. He was the man in the passenger seat. They drove into a roundabout and he was killed outright.'

I shook my head. 'But why would Millie be driving his car?'

'According to the police, by the smell of him, he was absolutely blotto. Your mother would have been the fittest driver of the two. Of course, neither of them should have been behind the wheel.'

We were all quiet for a moment.

'But I don't understand!' I said. 'What was Millie doing in a car with Mr Glinka in the first place?'

Hugh and Edward just looked at me.

Edward was the one to speak. 'We can't know for sure, Freya. But whatever the reason you think, it's probably that.'

My father's arms hung limp by his sides but his fists were clenched. 'Just shut up, Edward! For once, can't you see this is none of your bloody business!'

Edward stood stunned. 'Hugh! I just wanted... I'm trying to do the right thing.'

'You've done quite enough already.' My father sat and bowed his head.

Edward and I left him there alone in the hospital. We drove home in silence.

The first forty-eight hours were the most important, apparently, and since Millie didn't wake up within a couple of days, it got less and less likely that she ever would. But they took her off of the respirator and she kept on breathing, which meant there was enough left of her brain to do something at least. After a week, she opened her eyes. Then, when Edward came into the room, she said, 'You need a haircut.' They said she was still in a coma, which made no sense. But she couldn't walk or swallow, so she had to be in bed, with a feeding tube into her stomach.

The doctor told us she looked better than she actually was.

'She's in what we call a minimally conscious state. Not awake, not asleep.'

When I approached her, she looked as though she knew me.

The doctor frowned. 'Involuntary eye movements are common, but not necessarily significant.'

Because Mr Glinka had once been famous there was a story about the accident on page three of the Cambridge Evening News. It mentioned Millie, too – that she was a neighbour who'd been driving when they crashed. The article didn't say anything about how Millie had two husbands already and was having an affair with Mr Glinka as well, just because he was there – just because she could. Mr Glinka's funeral would be held in one of the university chapels, but Hugh said I couldn't go, because the situation was delicate.

My father didn't cry, not that I saw. Millie always said he was stoical and so was I, I suppose, because I didn't cry either. I didn't know what to cry about. Edward wept all day, though. Within a couple of days, his clothes were loose.

He went to the doctors and they gave him Valium to get through the day and temazapam for the night. 'D'you want any?' He waved a little plastic bottle at me.

'I'm fine, thanks,' I replied. I acted like I was above all that, when actually, I'd pinched Millie's stash of Mogadon from her bedroom. Just half a one with a glass of brandy was fine to get me to sleep. Since my mother was in hospital, she wouldn't need them. In there, they gave her all the drugs she needed.

One morning Hugh turned to me and said, 'You need to go back to school, Freya. Business as usual. I'm popping round the office today. We can't just stop. It's not what your mother would have wanted.'

'I'm not going back.' It wasn't that I wouldn't go, but more that I couldn't. My legs would never be able to pedal there again. Besides, until Millie woke up and things were back to normal, exams and stuff didn't really matter.

'You like school,' said my father.

'No, I don't. Never have. And not St Joan's. Never wanted to go there in the first place.'

'Did something happen?'

I couldn't tell him about Connie and Jessica. He'd be upset and there was always the risk he'd tell me to just bloody get on with it.

I thought he was going to get cross, but he didn't. He thought for a bit. 'We'll work something out.'

The thing about Hugh was, he didn't know very much about my life – not like I knew about his. He didn't understand about me and Mrs Glinka. The thing that had happened, it had nothing to do with me or her. We were innocent. Besides, Sasha would be back from France for the funeral, and I needed to tell him how sorry I was. That didn't mean we were going out or anything, but it'd be a nice thing to do, just as a friend.

The day before Mr Glinka's funeral, when Hugh had popped to the office and Edward was upstairs in his room, crying, I got on my bicycle to see Sasha's mother.

It was only a fortnight since I'd been there last, but in that time, the season had changed. Lavish summer had worn away to shabby autumn and the Glinka house was an ugly button sewn onto a threadbare rug.

As I stood by the front door, I reminded myself that true friendship was like true love – it endured anything. I knocked on the door and waited. Footsteps approached, then stopped. Then the door opened and Mrs Glinka stood before me. A thin white line splayed either side of her centre parting. I waited for her to move aside and let me in, but she stood still. 'Are you OK?' I asked.

'Freya.' She pronounced my name like it was significant.

'I wanted to come before. I wanted to talk to you at the hospital but Hugh wouldn't let me. He said to leave you alone. But I knew you'd want to see me, maybe not now, but eventually.'

'Your father has some sense. Poor man.' She wasn't looking at me, but through me, a bit like Millie did now she was in a coma.

'And Sasha... I wanted to tell him I was sorry. It's not like I knew Mr Glinka well, but...' Mrs Glinka's face grew red while I was talking, so I thought I'd better stop.

'My son?' she screamed. 'You stay away from my son. He told me what you tried to do. You pretend to be a nice girl, and in truth, you're no better than your filthy mother.'

I couldn't believe Sasha had told his mother about the summer ball. It wasn't the kind of thing you blabbed to your parents. And besides, I'd never let on about what he got up to, about the drugs and stuff. 'He kissed me!' I said. 'I never did anything wrong!'

Mrs Glinka's face twisted into a half-smile. She leaned against the doorpost. 'Without you, I would have my husband. Without you, I would have my house. My life. My heart.'

'You still have your house.'

She shook her head. 'The bank owns the house and interests rates... Well, you're too young to understand. To keep the house I have to work in Roman's shop. And I can't do that.'

She'd be rather good in retail, I suspected. But Mrs Glinka wasn't like my mother: the world outside the home was not for her.

'Perhaps you could get a lodger.' Although soon as I said it I thought of Edward and I knew what Mrs Glinka must think of him.

'The house was picked out by the university as the sanctuary of a great poet. And now the great poet is dead...' She blew into the air, as if the house was being blown away.

'You can't go.'

'This town has poisoned me. People like you and your mother.'

I leaned towards her, tried to take her by the shoulders, but she brushed my hands away. 'Please!' I cried. 'You're my best friend in all the world!'

I'd vowed never to humiliate myself like this. I'd not abased myself before Jessica and Connie. I'd accepted their rejection and walked away, eyes straight, moral high ground conquered. But Mrs Glinka was different. She was a grown-up, so she should be looking after me, and there she was, looking at me like I was nothing or evil, like we'd never spent day after day for two years telling each other everything in the universe.

She retreated behind the door till it was almost closed and only her face poked through. When she spoke, her voice was measured, exhausted. 'I realise you might think that it's my grief talking. But I'm telling you – never come here again. Sasha and I, we never existed. You never existed. The badness is in your blood. I thought I could purge it, but I can't. Goodbye, Freya.'

Gently, she shut the door in my face.

I stood for a while on her doorstep, waiting to see if she'd change her mind. I thought of all the things I'd say to her when she came back out, like that Millie wasn't filthy. Mr Glinka must've been lonely if he'd been going around with my mother and that was probably Mrs Glinka's fault for being mad and not doing anything about it. But mostly I thought how I'd miss sitting at her kitchen table, being listened to and praised. Mrs Glinka had taught me how to be alive, how to be a woman, things my mother never had time to tell me about, because she was too busy doing them herself.

At Sasha's bedroom window, an invisible hand drew shut the curtains.

For ages, I stared at the place the hand had been, willing it to reappear. I couldn't even know if it was Sasha, but who else could it have been? The house would be empty except for his mother and him, now that my mother had killed his father.

I remembered the roughness of his kiss, the stroke of his forefinger along the back of my neck. I thought of all the jokes he'd never make that I'd never get to laugh at. I knew I'd never love another boy like I'd loved him. And I knew I'd never see him again.

Back home, I dragged myself to my room and wept. I cried all evening, until a Mogadon sent me to sleep. Then, in the morning, soon as I was awake enough to remember I wasn't dreaming, I wept again. My soul weighed heavy as the rock in a sack of drowning kittens.

When I came downstairs, without appetite, eyes piggy with inflammation, my father looked relieved. 'It's good to get it out,' he said.

Edward gave me a sympathetic glance. I didn't have the heart to tell him that we were mourning different lost loves, but pain was pain, I supposed. For whatever reason, in the weeks – maybe months – to come, we might as well suffer together.

The next morning, I came across the expensive shopping bag my shocking pink birthday dress had come in. Inside, on the receipt, my mother had written one of her lists.

Freya, darling. You're going to look so grown-up in this frock, but isn't that what you wanted?
1. When buying formal wear, think to yourself – legs

or tits, not both at the same time.

2. Every time you step out the front door, whatever you're wearing, however you feel, just remember you're the most beautiful girl in the world.

✳ epilogue ✳

Now, when I return to Cambridge to see my two fathers, my friends say it sounds incredibly glamorous and beg to come with me. When sometimes I let them, they are disappointed to find two middle-aged men who don't even sleep together, living in a normal, if rather over-designed house. I don't believe that either Hugh or Edward have sex with anyone, but if they do, they're terribly discreet about it. Hugh's affair with Jackie his secretary turns out, now I'm allowed to know the details, to have been platonic, more or less. Just shows there's no point concealing things from children: what they imagine will always be far more lurid than the truth. I'm not sure that either Hugh or Edward ever had much of a sex drive. Millie was the one who was keen on that sort of thing. I think – or dread, perhaps, is the better word – that I may have inherited her genes, not my father's. It's a bit early to say. I'll have to wait till I'm forty, I expect, before I bear the full brunt of that eventuality.

I never go straight home. Instead, I park in Lion Yard and have a stroll round the city centre. The colleges remain the same, except for new accommodation blocks which, I notice, are becoming less experimental, more retro – faithful pastiches of earlier architectural styles. The graffiti I remember has been painted over. No longer does it read 'JACK THE BISCUIT IS SKINHEAD OK' over the Mill Road railway bridge. Probably Jack is no longer known as The Biscuit. And if he is a skinhead, it's through male pattern baldness rather than style statement.

Even nowadays, when no one's as rich as they'd like to be, and my generation is the first in history who may never be as wealthy as our parents, my town, always affluent, now borders on the chi-chi. We have an olive oil emporium, a fudge maker's, and a deli which sells bacon so costly, it must come from golden pigs. The stinky pub where I drank my first ever legal pint is now the purveyor of fine wines, for consumption on and off the premises. Millie would've enjoyed owning somewhere like that. I'm sure, had she continued working, she'd have started up on her own. With Hugh and Edward being financially secure at last, she'd have had the freedom.

Though I haven't lived in the town, not full-time, for years, I still bump into people I know. Occasionally I see Connie, who always blanks me. I smile at her briskly and say 'hi', to show that not only am I untouched by her cruelty, but that I am happy. The best revenge is living well – supposedly. Connie looks as though she's living pretty well herself. She's grown up tall, whereas I never grew a millimetre after I was twelve. She dresses exquisitely and fits into the tiniest of jeans, but her face already shows signs of wear: she's aged before her time.

Last time I came back, I saw Jessica. She was in Gap, her frustrated fingers rummaging through a table of knitwear. She couldn't seem to find what she was looking for, which was just as well, I thought, since polo necks had never suited her anyhow. She'd piled it on a bit since school, but her face – round, glowing, warm-eyed – was prettier than ever.

'Freya!' Excited, she waved to me as soon as she spotted me.

'Hi, Jessica.' I submitted to her hug, felt her large round breasts squash into my chest.

'I can't believe I've never bumped into you. Not once, not since...' Her eyes grew teary, her voice plaintive. 'I never imagined you wouldn't come back to St Joan's.'

'Turned out Braxton Girls' had a free place. I'd always wanted to go there, but we couldn't afford it. I had a great time.'

This was a lie. I didn't have a great time at Braxton Girls'. The girls were just as cliquey, standoffish and self-absorbed, but at least they were different girls, who knew nothing about me. At Braxton Girls' they taught real Latin instead of Class Civ, and the careers advisors wanted us to become doctors and lawyers, not nurses and teachers. When I refused to go back to St Joan's, Hugh took one look at the state sector and rejected it out of hand. It turned out that Edward had a cousin who was a head of year at St Joan's superior rival. He played the personal tragedy card, and I secured a bursary. I was cross with Hugh for never getting me a bursary to Braxton Girls' in the first place, but Edward explained that bursaries were discretionary awards, not necessarily advertised, and therefore only available to those in the know. I'd no real grounds for complaint. At least I never had to return to the site of my former torment.

'I hope you didn't leave because of me, Freya!' Jessica was sobbing now.

'Course not.'

'I always really really liked you. Whatever Connie thought, that had nothing to do with me.'

'Difficult, though, when your friends don't like your other friends.'

'Oh, Connie can be tricky. Don't have to tell me that. When I got engaged…' She flashed a modest diamond. 'She didn't speak to me for a month. But she's not really a friend, more like a sister. She's had an awful time, you know. Maybe not as awful as… You have to forgive people like that.'

I wasn't sure that I agreed.

Reluctantly, I said I'd go for a coffee with her at Berlucci's, for old time's sakes.

As we pushed through the door into the steamy interior, I realised I hadn't been there since the day we saw Sasha and his friends. I hadn't dared go in case he was sitting at the corner table, juggling with salt and pepper pots.

But of course, Sasha wasn't there, nor was he likely to be, since he'd moved away. After the summer ball I'd never seen him again, not apart from his hand at his bedroom window, which didn't really count. I'd always promised myself that I'd look him up one day – it wouldn't be hard to find someone with an unusual name like his. But I'd decided to wait until I was perfect — exactly the person I wanted to be. As yet, that day hadn't quite arrived.

Berlucci's was a third of its former size. Our old haunt was no longer a slouchy café where customers could hang out for hours, nurturing their lattes. It'd become a cramped cafeteria, where trays of congealed penne sweated under hot lamps. The tables, once round, were now square. This was a place to sit up and eat, not lounge about and drink. The waitresses were still Italian, but different ones. I scanned their faces, searching for a family resemblance to the ebullient Rosalina. I wondered if Rosalina still dressed like Madonna and whether, like Connie, she lived her life according to Madonna's imagined rules. Someone told me that Rosalina had got sick and died. I couldn't believe that was true.

As we sipped our cappuccinos, which were nothing like as fluffy as I remembered, Jessica told me about her work as a speech therapist and how she was planning to marry a junior osteopath.

'You'll come to the wedding, won't you? The colour palette is peaches and cream with a hint of raspberry. We're even having pavlova for dessert.'

We exchanged addresses and phone numbers and I promised to keep in touch, knowing I had no intention of doing so. I had new friends now — ones who'd never betrayed me.

At the university bookshop, as I passed by the Local Interest section, I saw copies of Roman Glinka's book, prominently displayed, even years after his death. When the slim volume first came out, being published posthumously made it special, even more so since the author had died tragically, never managing to see the glorious events for which he had waited almost three decades – the fall of the Berlin Wall and the collapse of Communism. If he'd lived, he could have become a grand old man of Russian letters. He'd have found new things to rail against – the rise of the plutocracy, the loss of idealism. I'd never been able to face reading the book, but this time I picked up a copy and flicked through. Roman Glinka's Wild East drew the rather trite comparisons, I thought, between the flatness of The Fens and the level expansiveness of the author's native land. The poems had all been originally written in Russian, then translated into English. Mr Glinka had done most of the translation himself, but his wife completed the task after his death.

Wild East had engendered further interest because of a series of sonnets dedicated to a dark lady. All of these had been written in the summer before the poet's death. The Russian critics said they were an allusion to Shakespeare's sonnets and declared that Glinka had surpassed his Western model. Some of the reviews mentioned Millie's name, but most did not. After all, my mother was still alive and married, and nothing had ever been proven. As far as the inquest was concerned, my mother was a neighbour giving another neighbour a lift when, being a heavy drinker, she'd no idea she was over the limit.

As soon as I came to the poems in question, it was clear to me that no mystery existed. The slim thighs, white as sugar, the dirty man's laugh, the fingers tinged with the bitter caramel of nicotine, all these belonged to my mother. Was she aware of the strength of the passions she inspired? At the time, I considered her vampish and unsavoury. She preyed upon men, I thought, and exploited their weakness. But now I am half-proud that that a saleswoman the wrong side of forty could have been not only the muse of a poet, but the wife of two fine men, and the object of adoration for many more. She achieved something extraordinary in her life, which was to transcend not only her station, but her gender.

I've spent many hours speculating as to why she behaved in the way she did. I've come to the conclusion that she simply needed lots of attention from men, sexual and otherwise. When my father as well as a younger live-in lover failed to satisfy, she simply looked further afield. She hadn't reckoned on the fact that Edward, like Hugh, was, as far as romance goes, a cactus, who needed watering only a couple of times a decade.

Of course, Hugh and Ed do have another woman in their life – that woman being me. I am spoilt, yes, but no one can accuse me of never having known hardship.

The reason I never go straight home to Hugh and Edward is because soon as I'm in the front door, I never want to leave. Edward makes me my favourites. His lasagne, always decent, is now superb. They tell me how thin I've become and they tut-tut at my hemlines. They demand to know about my work and give me advice about boyfriends – advice I always ignore. They even have a cat now, which Hugh had always wanted, but Millie would never allow. If they didn't insist on spending the whole of Saturday afternoon watching sport – football, rugby or cricket – they're not fussy – our home would be paradise on earth.

I worry sometimes that they don't socialise as much as they should. It's not as though they don't get offers, since they are accepted, pretty much, for who they are. The Harmisteads next door have never spoken to them again, not since Hugh's party, but Hugh and Edward got their own back by buying a set of table tennis and playing it in the back garden all summer. They know from the Lewises next-door-but-one that it drives the Harmisteads mad.

My mother's nursing home is a Nineteen Thirties cruise liner floating on a sedate beech-lined avenue. In the room next door lives a Maths professor with pre-senile dementia, and down the corridor is the wife of a former cabinet minister, immobile through motor neurone disease. In death as in life, Millie has only the best. When I pad along the cool pink corridors, I don't smell sickness. This is less a medical facility – more a hotel for those at life's last staging post.

After the accident, Millie stayed in hospital as they waited for her skull to heal. The scans revealed considerable brain activity.

'We haven't the foggiest, really,' admitted the consultant. 'She's done terribly well to get this far. She's got fighting spirit, that's for sure.'

A few months on, they moved her to a rehabilitation unit.

The doctors said, 'She's fine now, medically speaking, or stable, at any rate. Now it's a question of the long haul.'

But in rehab, nothing much improved. Still no walking, no swallowing. But they found if they put a pad of paper and a pencil under her hand, that she could write. 'Why new curtains?' she scrawled furiously, when they replaced the blinds in her room. Her desire to write lists must be located deep within her psyche. She also draws – mainly abstract designs, but sometimes cars and houses. She never did this before. They tried her on needlework, too. She managed to embroider a handkerchief with tiny squiffy silky flowers.

'She never used to do needlework,' I told the nurse. 'Does that mean she can still learn?'

But the nurse shook her head. 'Doubt it. She must've learnt to sew when she was a little girl. There's still someone in there, but we just can't get to her.'

Researchers all round the world are working on cases like my mother's, so you never know. People recover from all sorts of things, sometimes decades later. One day, I'm sure, she'll be restored to me, good as new. I'll never give up hope.

Millie, in her half life, is in some ways more beautiful than ever. As soon as her bandage was removed, her shaved hair grew back lustrous as before. The grey which illuminates the darkness gives her a continental sophistication she never had when she applied her fortnightly chestnut rinse. Since she never goes in the sun, her skin remains pale, ethereal. Gone are the lines of frustration which had started to form between her eyebrows, at the corners of her mouth. She now has two facial expressions – nothing and happy. When she sees me, she is happy. 'You've come!' she says, although she never says my name. I'm not even sure she knows I'm her daughter. The nurses say that the family contact is therapeutic for her because it keeps her emotions alive. That's why Hugh visits every day. Now he's more of a silent partner in the business, he has the time. 'Very soothing it is, too,' he tells me. 'She's much easier company like this.'

He's joking when he says that, but only half. Millie now has a calm radiance, a satisfaction. In life, she always needed more than she had, but now her life exists in one room, is expressed on pieces of paper and scraps of cloth – seemingly, at last, she has achieved contentment.

My father's existence, always complicated, is now simple. I think he has spent his life in terror. When he was growing up awful things kept happening, so as an adult, he'd do anything to avoid the worst. Then, after Millie had the accident, there was nothing more to fear. Nothing would ever be so terrible again.

That day I sat at her bedside and told her about my property business. I think she supports my deciding not to join the family firm – at least, not yet. She worries, of course, about my security, but she can hardly fault me for wanting independence. I told her some funny stories about an ongoing row I was having with my builder and she couldn't help but smile.

Best of all about my mother is the readiness with which she accepts affection. I can sit for hours holding her hand, stroking her hair. She likes to be hugged and kissed, where before she'd pull away and make me go to Hugh instead. She smells nicer now she has given up smoking and drinking. I nuzzle into her neck, inhaling the scent of shampoo and medicated soap.

I am sorry for all she has lost. I wish I could return to that night and not give her reason to drink herself silly then escape for the evening with her lover. To give myself life, had I found it necessary to deprive my mother of hers?

Now, as always, I cling to every moment we have together. If I've learned one thing from my mother, it's to take all the happiness I can, wherever I find it. In some respects, our relationship has never been better. Too late, perhaps, I've realised how easy she is to love.